THE ROAD TO HELL

THE ROAD TO HELL

SHEILA QUIGLEY

www.tontobooks.co.uk

Published in 2009 by Tonto Books Limited

Copyright © Sheila Quigley 2009

ISBN-13:

9781907183034

British Library Cataloguing in Publication Data:
A catalogue record for this book is available from
the British Library

Cover design by Elliot Thomson at www.preamptive.com

Printed and bound in the UK by
CPI Mackays, Chatham ME5 8TD

Tonto Books Ltd
Blaydon-on-Tyne
United Kingdom

www.tontobooks.co.uk

For

Rita Davison

A light in the dark.

PROLOGUE

The bus from Newcastle to Houghton-le-Spring was packed solid; large bodies, small bodies, all sweating in the overpowering heat. They had reached the Washington Galleries shopping centre when he spotted her.

She was dragging a large suitcase on to the bus. In her other hand was a pack of sandwiches. He couldn't read the label, though he knew what it would be, what it had always been: tuna and sweetcorn. She didn't so much walk down the aisle; more like she strode, head held high with a slight tilt to the right, the way she'd always walked, her *Fuck you world, I'm different, dare to take me on* stride.

She sat down on the side seat, facing him across the aisle. He watched her out of the corner of his eye as he felt the excitement building in his blood and prayed he would be able to contain it. Control was everything. The right time would come soon. His breathing quickened and he tried to regulate it by breathing deeply through his mouth. A middle-aged man looked over in his direction and their eyes locked for a moment. He stared into the older man's eyes as if staring into his very soul, seeing everything and taking whatever he wanted. The older man gave an involuntary shiver before breaking contact, knowing he'd lost the battle.

She hadn't changed one bit in the last fourteen years. Of course, she wouldn't recognise him: he had changed – a lot. He would introduce himself when they were alone, then she would remember him … just like the others had. She would know. A smile formed as he played the scene out in his mind.

Detective Inspector Lorraine Hunt could see the flashing lights of the police vehicles from the top of Newbottle as they drove down towards the dual carriageway. Detective Sergeant Luke Daniels was driving. They had both been enjoying a meal at the Sun Inn when the garbled call came in from Carter. A farmer had found a body in his field. Lorraine preferred to drive, but she'd had a couple of glasses of wine to chill out, and would rather not take the risk. It seemed that Superintendant Clark had never been off her back for a month or so, but Luke was adamant she was imagining it, blaming everything on this damn oppressive heat. She blew air out of her cheeks as she lifted her long dark hair off her neck.

Until a week ago Lorraine had been blonde. Then, without even telling him, she'd dyed her hair, saying she fancied a change. She suited it, he had to admit, her blue eyes seemed to sparkle more than ever, but it had been a shock that still threw him off guard now and then.

'God, I can't stand this much longer.' She fanned the back of her neck with her hair. 'It's nearly bloody ten o'clock at night, and if anything it's getting hotter.'

Concentrating on his driving, a thin film of sweat on his dark brow, Luke nodded, his thoughts elsewhere.

'Are you listening to me?'

'Yeah, sure.' He glanced quickly at her, then swung his eyes back to the road.

'OK. What's the problem?'

'Nothing,' he replied quickly.

Too quickly for Lorraine's liking. Luke was one of the easiest people in the world to read and this was why Lorraine loved him.

'Yes there is. You've been prickly for a few days, so spill the beans.'

They reached the dual carriageway before Luke answered. Swallowing hard, he said, 'Well you know, I, er … I think Selina … I think Selina and Mickey might be, you know what.'

'What's "you know what"?' Lorraine hid a smile. Luke could be so old fashioned at times. Selina, the daughter he had not known existed, had turned up nearly a year ago with obvious past history but, after a rocky start, they had sorted their problems and now Luke behaved as if she'd been with him all of her life and was an angel.

The truth was, Lorraine thought, glancing sideways at him, that Selina was an angel with dusty wings. She'd turned out good; she'd only needed the chance and the stability Luke had given her.

'Are you trying to say that they're sleeping together?' Lorraine asked dryly.

'Well, I wouldn't put it … '

'Get a life, Luke. They're both nearly eighteen for God's sake.'

'I just don't want her making the same mistake …'

'That you and her mother made,' Lorraine put in before Luke could finish.

Luke squirmed in his seat as they pulled up at the field. 'And don't,' Lorraine added as they got out of the car, 'go putting your oar in. Selina and Mickey are fine and far from stupid … Ah, I see Scottie got here before us.'

The crime scene was lit up with arc lights and it wasn't hard to miss Scottie's large frame in the white forensic suit making his way towards them. He held two parcels in his hand and offered one each to Lorraine and Luke when he reached them.

'Sorry love,' he said to Lorraine, 'but this one's really messy.'

Lorraine took the offered parcel with a groan. She hated wearing the damn things, a job to get them on and an even bigger job to get them off. Especially when wearing a dress.

'Might I just say, dear, that red is certainly your colour. Even more now that you look so Italian,' Scottie said admiringly.

'Flattery will get you everywhere, Scottie,' Lorraine winked at him.

'Hi, Scottie,' Luke smiled, stepping between them and taking his parcel.

The here was no answering smile on Scottie's usually friendly face, which gave Luke a queasy feeling that this was something out of the ordinary. He knew that Lorraine would have realised as well. They got suited up and made their way over to the crime.

'So, what have you got for us so far?' Lorraine asked. Lifting the yellow incident tape up and holding it until Lorraine and Luke stepped under, Scottie said: 'Female, early thirties, cause of death ...' He paused a moment and Lorraine looked at him oddly. 'Probably strangulation.'

'Probably?' Luke asked, one eyebrow lifted in question.

Lorraine frowned. She knew it wasn't like Scottie to be so evasive; he was usually straight to the point and ninety-nine per cent correct.

With a sigh, Scottie swung his head back to Lorraine. 'Before you take a look I have to warn you she's in a bit of a mess, Lorraine.'

Lorraine nodded, steeling herself. She'd seen quite a few bits of a mess, and sometimes, just sometimes, when faced with the depravity of the human race, she felt like throwing it all in. It was at these times her determination to bring the culprit to justice kept her going.

They stepped into the tent, Scottie in the lead. Inside was well lit and when they were circled around the body Lorraine stared at the dead girl's face, hearing Luke gasp beside her. The police photographer, a small dapper man with old-fashioned black-rimmed spectacles that kept slipping off his nose (Lorraine had often seen him picking them up from the ground), was just finishing his work and with a grim face, not meeting Lorraine's eyes, he left the tent to give them more room.

The woman was naked, her arms and legs spread wide apart. She had bite marks all over her stomach.

'Dear God,' Lorraine muttered.

'She's been repeatedly raped, alive and dead. See how much blood the poor lass has lost.' Scottie pointed at the blood pooled around her body. 'Because there's been no rain for nearly a month the ground's so hard and dry it's like concrete and the blood is only now starting to seep into the soil.'

'Dogs, you think?' Luke asked, the revulsion plain on his face as he stared at the bite marks on the woman's stomach.

'Human ... This is one sick Joe, guys.' Scottie hesitated for a moment, looking at Lorraine, not noticing Luke start to gag, as he said to Lorraine, 'You alright, love?'

Lorraine hadn't moved. She was still looking down at the woman's face, her own ashen in the strong light.

'What's wrong?' Luke asked, concern in his voice.

Lorraine didn't answer for a moment, then she said quietly, 'I ... I know her.'

'You know who she is?' Scottie asked.

Lorraine ran her tongue over her dry lips, her hands started to sweat and she could feel her body trembling. *Shock*, she told herself, then spun round and quickly ran out of the tent.

When the men followed they found her next to a tree, vomiting. Luke put his arm around her shoulders as he handed her a paper handkerchief, and after wiping her mouth and taking a few deep breaths she turned and rested her head on his shoulder for a moment while Scottie looked on, deep concern written on his features.

Her face deathly pale, Lorraine sighed. 'She's an old friend ... I grew up with her ... Her name ... Her name is ... was ... Amy Dawson.'

'I'm so sorry, love.' Scottie patted her back.

Lorraine straightened up and stepped away from Luke. Shaking her head and looking from one to the other she went on. 'You don't understand. She's not the first.'

PART ONE

THE BEGINNING

1994

CHAPTER ONE

Midnight, and a hush had descended over the hospital. For a brief time in the warm summer night there were no screeching sirens, no taxis or ambulances dropping beaten-up drunks at the door: all was peace and quiet.

On the second floor a dying woman lay on her bed, her two oldest children at her side. Nineteen-year-old Leanne Knightly gently stroked the back of her mother's hand; looking at her face she saw a tear slide out of her eye. Dorothy Knightly was forty-one years old and looked easily twice her age. Gone was the lush dark hair that her children had inherited, and her brown eyes had lost the sparkle that her husband had loved. For the last six months she had been fighting a battle she couldn't ever hope to win. The cancer had its icy tentacles weaving around her body long before it was ever detected.

Leanne, her thick black hair cropped very short, glanced across the bed to her brother, who had not taken his eyes off their mother's face for most of the time that they had been sitting there. Sam was a year older than Leanne and had been, in title only, the head of the family for the last two and a half years, since their father had died from the same terrible disease a week after the youngest Knightly, Andrew, was born.

Dorothy's fingers twitched on her right hand, disturbing the gold cross on the thin chain that was wrapped tightly around her fingers, causing it to sway gently from side to side, and a moment later her eyes opened. Slowly, pain etched in every line of her face, she moved her head from her daughter to her son.

'Promise me, Sam,' she whispered. 'That you will look after your sisters and Andrew. Promise me, please Sam. Don't leave it all up to Leanne.'

For a moment she feared her pleas were falling on deaf ears; then Sam swallowed hard as he wiped his sweating palms on his jeans. He'd thought about this moment while he'd lain awake all last night, he knew there was no point in shushing her and telling her that she would soon be better. His mother had known for a good long while that it was only a matter of time.

This was the third time this month that she had been rushed into hospital, the second time in this very bed, then demanded to be taken home after a few days. The doctors had assured him and Leanne that this time she would not be going home. Her next move from this bed would be to her grave.

'I promise, Mam,' he said finally, after a very long moment in which Leanne had inwardly willed him to give their mother the right answer. 'I promise.' His voice was hoarse with the endless chain-smoking he had done through the night. He rubbed her hand gently. 'I promise.'

Sam was a handsome young man who always reminded Dorothy of her husband. He resembled him in more ways than one, apart from the anger. Her Samuel had never possessed the rage that young Sam seemed to have been born with. He took another long moment, then bit into his bottom lip as he met her eyes and nodded.

Dorothy gave a slight nod in return, then moved her eyes to her daughter. 'Promise me, Leanne.' She used her fingernail to scratch Leanne's hand, but the effort had no strength behind it and only succeeded in wringing a sob from the young girl, soon to be forced into motherhood.

'Yes, yes,' Leanne said quietly a moment later as she let go of her dreams and took up the reins of her two sisters and baby brother. 'I promise ... I promise, Mam.'

Dorothy's lips twitched into a slow smile, then, content that the little ones would be safe, she let go and slipped slowly into a pain-free peace.

At the door two-year-old Andrew looked from his mother's still, quiet face to his sisters. Seven-year-old Tammy was squeezing his right hand and nine-year-old Stacey was squeezing his left even harder.

He looked back at his mother and sensed something terrible had happened, something so incomprehensible that he had no words for it. He screamed then, a high-pitched warble that reached the ceiling and echoed around the room. Almost at once his sisters joined in.

That had been six months ago and Sam's promise was evaporating as quickly as early morning summer mist. Eyes bulging, his usually handsome face contorted into a mask of red rage and fists clenched tight against his sides, he viciously kicked the bedroom door. He kicked it again and again, but still enraged he lifted his right hand and punched a hole in the top panel.

'Shut up now!' he screamed. 'Fucking shut up! ... Just shut the fuck up ... For God's sake, shut up, I can't take any more.' He punched the door again, leaving a matching hole in the other side. 'SHUT UP!'

Terrified by his brother's rage, and not understanding the reason, knowing only that it was directed at him, little Andrew Knightly stood at the end of his cot, his back pressed against the bars, his blue pyjamas wet with the tears he'd cried for the last hour. His eyes were wide with fear, his body shaking uncontrollably, his sobs tearing at his sisters' hearts.

Tammy and Stacey huddled together on their bed in the next room, the quilt pulled over their heads, both of them crying softly and praying as hard as they could for Leanne to please, please come home soon.

Andrew howled even louder a moment later when, glaring at him, Sam pushed open the broken door and stepped into the room.

'Lee, want Lee, me want Leanne,' Andrew whimpered, looking up at his brother.

For a long moment Sam stood amongst the shattered remnants of the door, the rage inside of him burning like a living being, fuelled by his brother's sobs, urging him on, demanding a release. His fists were still clenched, his arms held stiffly by his side, Andrew's face filling his eyes, his screams filling his ears, until all he wanted to do was destroy. Destroy and run, run free from his godforsaken chained existence.

Fighting for control, he sucked air into his lungs, long, harsh, ragged breaths. Deep down inside of him, at the core that was Sam, the last thing he wanted to do was hurt Andrew. *I love the kid, for God's sake. But it seems like the brat has never stopped crying for fucking months now, ever since the day that we buried Mam.*

'Oh, God.' His mother's pain-filled face hovered in his mind's eye; he hung his head in shame, and sobbed even louder than Andrew. 'Sorry, Mam ... So, so sorry. I can't ... Oh, God.'

Quickly, before his temper rose again, and with a guilty backward glance at Andrew, who had momentarily fallen silent and now watched him with huge, dark, sad eyes, Sam hurried out of the bedroom and ran down the stairs, nearly tripping over Thomas the Tank engine at the bottom. 'Bastard.' Viciously, he kicked the toy train at the wall; it bounced hard, leaving behind it a red and blue smear on the pale green paint. Andrew started to cry again, huge retching sobs that could be heard clearly by his sisters.

Stacey patted Tammy's head as she whispered, 'Wait here Tammy, I won't be a minute.'

Jumping out of bed she ran into the next room and grabbed Andrew out of his cot. 'Shh, shh,' she whispered in his ear, soothing him, as Andrew, his heart racing desperately with fear, clung tightly to her, his fingers hooked on the collar of her yellow pyjamas. She quickly took him back into their bed.

Feeling safe amongst his sisters, Andrew chuckled between sobs as he snuggled down between Tammy and Stacey, drained and exhausted, but now, feeling safe, he quickly went to sleep.

'When is she coming home?' Tammy hissed angrily. 'She promised she wouldn't be late, she promised ... I ... I hate our Sam now ... I hate him. I *hate* him. And I hate her an' all ... I want our Mam back.' Tammy grabbed the sheets and began twisting them, wanting to cry and scream as loudly as Andrew had, but knowing, as young as she was, that it would probably send her older brother way over the edge.

'We all do, Tammy, but Leanne's doing her best to keep us together, you know she is, and she's not even late,' Stacey whispered back, defending Leanne. 'It's not even ten o'clock. And she hasn't been out for ages. He promised she could go to the party, didn't he? And he said he would go when she came back, so it's not fair to blame our Leanne.'

Tammy tutted. 'He says anything he wants and ... and all he ever does is shout all the time, he's nasty. Shout, shout, shout ... I hate him. And I'm hot in here now, Andy's got all the bed.' She wriggled and raised herself up on one elbow and made to push Andrew along the bed with her free hand.

'Don't you dare wake him up,' Stacey hissed.

Tammy tutted again, then, pulling a face at Andrew, she buried her head in the pillow.

Downstairs Sam was pacing the floor, punching the palm of his left hand with his right fist. 'Where the hell is she? Where the fucking hell is she?' He went to the window, pulled the net curtain along and glowered into the street, his fingers impatiently tapping out a drum roll on the windowsill.

Got to get to the party.

Everybody's gonna be there but me.

The party was for Lorraine Hunt, who was leaving for a university in London tomorrow. They had all been together since the first day of infant school. She would be the first one of their gang to leave the small town, probably the only one, the others felt, with any real brains.

He punched his left palm again and again, unaware of the blood dripping around the splinter in his knuckle and the trail of blood he was leaving behind him, feeling nothing but the burning need to escape from this claustrophobic house and screaming kids that he'd been saddled with.

'It's not fair, it just not fucking fair.' He kicked out at the wall, close to the coloured scuffmark left by Andrew's toy train.

I'm only young, for God's sake. Fucking hell, I've got a life to live. Places to go. It just isn't fair. No way should I be stuck here looking after a bunch of stupid kids.

He clenched his fists as his dreams faded, visions of backpacking in Australia cracked and frayed at the edges. *Australia, that's where I wanna be, not stuck in this dump, babysitting for the rest of my life. No way.*

'Fuck.' He had to get to the party, and soon. He was positive that bastard Randy McCade was going to say something tonight. He had to get there before he opened his big fat mouth and spoiled the dream.

Sam shook his head, seething inside with pent-up rage. 'Friend or not, I'll fucking kill him if he does ... I'll tear his fucking head off and stamp on his guts, the bastard.'

His mounting frustration drove him to the door. His motorbike parked on the street, chrome shining in the lamp light, called to him. He peered up the stairs, strained his ears, paused for a moment, and could hear nothing. He looked back at the door.

He longed to be gone, yearned to feel the wind on his skin, the power of his bike between his legs. He ached to be free. It was a living pain that tortured him.

He glanced once more up the stairs. 'Little bastard must have fallen asleep at last,' he whispered.

Why should I stop in the bloody house and be saddled with a pile of brats at my age? Who the fucking hell needs the hassle?

'I should be out, out enjoying myself with mates, not stuck in here. For God's sake!'

He looked at his black leather motorbike jacket hanging on the banister with intense longing, stood for a moment longer, his need to be free fighting his guilt at leaving the kids alone. Then, 'Fuck it ... I'm not being trapped here like a mug any longer.'

Grabbing the jacket off the banister he shrugged it on quickly before he changed his mind, yanked the zipper up to his chin, picked his blue helmet up from under the chipped hall table and grabbed his keys from the table top.

His blood burning with the sense of freedom, he quietly opened the door and crept out. Not once going down the path nor even when he reached his motorbike and kick-started it did he give the house a backward glance.

Andrew slept through the soft snick of the front door closing behind Sam, Tammy snored gently, unaware that they were soon to be alone, but Stacey heard and knew that their brother, their protector, had gone, leaving them in the darkness of the night and with the fears that prowl a young girl's imagination.

Slowly, quietly, so as not to disturb the others, especially Andrew, she slipped out of bed and went to the window. Gently she pulled the net curtain across and watched as Sam started his bike and drove off.

She was still staring sadly out of the window a few minutes later when Jason Smith walked down the street. Stacey gasped and her heart began to race, her eyes wide with fright and fear nailing her feet to the floor. She was unable to move as she stared down at him. All the kids talked about Jason Smith, he loved to frighten them, he was a bully and nobody liked him. She'd heard her sister Leanne talking to Sandra Gilbride and Sandra had said that the black eye Dolly had a few months ago was off Jason Smith and he had slapped some of the kids around.

With the homing instinct of a pigeon, Jason Smith looked up at the window and stuck his middle finger up. Stacey shivered. She loved Dolly, Jason Smith's mother, to bits, but nobody in the street liked fat, greasy Jason, who shouted at the kids all the time and even slammed the door in your face when Dolly had told you to come over for a piece of her corned beef pie, or even a yummy chocolate fairy cake that she sometimes let you help her make.

Dropping the curtain, Stacey stood with her back against the wall, her arms folded across her thin chest, remembering the other day in the park when the kids were saying that if Jason Smith was in a bad mood he liked to bite you.

'Please, baby Jesus, don't let Jason Smith know that we are all by ourselves,' she whispered, as huge fat tears slid down her face and dripped slowly on to the cold canvas floor. 'Please don't let him come in and bite me.'

CHAPTER TWO

Leanne arrived back home ten minutes later than she had promised and feeling very guilty. She hurried up the path to the door, panting from running nearly all the way and cursing the blisters she could feel forming on both feet, her black sling-back high heels, the first new pair of shoes she'd had in over two years, clicking loudly.

The heavy scent of Mr Skillings' roses drifted over the hedge in the warm night breeze. Roses always reminded her of Mr Skillings and how kind he was, even to taking Andrew along to the shop every other day, or for a walk up the park just to get him from under her feet for a while.

She hurried closer. In her heart she knew that Sam would be angry even though she was just a few minutes late. Sam was always angry.

'Hope he hasn't taken it out on the girls,' she muttered, fishing around in her handbag for the key and finding it strange that he wasn't actually waiting at the front door for her, demanding to know why the hell she was so bloody late.

It had been hard pulling herself away, she was having such a good time catching up with friends she hadn't seen in ages, but she'd promised.

Sam never keeps his promises though, a voice whispered in her head as she opened the door. *Sandra Gilbride's right, I should get out more, I'm only young; I should be out enjoying myself and Sam should take his turn with the kids instead of leaving everything up to me. He's a selfish streak a mile wide.*

'And I promised Mam,' she whispered to the night as she opened the door. Thank God the girls were pretty well all right, though Andrew was definitely a handful, but the social worker did say that he should start settling down soon.

She nodded her head as she stepped over the threshold. Pretty soon he would be at school. *Can't wait for that day to come!*

They said she was doing a really good job. Yeah, but what they didn't know was that when they closed the door behind them and went away, leaving her all alone to cope with everything, all Leanne wanted to do was cry.

'Sam?' she said quietly, feeling the emptiness as she walked into the kitchen, then through into the silent, deserted sitting room where the absence of a blaring television told her immediately that Sam was not in the house.

Oh God. The kids.

Upstairs, Stacey had heard the door open.

What if it's Jason Smith? What if he saw our Sam go out and leave us on our own?

Her eyes wide, her body trembling with fear fuelled by a child's active imagination, she looked around for somewhere to hide, but the room was tiny and even for a small girl there was nowhere.

Under the bed, maybe? She glanced at her sleeping brother and sister. *If I hide, he'll get them.*

Tears of fright and frustration ran down her face. Not knowing what to do she knuckled the tears away and sniffed. A moment later she froze when she heard a soft footstep on the stairs, followed quickly by another. The hairs crawled on the back of her neck, she felt sick and then ashamed when she wet herself.

Terrified, she felt her legs start to give way. She started to sob and couldn't stop shaking.

Jason Smith is coming to get you.

A low moan of absolute terror escaped from her lips just before she fainted and collapsed in a crumpled heap on the floor.

Leanne reached the top of the stairs without knowing that in her rush to see the children her hand had picked up spots of blood from the handrail. She hesitated, as if she couldn't decide which room to go to first, then turned to her left and saw the broken door. Her heart racing, she rushed into Andrew's room.

For a long heart-stopping moment the sight of an empty cot terrified her. She froze, her blood pounding in her ears, a scream building up in her throat, her heart filling with the dread any parent or carer of the very young always carries with them: the fear of an empty bed.

Then utter panic took hold. She spun round and ran into her sisters' room, fearing that something might have happened to all three kids.

She saw Tammy's dark curls first, then Andrew, bottom up, snuggled into Tammy's back.

'Thank God,' she murmured, breathing quickly and feeling as if she was going to faint.

'Uh oh,' she uttered a moment later, her knuckles finding their way to her mouth as the turmoil started all over again. *Where's Stacey?*

Her heart lurched when she heard a low moaning sound coming from behind the bed.

'Stacey?' she whispered. Falling back into place, her heart began to hammer in her chest. 'Stacey? Are you alright, baby? Where are you,

Stacey?'

She felt a scream welling up inside. *Please be alright, pet, please girl. Please, oh please.*

She wanted to move fast, tried to, but her feet refused to co-operate; she was terrified of what she would find. Had someone hurt Stacey? *Please God, no.*

It was obvious to her now that Sam had gone and left the kids all alone. The selfish bastard, ten minutes late, that's all, as if he couldn't have waited a bit longer. And he'd been out all afternoon riding that bloody bike when he'd promised to take Andrew to the park. *Oh God, had someone seen him leave and then come in?*

'Oh, please let her be alright,' she whispered, trying to divert her thoughts away from the picture that was building there.

Reaching the end of the bed and fearful of what she might find, her hands shaking, she took hold of the bedpost and noticed the blood. Recoiling, she thought, *The door, the blood, it has to be Sam.*

Anything else was unthinkable. Praying she was right and that a maniacal stranger was not lurking in the house, she peered over the edge of the bed. Stacey was lying on the floor, curled into the foetal position. A soft, low moan drifted out of her mouth.

'Stacey!' Leanne gasped, moving to her sister. 'What the hell?' Falling to her knees, she cradled Stacey's head. 'Please say you're alright, Stacey, talk to me! Please,' she begged, 'talk to me, Stacey.'

Stacey moaned again then opened her eyes. Blinking twice, she whispered, 'Leanne?' Her eyes, wary and frightened at first, lit up when she recognised her sister. 'Oh Leanne,' she sobbed, her arms reaching out for her.

'What happened, love?'

But Stacey couldn't speak, she buried her head deeper into Leanne's chest and clung on tightly.

Leanne gave her a minute but she had to know what had happened. Had to know if she was alright. Prising Stacey's grip loose she held her at arm's length.

'Oh dear me, love, are you alright? What happened?' Leanne suppressed the desire to shake Stacey in her eagerness to find out what was wrong. 'Come on sweetie, tell me what happened.'

'I thought it was Jason Smith.'

'What?'

Stacey sat up and stared at Leanne for a moment before running her fingers slowly over her sister's face. She started to cry again. 'I ... I heard somebody on the stairs. When ... when our Sam went out, 'cos, 'cos our Andrew was crying all the time, he just wouldn't stop.' She started to sob. 'And ... and he smashed the door.'

'Take it easy love, just breathe nice and slow, you can tell me in a minute.'

As she was feeling a little better in Leanne's presence, Stacey's breathing eased from a harsh rattle. She took another moment, then went on with her story. 'Jason Smith came along the street and saw me at the window. I thought it was him coming up the stairs, I was frightened, Le ... Leanne, and, and I, I think I must have fainted or, or something.' Her bottom lip quivered and she started to cry again.

Leanne held her tightly. 'Come on love, must have been me you heard. Jason wouldn't really hurt you, he's just a bully and likes to frighten the kids.' She rocked Stacey back and forwards for a few calming minutes. 'We'll go downstairs. I'm here now, nothing can harm you when I'm here. Come on, quietly now, we don't want the others awake, pet.' Leanne gently helped Stacey up.

Outwardly calm for Stacey's sake, inside Leanne was seething with anger. *How dare he? How dare he go and leave them!*

Half an hour later Stacey, calmed down and in a clean nightgown, was tucked back up in bed. Leanne sat downstairs staring at the blank television screen, wanting nothing more than to put her hands round her brother's neck and choke the life out of him.

'The bastard,' she muttered angrily. 'Where the hell does he get off, leaving the kids alone?' She flicked an angry tear away.

But all he ever wants to do is go out, get drunk, get sober, meet his mates and ride that flaming bike. Like I'm not supposed to have any mates, have any fun? Life's all about Sam and what he wants!

Never mind me.

Well, he's had it all his way for too long now.

She folded her arms across her chest, her anger building all over again.

The bastard.

She pictured him sitting in the hospital and promising their dying mother that he would help look after them all.

Enough of this, I'm sick to death of him leaving every bloody thing to me, time he faced up to the fact that we have three kids to bring up. I'll die first before I'll let them end up in a home. When he gets in tonight things are gonna be sorted, he can moan as much as he likes. Selfish, that's what he is, always bloody well has been.

A stubborn look on her normally placid face, she prepared herself to wait for her brother to come home.

Things will be sorted tonight.

'And that's a fact,' she muttered adamantly, her face set in a stubborn mask.

CHAPTER THREE

Randy McCade, tall, fair haired and slim, looked in the mirror and popped an extra-strong mint into his mouth. His hazel eyes looked back at him for a moment, then his gaze dropped as he pulled his lips back and examined his teeth. He was proud of his strong white teeth and smiled as often as he could, sometimes when he didn't want too, though if he was honest there wasn't a lot to smile about lately. He never did get the job he wanted. Instead he'd ended up fiddling for his older brother, Tony, in his gambling den.

He sighed. *I'm fed up giving slot machine change to bloody idiots who should know better than to put all their money in the friggin' bandits.*

After a year he'd grown immune to their cries of 'What am I gonna do?' when they had gambled every single penny they possessed and looked at him with desperate fear in their eyes, another week until giro day or pension day, no food in the house, last week's debts still to pay and the fear of the money lender banging on the door.

He told Tony that he wasn't bothered, tried hard to tell himself the same, but secretly he did feel sorry for them. He kept quiet about it because the first time he'd mentioned over the supper table that old Meg Healey had no money left to put her heating on the others – his brothers Patrick, Tom, Tony, Pete and his cousin Mick, who lived with them because he'd been thrown out of the house, and his sister Jenna – had looked at him oddly. Even his mother had called Meg a silly old fool, and Tony had laughed his head off and called him a soft pussy. Patrick though, Patrick hadn't laughed, Patrick had sneered nastily at him and said nothing, and somehow that had felt far worse than Tony's laughter.

Still, Randy was pleased that the job of collecting money owed had fallen to his cousin Mick, who was more suited to frightening pensioners and teenagers alike if they were a day late in paying, or a penny short.

He sighed. Why he hadn't been born into an ordinary family instead of the bunch of villains and rogues that the bloody lot of them were? His dad wasn't a villain, but he'd lost control of the family years ago.

He knew there was no point going to him with anything, the old geezer was terrified of Patrick, who was quite content to let Tony be the front man. He knew also that Tony was the brainbox and perhaps a match for Patrick with his fists and sadistic ways; only Tony had a longer fuse. Patrick's fuse was non-existent.

Randy didn't dare tell them yet that he was thinking of joining the army, it being the only escape route he could think of.

He ran his tongue over his teeth.

I need to run it past Jacko, see what he thinks, maybe we could join up together, maybe even Dave and Sam might go for it, now that would be great.

But first things first, worst of all I'm now going to lose me girl. She's going to university. We're all gonna miss her, we've been together for years, inseparable, that's what the teachers used to call us.

Never thought I would feel like this about her though. Never in a million saw this coming.

He fastened the buttons on his new denim shirt and posed one way, then the other. 'How can she bring herself to leave me?'

Well, apart from that bloody spot that's threatening to burst on the end of me nose, like.

He carefully rubbed some of Jenna's makeup that he'd nicked from her room over the offending spot.

Strictly speaking though, he thought, giving himself one last glance in the mirror, making sure every hair was in place, *she's not* my *girl, she doesn't belong to any of us. She just treats me the same as the rest of them.*

Just like a mate.

But I love her.

He looked up and sighed.

And I know Sam thinks he does as well ... I can tell.

So tonight I'm gonna ask her, before it's too late and she meets one of those university blokes.

Or before Sam gets there first.

Should have asked her before now.

After all, it's my bike she always rides on. Well, most of the time anyhow. OK, so I've got the best bike, Jacko's is always breaking down and Sam's isn't much better, and Sara mostly rides on Dave's bike, Amy has her own, but her folks are rich. Lorraine rides mine because she likes holding on to me. He nodded to himself in the mirror and grinned.

'Well, how could she resist?'

Full of confidence, he smiled as he ran downstairs, grabbed his gear and quickly went through the front door before Tony or anyone else knew he was gone.

With a determined look on his face Randy jumped on his motorbike and headed towards the party.

CHAPTER FOUR

Mavis had really done her daughter proud. Everyone said so. The Miners' Hall was decked with glittering banners wishing Lorraine good luck. Pink balloons floated around the room and at the front of the hall a large table was packed to overflowing with finger food.

Peggy, her red hair in a shoulder-length bob and looking trim and smart in black, stood with her arm around Lorraine, whose denim skirt was only an inch shorter than her own. Peggy's eyes were on the DJ as 'Step On' by Happy Mondays faded in to Blur's 'There's No Other Way'.

'Hasn't he got a nice little bum, Lorry?'

Lorraine didn't have a chance to reply. Her mother was in earshot.

'You should be ashamed of yourself,' Mavis said, one eyebrow arched as she walked past them with a plate of sandwiches in her hand, her flowing lilac dress sweeping out behind her. 'He's half your age.'

'What?' Peggy asked, feigning stunned astonishment.

Lorraine grinned. She was used to her mother and godmother's little fights. Peggy arrived at infrequent intervals, then disappeared for months at a time, though she always kept in contact by phone.

Turning, Mavis headed back to her daughter and friend. 'You know what. It's written all over your face and half the room heard what you said.'

'Eee, Mavis love, you're not suggesting that ... Anyhow, he's not half my age. Cheeky bugger.'

'He'll be twenty-five if he's a day.'

'Well ... That doesn't make him half my age!' Peggy replied indignantly.

Laughing, Lorraine disentangled herself from Peggy, 'OK guys, gotta talk to some people.'

'That's OK, girl.' Peggy patted Lorraine's arm. 'You tottle off now and mind you behave yourself.'

'Oh, and thanks for the watch, Peggy.' Lorraine waved her wrist in the air, showing the silver watch Peggy had bought for her, then kissed her cheek.

'That's alright pet, glad you like it ... And remember what I said: when you're away from home, keep your hand on your tuppence. Don't want no little Lorraines wandering around yet, making me and your mam older than we are.'

'Peggy!' Lorraine cried, shaking her head, her face pink with embarrassment, but unable to hide a smile. She walked over to where Jacko Musgrove and Dave Ridley sat, each nursing a half glass of lager, stopping here and there on her way to have a brief word with family and friends.

'You look gorgeous, petal,' Lorraine's Uncle Harry said. 'Midnight blue is your colour, girl. Pity karate suits aren't made in that shade, you'd knock 'em dead without making a move.'

Lorraine laughed. 'Yeah, says who?'

'Me!' Harry leaned forward and kissed the same cheek that Peggy had. 'Do us proud, girl,' he whispered in her ear. 'And don't forget the name of that Sensei down there, I had a word with him the other day, he's expecting you.'

'I will and I won't,' she nodded, and moved on, her blonde ponytail bobbing as she moved. Catching Dave's eye she gestured with her head for him to follow her outside.

Slithering through the crowd and glancing back to check that her mother's eye was not on her, Lorraine made it safely outside. She was standing in the doorway looking up the street when Jacko and Dave joined her.

'Oh, thank God. Give us a fag, Dave.'

Knowing exactly what she had wanted, Dave already had his cigarettes in his hand; he took two out, lit one for Lorraine, then handed it to her before lighting one for himself. He was struggling with a raging case of acne. His mother had spent a fortune on acne cures but nothing seemed to work. And what bugged him lately was the fact that he already had to look up at Lorraine – it seemed as if every one of his friends was growing except him.

'I'm pleased to get out here for a bit. That Darren Watts keeps staring all the time. He actually asked if he could dance with me, I mean … him? Come on.'

'He's been trying to be one of us for years, and he still hasn't got the message.'

'He gives me the creeps,' Lorraine shivered. 'And he stares at Sara all the time. She hates him. He's even,' Lorraine looked quickly around then said in a loud whisper, 'tried it on with Amy.'

'Never! But everybody knows Amy's like, you know …' Dave said.

'Surprised she didn't black his eye,' Jacko laughed.

'Aye, me an' all … Sure you don't want one, Jacko, mate?' Dave held his packet of cigarettes out to Jacko.

Jacko Musgrove was the tallest of their little gang. He'd been tall in infant school, and when Lorraine had been looking for her friends she'd always looked for Jacko: his dark head had been way above anyone else's.

'How many times do I have to tell you? I don't and won't ever want one. Smells like donkey shite. Anyhow, they're bad for you.'

'Says who?' Dave asked.

Jacko shrugged. 'Somebody.'

Lorraine took a deep draw, held the smoke in her lungs for a moment, then let it out and watched as the smoke drifted off into the night before saying, 'It's a real downer that Amy couldn't make it, but since her stupid dad found out and banged her off to her aunt's to cure her ...' Lorraine shook her head. 'As if it was some sort of disease.'

'He's a dinosaur, that bloke,' Dave said, then laughed. 'Wonder what he'd say if he knew she'd met someone down there.'

Jacko chuckled. 'Probably have a stroke. Anyway, it's not like she's going to be away forever, is it?'

Lorraine smiled. None of them had really been surprised when Amy came out to them. They treated her as they always had, what she was, one of the gang. Even though in college she'd made some new friends, she still hung out with them a lot of the time.

'Where the hell's Randy and Sam? Is one of them picking Sara up? And Leanne's already gone home!'

'Don't know about Sara, she never asked anyone for a lift, thought she was coming with you?' Jacko turned to Dave.

Dave shrugged. 'I thought she was coming with Lorry. I went for a ride up Waldridge Fells this afternoon.'

Lorraine frowned. 'Yeah, she was supposed to be coming to mine. We couldn't wait any longer for her.'

'She'll probably be on her way.' Dave sighed and took a deep draw before nipping his cigarette and putting it in his pocket for later.

He'd had a crush on Sara Brown for years, but lately she'd not been very nice to him, jumping on Sam's or Jacko's bike when she always used to ride on his.

'They'll all be on their way. Randy won't have finished work until late. You know what their Tony's like, wants every ounce of blood he can get and that's out of his own,' Jacko said. Then, looking down the street for a moment and straining his ears, he swung back to Lorraine. 'Hang on, might be Sam I can hear. Tell you what, if he doesn't get that exhaust sorted soon he's gonna get pulled, bet you anything.'

'Sick of telling him.' Dave decided to relight his cigarette. He'd borrow off his mother if he ran short. He'd spent most of his cash on a present for Lorraine. He flicked the dead match over into the bushes and went on, 'But you know Sam.'

A moment later, Sam came up from the Burnside as Randy appeared in the opposite direction at the top of the street. Neither of them had a passenger. They pulled up outside of the Miners' Hall practically together.

Both were hardly off their bikes and in the act of taking their helmets off when Peggy came outside.

'Thought I might find you lot out here. Come on Lorry, Mam wants some photos.' She sniffed the air and looked suspiciously at Lorraine. 'Hope you haven't been smoking mind, Lorraine, you know what she'll say.'

'No, no, it was me.' Dave rushed to Lorraine's defence.

'So what if I had?' Lorraine frowned. 'I am old enough, you know, it's not like I'm a kid anymore.'

'Oh yeah, wise old teenager who knows it all, just like we've all been ... Anyhow, come on. Photos. Oh aye, and that Watts kid keeps pestering me. Says you promised to dance with him.'

'You dance with him, you invited him.'

'We had to. His mam goes to your mother's pottery class ... The cheeky bugger asked for an invite.'

'Frightening.' Lorraine pulled a face.

'Yeah. So's his mother.'

As Lorraine's friends trouped past, Peggy whispered in Lorraine's ear, 'And another thing, kiddo ... The ciggies. Think I was born yesterday?'

Lorraine tutted, then hurried on after her friends.

Oasis were belting out 'Cigarettes and Alcohol' as they all went back into the hall and posed for group photos. Lorraine, cheered up slightly when Mavis promised to keep a couple of photos for later and Dave and Jacko lifted her spirits more as they messed around to the music.

When Mavis had taken enough to satisfy the most ardent photographer and was happily smiling at everyone, the five of them made their way over to the corner where Lorraine had spotted some empty seats, Dave stopping on the way to grab a plate of food off the heavily laden table.

Sam frowned as Randy pushed in front of him and made sure he sat next to Lorraine. Quickly Sam side stepped in front of Jacko and grabbed the seat on Loraine's left. His eyes burning into Randy, he sneered and said out of the corner of his mouth, 'Get me a pint Jacko, mate.'

'You've got the bike, you know the rules. No drinking and driving, especially not the amount that goes down your throat once you get started,' Jacko answered.

If no one else could feel the tension coming off Sam, then Jacko certainly could. He knew also that it was directed at Randy, and had been for a week or two now. Things were changing lately and Jacko didn't like it, he wanted everything back like it used to be not so long ago, when the only arguments they had were over Monopoly money or where to go to skateboarding, or which film to watch on a Saturday night. Three of them used to have paper jobs and subsidised the other four if they couldn't beg money from elsewhere to go to the pictures, or Amy used to wheedle money out of her tight-fisted father, but that was before he knew.

'So? I can handle it, Mother Teresa,' Sam snarled back at Jacko, although he was still glaring at Randy.

'Yeah, well get your own.' Jacko turned to Lorraine. 'See you in a bit, OK?'

'Tosser,' Sam muttered as Jacko walked away.

Randy scowled. 'No he's not.'

Dave put the sandwich he'd just taken a bite out of back on the plate and said, around a huge mouthful of ham and bread, 'What the hell's the matter with you, Sam? Seems all you do lately is moan and snarl at us all for nowt. You sound like a bloody old man, for God's sake.'

'Mind your own fucking business.'

'Sam!' Lorraine said. She too had felt the tension coming off him and she was thinking pretty much the same as Jacko. It made her feel uneasy. They had squabbles amongst themselves occasionally over the years, it was only natural, but they had soon made up. Jacko had once, when they were fifteen, refused to speak to Sam for over a month because he went out shooting birds with Jason Smith, but this was different. Sam had been getting digs in at Randy for a few weeks now, and sitting this close, she was certain she could smell whisky on his breath.

'What's the matter, Sam?'

Sam shrugged. 'Does there have to be something the matter?' He curled his lip. 'I only asked him to get me a friggin' drink, for Christ's sake.'

Dave, always the peacemaker, was watching Sam warily. He pushed the plate of food towards him. 'Want a sandwich? Or there's some crab sticks. You like crab sticks, don't you ... Aye?' He picked a crab stick up and practically shoved it under Sam's nose. 'Here, have a crab stick.'

Sam snatched the crabstick and threw it at Dave. 'Shove the fucking crab stick up your arse. Fucking tit.'

'No need for that,' Randy said quietly.

Sam was on his feet instantly, surprising all of them. He held his fists up. Glaring at Randy, he snarled, 'Wanna make something of it, do you?'

'No.' Randy shook his head.

'Come on, outside. Now.' Sam was so fired up he adopted a boxer's stance and urged Randy outside with his hands.

'Sam!' Lorraine squealed, her voice a mixture of disappointment and amazement.

Looking at her face, Sam held still for a moment, then slowly dropped his fists to his side and mumbled something that might have been sorry. Then, in a clearer tone and making eye contact with none of them, he said, 'Sod it, I'm going to the bar.'

He pushed past Dave, his anger evident in the set of his jaw and the heavy tread of his feet as he made his way across the floor, ignoring Jacko, who was talking to Uncle Harry. Sam passed them and went to the other side of the bar.

'Take no notice of him Lorry, you know what he's like sometimes. If things ain't going his way he's not playing,' Dave said, and Randy nodded his agreement. Dave went on, 'Don't fret, he'll be alright in the morning and be at the station with the rest of us to see you off, you know he will.'

'But what set him off in the first place?'

'Does anything have to? You know what he's been like this last year.' Dave reached for another sandwich then changed his mind; his fingers hovering over the plate he decided to go for a sausage roll. 'It's them kids doing his head in,' he nodded as he popped the mini sausage roll into his mouth.

Lorraine sighed and Randy took hold of her elbow. 'Come on, let's dance. He'll come round ... You're supposed to be the party girl, you know.'

'OK, might as well.' Lorraine rose awkwardly and pulled at the hem of her skirt.

'Nice legs, Lorry. How come I never noticed them before?' Dave grinned, as Lorraine playfully slapped the back of his head.

The Stone Roses were replaced by Pulp's, 'Do You Remember The First Time?' as they walked on to the dance floor. Randy smiled and opened his arms.

For a moment Lorraine didn't know quite what to do. She'd danced with the guys before, and Randy was certainly the best dancer of them all, with Jacko taking a close second. The others both had two left feet. But she'd never really danced up close like Randy was obviously wanting. Then she caught sight of the bar over Randy's shoulder.

Sam's eyes were evil slits, his mouth mean. He raised his glass and swallowed the whisky down in one gulp, then slammed the glass on the bar. From the other side of the bar, Jacko was watching Sam, a deep frown covering his usually friendly, easy-going face.

Darren Watts put his empty glass on the bar, accidentally knocking Sam's elbow.

'Watch it. Fucking creep,' Sam snarled.

Darren looked the other way, his face red as he muttered, 'Sorry.'

'I'll show you sorry.' Sam stepped towards him.

'Leave it,' Jacko said from across the bar as Watts walked quickly away.

'It's him!' Sam snapped at Jacko. 'Him, not me. *Him*. The fucking creep.'

On the dance floor Lorraine blinked, Randy was whispering something in her ear.

'What?' she stepped backwards.

Randy shrugged. 'Just thought you might like one last ride on the bike – you know, you're gonna be away for years.'

'Erm ...'

Randy grinned. 'You know what I mean. It'll be months before we all see you again.'

Why not, she thought. *I love Randy's bike and the party's winding down, we could go for a ride and Randy could drop me off at Sara's 'cos I really can't believe that Sara hasn't turned up to my leaving do, there's got to be something wrong, and her parents don't have a phone.*

Sighing, she looked at Randy. 'OK, give me a minute and I'll tell me mam.'

Randy nodded. Wearing the biggest smile ever he went over to Dave. 'We're going for a ride.'

'Where we going, like?'

'Not you, dumbo, me and Lorry.'

'Oh aye, where youse gonna ride too?'

Randy shrugged. 'Probs along the High Lane then over to the Ryhope road.'

'Come on.' Lorraine poked Randy's back. 'We can't be too long, the Hippy and the Rock Chick said I have to be back in half an hour to say goodnight to everybody. Thought they were gonna throw a fit when I said I was going for a bike ride. Jesus!'

'Come on then.' Randy tapped Dave's shoulder. 'See you in a bit, mate.'

'Yeah, we won't be long, Dave.' Lorraine smiled at Dave. On a sudden impulse she leaned over and touched Dave's cheek as if suddenly realising that this was the end of a chapter in her life and things were never going to be the same again. They were all growing up now, moving into the adult world.

Dave touched her hand as if understanding everything she was thinking. He smiled as he said, 'Aye, see youse.'

The door was closing behind them when Sam came out of the toilets. 'What the ...?' he muttered.

He looked over to the bar. Jacko was still there; having abandoned Harry, he was now chatting up Lisa Cotton.

Huh. No action there mate!

His eyes scoured the room, then he glanced back to their seats where Dave was talking to a couple of girls on the next table, both of them blonde, pretty, and obviously sisters. Lorraine's cousins from Newcastle. They had all met up before. Sam remembered fancying one of them like mad, a year or two ago, but they looked enough like each other to be twins and he couldn't remember which one it was.

So it was Lorraine and Randy going out the door. 'Bastards.' Sam clenched his fists and barely refrained from stamping on the floor as his temper soared.

She couldn't have gone for a fag 'cos Dave's still in here. He looked round the room again and gritted his teeth before muttering, 'What the fuck does Randy think he's playing at, the fucking prick?'

Fists still locked, he strode over to Dave, who was in the process of moving seats so he could sit a little closer to the cousins.

'Where the fuck they gone?' Sam demanded when he reached the table.

'What?' Dave was puzzled for a moment.

'Stop playing dumb, arsehole, you know who I'm talking about. Them two ... Lorraine and fucking Randy.'

Dave shrugged. 'Dunno.'

'Yes you fucking do.'

The cousins looked at each other, a silent message passing between them. Then they stood up together and, after giving Sam dirty looks which went way over his head, they smiled at Dave and promised to see him later.

'Now look what you've done,' Dave moaned when the girls were gone. 'I was in there!'

'Like fuck you were. Tell me where Lorry and that fucking prat are.'

'Told you, I don't know.' Nervously Dave reached for a sausage roll. Sam was his friend and had been for as long as he could remember, but Dave had always feared Sam's temper, which could flare up at any time, and lately it seemed to be getting worse. *It's like anything's setting him off lately*, he thought, his hand searching for his mouth.

Knocking the food out of Dave's hand, Sam grabbed his wrist. Squeezing hard, then twisting it savagely, he demanded once more, speaking each word slowly and menacingly as his fingers dug harder and harder. 'I'll ask you one more time ... Where the fuck have they gone?'

'Fuck off,' Dave squealed as he tried to reclaim his wrist, but Sam was by far the stronger. He twisted Dave's wrist again, feeling the bones begin to give under the skin. 'It'll be your fucking neck if you don't tell me. I promise.'

'Get off ... It's hurting, you prick.'

Sam squeezed harder, his fingernails drawing blood, his face showing neither mercy nor concern for his lifelong friend. Unable to bear the pain any longer and frightened in case something in his wrist was about to snap, Dave caved in.

'Alright, alright, I'll tell you, just get off me hand will you ... Get off!'

'Well?' Sam demanded as, wincing with pain and glaring up at him, Dave rubbed his wrist.

'Fucking hurry up,' Sam demanded, reaching for Dave's other hand.

'The High Lane. They went up there. OK, happy now?'

'Where else?'

Dave sighed again before blurting angrily, 'And on to the Ryhope road ... And that's all I know. For Christ's sake, they've only gone for a bloody bike ride, and what the fuck's it gotta do with you anyhow? You the boss now, eh?'

Sam glared at Dave and what he said next sent a chill through Dave's body, 'She's mine, right ... *Mine*. Understand? She always has been and she always will be, OK? And I'll teach the bastard to mess with *my* girl.'

'She's not your girl,' Dave snapped back at him, keeping a tight hold on his wrist. 'She's nobody's girl, she's a mate. Just like Randy's a mate.'

'Yeah? We'll soon see about that.' Sam spun round and hurried out of the hall.

Outside he ran into Darren Watts who sidestepped to get out of Sam's way, only it didn't work because Sam stepped the same way. 'Fuck off, creep.' Sam launched his fist at Watts, connecting with his chin. Watts went down and Sam stepped over him. 'You fancy her an' all, don't you? And the others. I've seen the way you look at her, dirty filthy bastard.'

He kicked Watts as he struggled to get up, the kick landed on his ribs. Watts grabbed his side and sinking back to the ground eyed Sam, hate singeing the air between them.

'They're only nice to you sometimes 'cos they feel sorry for you, fucking ugly creep. Understand, eh? Do you? But all *you* want to do is get into their knickers.'

'How do you know I already haven't?' Darren Watts muttered.

'What?'

'You heard,' Watts smirked.

'Bastard ... Lying bastard. No way.' He kicked Watts again and again, but Watts just kept on grinning.

With his rage at an all-time high Sam smashed his fist into Watts' face once more before running for his bike.

Jacko had seen Sam storm out and, with a puzzled look on his face, left the bar and went over to Dave, who was still rubbing his wrist and staring into the remains of the lager he'd had for over the past hour.

'What the hell's going on with him?' Jacko asked, his frown growing deeper when he saw the red marks on Dave's arm, guessing that Sam was responsible.

Dave shook his head, still staring into his glass.

'Dave?'

'I er ... I think ... I think I've fucked up royally this time mate,' he replied after a moment.

'How's that?' Jacko asked, the hairs on the back of his neck standing up.

'Sam wanted to know where Randy and Lorraine were, and ... And I told him. He's so mad he's practically foaming at the mouth ... And he's been hitting the whisky hard, downed three that I know of in no time.' He sighed and looked up at Jacko. 'I think he's gone after Randy, mate, and the mood he's in he'll ...' Dave shook his head. 'He's frightening, man. I think he's really lost it this time.'

'Shit.'

'Yeah, fucking deep an' all.' Dave reached for his glass and drained the dregs, slapped it down on the table and shook his head before saying, 'And I've dropped them right in it.'

'Come on.'

'Where we going?'

'To find them all before Sam does something really fucking stupid. God!' he snapped, and Dave shuddered. 'We should've seen this coming, Dave.'

The colour drained from Dave's face, making his acne stand out even more against the paleness of his skin. 'I shouldn't have told him. He's been acting crazy lately, hasn't he?' Shaking his head, he stood up. 'If anything happens it'll be my fault won't it? All my fault.'

Not one for pulling punches, Jacko said 'Yup' as he hurried towards the door.

His heart sinking fast, his mind going into overdrive thinking of what might, what could, what probably would happen, Dave followed Jacko.

Outside, Jacko stopped dead in his tracks. Nearly bumping into him, Dave moved round and saw the pool of blood.

'What the hell?' Dave said.

Jacko shook his head, then looked up the deserted street. 'Dunno what's happened here Dave, but I wouldn't be surprised if Sam's got something to do with it.'

Staring at the blood, Dave chewed his lip. *Is this my fault?* he wondered as he climbed on his bike.

CHAPTER FIVE

Lorraine clung to Randy, her arms tight around his waist, the smell of leather from his jacket making her nose tingle as the bike hurtled along the deserted road towards Ryhope. As they approached Burdon village Randy slowed down, then pulled the bike to a stop outside of a small copse of trees on their left.

Loosening her grip, Lorraine said, 'What have we stopped for?'

Randy jumped off the bike and, taking his helmet off, he licked his dry lips and everything he had planned to say melted from his head. He could only marvel at how beautiful she was in the moonlight as she stepped off the bike, took her helmet off and shook her mane of blonde hair loose.

Still waiting for an answer, Lorraine flinched a moment later when Randy grabbed her and pulled her roughly towards him and quickly, before she realised what was happening, covered her mouth with his.

Lorraine smelled spearmint chewing gum on his breath that totally failed to cover the garlic he'd had at dinnertime.

'Oi! Get off!' she yelled, pushing him as hard as she could. 'What the hell are you playing at, Randy?' she wiped her mouth with the back of her hand. 'Urrggg.'

Randy fell backwards, twisting his ankle, but he jumped quickly to his feet. Discomforted by the intensity of his glare, Lorraine said, 'Come on Randy, stop pissing about, I want to go back now.'

'But I don't, Lorry.' His voice was sullen as he looked at her from under lowered lids.

'Tough. Get on the flaming bike, will you?' Lorraine yelled, moving towards the bike. 'Or I'll drive it myself and bloody well leave you here to walk home.'

Lorraine had never seen Randy like this before, he had never in all the years she'd known him been sullen or violent in any way. She knew that Randy was kind, not like most of his family, who were into all sorts of trouble – even his sister was best kept away from.

If anything, she thought, Randy was even softer than Dave. Sam was the hothead, though even he was careful of Jacko, who could truly handle himself if he had to. Thank God Jacko was mostly even tempered and sort of the leader, if they had to have one.

What the hell has got into him?

Randy took the keys out of his pocket and jangled them in her face. Angrily, she snatched for them, but Randy was quicker. Not quick enough to avoid the hard slap on his face that came next though.

'What you do that for?' he asked, full of amazement as he stepped back rubbing his right cheek.

'What for? You're losing the bloody plot, you are. Where do you get off, trying something like that? Jesus.'

He sighed and the mask melted away, leaving the real Randy.

'You're right, I'm sorry Lorraine,' he said awkwardly a moment later. 'I was right out of order.'

'Huh.'

'Shit, no, *no*, please, I really am ... I shouldn't have ... *Shit*. It's just that you're going away ...' he ran his fingers around the edge of his helmet, looking at the ground, afraid now to meet her eyes. He reminded her of the day they had started school and he had offered her his blue lunchbox, practically forcing it on her because she said it was nice. 'And', he went on, still not daring to look up, 'I was frightened in case you met some other guy, and ... Well, you know.' He lifted his face.

Are those tears in his eyes? she thought, her heart feeling a tiny pang of guilt. *Damn!*

For a moment she didn't know what to say, she felt awkward and couldn't find the words. Randy was one of the guys, a mate, and that's what she thought of him as: a good mate she would do anything for.

Shit. What the hell should I do?

Tell him the truth.

She hesitated a moment, then her words came out in a rush, tumbling over each other. 'Oh Randy, I love you like a brother, I always have. You and the rest of the guys ... My four brothers. And Sara and Amy are like the sisters I never had, but us lot, we have something special ... You know this.'

'I know, *I know*, and you're right ... But who would have thought that the gangly five year old with eyes too big for her face, and plaits reaching to her waist, and who even then could climb trees better than any of us ...' he sighed, paused a moment, then went on quietly. 'Who would have thought you were ever gonna turn out like you have?'

'Now you're making me blush.' Lorraine was pleased that the situation was defused. She really had never seen Randy act like that before and it had slightly unnerved her. She batted him playfully with her helmet. 'Come on, Randy. Let's get back.'

Randy sighed again, feeling embarrassed now that he'd made a fool of himself and worried about what the others would think of him. 'OK. Er, Lorraine, you won't say anything to the others? Like, you won't tell them what I said?'

Lorraine smiled. 'Our secret, Randy.'

'Thanks, Lorry. You're a good 'un.' He smiled his relief.

Together they got on the bike, Randy revved up, then they were off. They'd just reached Reg Vardy's garage and were slowing down to cross the dual carriageway when Sam appeared across the road. He revved his engine when he saw them and, without looking either way, he screeched across the tarmac.

'Fucking hell,' Randy muttered under his breath. He knew exactly why Sam was there and what he was thinking. Quickly, and feeling fear in his gut like he never had before, he turned his bike and took off in the direction they had just come from.

'What's going on?' Lorraine yelled, fearing Randy was having second thoughts and was maybe trying to run away with her, but her words were snatched by the wind.

Jacko and Dave were a split second behind Sam and made it across the dual carriageway in one piece, catching up with the others just as Sam became level with Randy.

'What the fuck?' Jacko muttered under his breath as Sam edged his bike closer to Randy's.

'Oh my God!' Dave screamed, risking a quick look around Jacko's shoulder.

'Pull over, Randy,' Jacko yelled. 'For God's sake. Before the crazy bastard runs you off the road!'

But Randy couldn't hear, he panicked and his answer was to go faster. Sam, all caution gone and the speed fuelling his anger, accelerated to keep up with him.

Lorraine, absolutely terrified now, knowing the real reason for Randy's sudden about turn, was clinging on to him as if her life depended on it. The speed they were going and the fear in her gut told her it did. Her fingers were digging into his stomach, her nails drawing blood the way Sam had drawn blood from Dave, and she was praying for Sam to go away or for Randy to stop. Helpless, all she could do was to dig her knees tighter and hold on the best she could, frightened that at any moment she was going to die before she'd

really had a chance to live, crying tears that were dried instantly by
the wind.

CHAPTER SIX

The black Jeep came from nowhere. One moment the road ahead was clear, the next the huge, roaring 4x4 came soaring up a dip in the road like some huge primordial beast ready to devour them in moments.

Sam swerved to the left, the smell of burning rubber filling the air, the screech of his brakes harsh and frightening. His bike leapt out from under him, crash landing and skidding across the road, and he hit the ground rolling and continued over and over until he came to a stop ten yards away. Behind him, Jacko managed to slow, but not enough. Sam's bike was in the way and he hit it full on and went into a spin. Dave was thrown off and landed on the grass verge, which saved his life but broke his arm in three places. Jacko's bike dragged Sam's bike another ten yards down the road. The angry screech of metal scraping against the tarmac seemed to go on forever. It ended when both bikes landed on top of Jacko.

Randy hit the 4x4 dead centre. Lorraine, her screams filling the night, was flung off in the same way as Dave had been and landed in a field.

The driver of the 4x4 – a middle-aged woman named Brenda Sweeny – was too shocked to make a sound, though her mouth hung open in a parody of a scream. She feared that everyone around her was dead, but knew without doubt that the young man who had hit her was. She was staring in horror at his decapitated head in her lap and feeling the blood, his blood, a young life's blood, run down her legs. She looked from his head to the shattered windscreen, visualising the shocking moment of impact. A low moaning sound came from deep inside of her, building momentum until it left her throat seconds later. The sound tore the fabric of the night.

She knew deep inside of her panic that she needed to get to her phone, which was in her bag on the back seat. Slowly, her hands trembling erratically, her heart pounding so hard she thought it was going to burst at any minute, and trying as hard as she could not to vomit, she reached for the head. Controlling her instinct to push it off her lap and thanking God it was face down, she picked it up and the scream erupted again.

For a frozen moment, she couldn't move. Then crying, screaming, shaking, she placed the severed head on the seat next to her, turning quickly away as what she was praying not to happen did ... the head rolled over. But she was not quite quick enough and the image of the mangled flesh that once resembled a face would haunt her for as long as she lived.

She sobbed frantically as she called the ambulance amidst the heavy, sickening smell of petrol and the deathly silence just before the birds took flight and blotted out the stars.

Dave shook himself and groaned loudly as pain shot through his arm from his elbow to his wrist. Instinctively he knew it was broken, the same arm had been broken a few years ago in football practice and the pain was identical. For a moment he lay still, then, pretty sure it was just his arm, apart from a dull ache in his left knee, he sat up hugging his arm to his chest and groaning with the strain of it.

The first thing he saw was a tall, thin woman, dark hair wiping her face in the wind that had sprung up, holding one of those huge mobile phones to her ear. She was screaming something into it but his own ears were still ringing and he guessed she was calling for help. The next thing his senses alerted him to was the stink of petrol. He looked around and nearly bit his tongue off when he saw Randy. The front half of his friend's body was through the windscreen and lying inside of the 4x4, his legs and arms splayed open and unmoving on the bonnet.

He tasted blood and spat. 'Oh, God, no. Please! Please. Randy. *Randy!* he yelled.

He knew deep inside though that prayers were no good, it was too late. Randy was dead. No one could have gone through that windscreen and lived.

'Could he?' he muttered. 'People have survived worse. Haven't they? Course they have ... Randy!' For a moment his heart lifted and he yelled with all the strength he could find. '*Randy!*

Forgetting all about his broken arm, he let it flop as tears streamed down his face, and nearly passed out when his wrist, the same wrist that Sam had tortured, hit the ground.

Trying his best to ignore the pain, he began yelling, 'Randy ... Somebody help Randy!' Wildly, his heart pounding, he looked around for the others, but there was no sign of Lorraine, Sam or Jacko. He shivered and blinked rapidly when he saw the bikes piled on top of each other, as if lying abandoned and unloved in an old scrap yard.

He looked at the woman who, phone tucked away, was now coming towards him. Then his eyes caught up with his brain ... Something had moved under the bikes. He froze for a moment. 'Shit, the petrol!' He clambered up just as the woman reached him.

'No, no! Sit back down, you mustn't move.' Placing her hands on his shoulders, she gently tried to ease him back down into a sitting position; as agitated as he was he could still feel her hands shaking through his jacket.

'No!' he yelled, panicking. 'Somebody's under the bikes! The petrol ... the petrol could blow at any time!' He pushed her away with his shoulder and, holding his arm, ran in a painful lopsided hobble towards the bikes.

The woman hesitated, knowing the risks, her body swaying forward then back. Making her mind up, she swallowed hard, then, as if on an invisible string, followed Dave.

'It's Jacko. Oh, God, it's Jacko ... Jacko, are you alright? Please say you're alright. Talk to me, Jacko. For God's, sake talk to me ... Wake him up, wake him up!' he yelled to the woman, panic lifting his voice to a squeal.

Jacko was in no state to talk to anyone. He was unconscious or dead. Dave wasn't quite sure which. He could see, though, that part of his face had been nearly torn off, blood was seeping everywhere, and one of his legs was trapped under the first bike and twisted in a fashion that neither God nor nature had intended.

'Doesn't it mean you're still alive if you're bleeding?'

Dave looked up at Brenda Sweeny, begging in his heart for her to say yes. He knew that he was lying to himself about Randy. No one could anyone have gone through that windscreen and live.

Could he? And Lorraine and Sam, where were they? Where the fuck were they?

Brenda Sweeny's face held no answer for him. There was nothing to read there but a blank, dazed space. She gave a slight shrug along with a deep sigh, and said as she watched the steady trickle of petrol dripping from the top bike, 'We can try to get him out, but we have to be quick.'

Together, they managed to get the first bike off, mostly by Dave using his feet to kick it upright. With Jacko free from the chest up, Brenda dropped to her knees and put her ear to his chest, unaware that the hem of her coat was soaking up petrol.

At last, after what seemed forever, she stood up, turned to Dave, who had been holding his breath in fear, and nodded.

'Oh, thank God.' Dave's knees went weak with relief, 'Thank you, God. Come on, come on, we have to move him even though you're not supposed to.'

Slowly they lifted the other bike, with Dave crouching underneath and taking the weight, even though the pain in his arm was nearly unbearable, and praying hard for her to be quick. Brenda dragged Jacko's body away from the bikes and petrol. Dave gently eased the bike down to the road. He was about to stand up when he saw an eyeball staring accusingly at him, caught on the twisted handle bar.

Oh ... No, he thought, biting down on the sudden, frightening urge to giggle. *NO!* Forgetting all about his broken arm he quickly scrambled backwards and didn't even feel the pain when his shoulder hit the ground. Jacko's eye continued staring at him.

'Help me,' Brenda Sweeny shouted at him. 'Hurry up, the lot might blow.'

Rolling over on to his good side, Dave eased up into a sitting position and from there managed to rise. Reaching Jacko and Brenda, he shoved his good arm down inside Jacko's coat and caught hold of the belt around his waist, unable to look at his friend's face, knowing what was missing under that swell of blood and torn flesh. He dragged Jacko along the road, with Brenda gasping but doing her best to carry Jacko's ankles. In the end her own pain was so intense she had to give up.

A few moments later they were far enough away to feel safe. Gently they eased Jacko, who had been unconscious throughout, on to the grass verge. Slowly, with trembling fingers and huge, heart-rending sobs, Dave eased the flap of flesh that was the side of Jacko's face back into place. Both he and Brenda heaved sighs of relief when a moment later they heard the sound of sirens in the distance. Dave flopped on to the verge beside Jacko, his good hand still holding on to his friend's face.

The first bike, never really steady, began to slowly slip, gathering momentum on its slide. The metal handle bar hit the ground. It was then, with a sudden loud thump and a violent roar, that the bikes blew. Throwing herself down next to Dave, Brenda screamed as they watched large tongues of yellow and red flames race each other for the sky as if they were trying to escape the very jaws of hell.

'Run!' Dave yelled, mesmerised by the display in front of them. 'There's petrol on you. I can smell it.'

Brenda's heart lurched, gamely she tried to run, but her chest hurt and, gasping for air, her whole body shaking with fear, she slid down on to the road clutching her left arm.

'Shit!' Dave scrambled up, staring in terror at the tongue of fire that was snaking along the road towards them.

CHAPTER SEVEN

Dave grabbed hold of Brenda and, heaving with the weight of her, he managed to get her upright. Moaning, she immediately bent over and clutched at her chest.

'Oh, dear God.' Guessing that she was having a heart attack, Dave panicked and laid her quickly back down on the verge next to Jacko. He swung his head round to the road and gasped as the fire bobbed and weaved ever closer.

What to do?

There were tears in his eyes as he looked around for something, anything, to put out the flames. Then he gasped. 'Soil!' he muttered, and was answered by another moan from Brenda.

Frantically looking around for something to use and finding nothing, he grabbed a handful of the dark earth, cursing the fact that he could only use one hand. He took the few steps to the leading flames and deposited the soil a few inches in front of it then hurried back for more. As the flames were licking at the first drop of soil he threw another handful on top and watched, his heart pounding as they started to fizzle and die. Quickly he hurried back to Jacko and, wiping his hand on his jeans to rid them of the soil, he again picked up the flap of skin and flesh and gently eased it into place.

The ambulance finally arrived, the male driver and a female medic jumped quickly out of each side. Dave's whole body was now shaking uncontrollably, but he insisted on looking for his other two friends. Gently, he moved his hand from Jacko's face. 'You stay with him,' he said to Brenda, who although ashen faced was now sitting up. 'Sit here and keep hold of his ... his ... I'm gonna look for Lorraine and Sam.' He glanced over towards the 4x4 and Randy still spread eagled across the bonnet, sniffed loudly, then hung his head.

Watching him, Brenda Sweeny sobbed, remembering the young man's face as in her mind his head slowly turned and stared up at her. She knew for certain that she would see that image forever. It was imprinted on her mind now and would never go away. 'He, he's dead,' she muttered.

The medics reached them and started work on Jacko. The woman heard what Brenda had said and glanced at Randy.

Dave looked at her and saw in her eyes that there was no doubt at all. Tears rolled unchecked down his face. 'It's all my fault,' he muttered. 'All my fault.'

Turning to Brenda, he said, 'And there's loads of glass in your hair.' He then went to look for his missing friends, fearing the worst with each step he took.

'I know,' Brenda said miserably to Dave's retreating back. She could feel blood running down her neck, and had done since she got out of the Jeep.

'Where's the other one?'

Dave stopped, knowing she meant Sam. He looked up the long winding country road. Sam was nowhere in sight.

Brenda shook her head, showering tiny shards of glass everywhere.

A moment later they both froze as an ear-piercing scream from the field across the road startled them.

'Lorraine,' Dave whispered, looking in fear in the direction that the scream had come from, as it came again and again.

CHAPTER EIGHT

Unable to sleep, Leanne prised the lid off the old green and gold baccy tin with her thumbs. It was bashed and faded but it had belonged to her father. She kept her supply of fag ends in there and rolled the tobacco when she had nothing else to smoke. It tasted lousy but anything was better than nothing.

Slowly trying to keep calm, she rolled a cigarette. As she was putting the lid back on the tin there was a noise at the back door. She frowned. There had been no sound of his bike. Hurriedly, she put the cigarette back in the tin, shoved it down the side of the settee and watched the door.

Still waiting a few minutes later without an appearance from Sam, she decided to go and look in case someone else had taken the opportunity of an unlocked door and was now raiding her kitchen. She glanced at the poker. *Should I?*

'No,' she answered herself, shaking her head as she made her way to the kitchen. 'It'll be our Sam playing silly buggers.'

I'll silly bugger him she thought, going through the kitchen door. 'Oh my God,' she yelped a moment later. 'What the bloody hell's happened to you?'

She hurried over to her brother, who was sitting on the chair, one leg resting on the table, trying to pick grit out of his skin. Judging by the huge amount that she could see, he would be there until next Christmas.

'You've come off that damn bike, haven't you? I warned you that would happen. Now look at the bloody state of you.'

Sam shrugged, his eyes narrow with pain as he kept on plucking the tiny stones out of his leg. His jeans were in tatters and his arms and legs were covered in blood.

He winced as a deeply embedded stone came free. Leanne hurried over to the sink and filled a bowl with warm water. Grabbing a cloth she went to him.

'Are you gonna tell me what happened or not?' She pulled a chair over, sat down and began bathing his leg, giving a wary eye to the other leg, which looked just as bad. His leather jacket was shredded and looking through the tears in the leather she could see his arms had not fared much better.

'Fell off. That's all you need to know,' he replied in a tone that stated 'and that's all you're getting to know'.

'Where's the bike?'

'Wrecked,' he said angrily.

She tutted, then snapped quickly back, 'I hope you weren't bloody racing.'

'I said ...' he snarled back at her.

But Leanne had borne enough. Even if he was injured, his whole attitude stank lately, plus he'd left the kids alone and that really riled her. *And the idiot could have been killed, plus that fucking bike eats more petrol than we eat food. And the door! The fucking door, damn it.*

She pictured the broken door and screamed at him, 'Fuck off with what you said. Everything's about what you said ... What you want to do.' She jumped up, knocking the chair over behind her. 'You left the kids on their own tonight, Sam. Anything could have happened. Anything. Do you understand? I came back and Stacey was terrified to death. What did you leave them for? And I can smell the bloody whisky on your breath, you know what that does to you.'

Sam looked up at her, his eyes narrowed. For a moment there was silence, then he snapped, 'Yeah, and do *you* want to know something?' He yanked his leg away and stood up, towering above her, but Leanne held her ground and his glare as he yelled, 'I'm leaving all of youse, pissing off for good. Now. Tonight. Got that? OK.'

'What?' Her jaw dropped open.

'You heard what I said. I'm fucking sick up to me neck, can't take any friggin' more, and as soon as this mess is cleaned up I'm off. And if anyone comes knocking, you ain't fuckin' seen me and know nowt. Got it?'

Leanne's heart sank. This she had not expected, but a small voice in her head said, *I knew all along he wouldn't stick around.*

'You can't leave ... You can't leave us on our own, you can't, what'll we do?' Fear churned in her stomach.

How will I cope?

What can I do?

Sam was adamant. 'Watch me.'

'But why, what have you done that's so bad you have to run away?'

'Nothing. You deaf or what?'

Leanne's heart raced. 'Yes you have, you *have*, 'cos it's not me and the kids, you're using that as an excuse. It's something you've done, isn't it? *Isn't it?*' She put her hand to her mouth, her thoughts racing as fast as her heart.

'Shut up!' he yelled at her.

'Oh my God, you've ran somebody over, haven't you?' Her voice rose with every word. 'You've killed somebody!'

'I haven't done anything!' he yelled again, but Leanne could see the faint shadow of fear in his eyes. 'Whatever they say, it was an accident. I didn't mean for it to happen. That's the God's honest truth, Leanne I ... I just wanted to frighten him, that's all ... You have to believe me. Whatever they say, it was an accident, understand? An accident.'

'Frighten who? Who the hell were you trying to frighten?'

'Nobody, it doesn't matter. I already told you. It was an accident, a stupid, stupid fucking accident.'

'What was an accident?'

'Fucking shut up!' Sam put his hands over his ears. 'I can't fucking stand it no more! The lot of youse are doing me head in. You, them ... I can't think straight around here anymore. I'm not wasting my life looking after a bunch of kids. Every day me fucking head hurts more than the day before. Shoes, food, clothes. Can't hack it no fucking more.' There were tears in his eyes. 'How the hell can they go through so many fucking shoes?'

'But you promised our mam!' Leanne's voice was even quieter now as she practically whispered, tears running down her face. 'I can't do it on my own ... You promised.'

'NO!' Sam hurried out of the room. Leanne, all energy drained out of her, sank into the kitchen chair.

Five minutes later he was back, wearing fresh jeans, a brown checked shirt, an old blue denim jacket and had a beaten-up rucksack over his shoulder. Leanne had not moved.

Sam looked at her for a moment before going to the back door. Hesitating briefly he turned and said, 'I'll get a job, send some money ... I won't forget you. I promise.'

'You already have,' she replied in a quiet voice.

He looked at her again as if taking a photograph to store in his mind; then without another word or a backward glance he was gone, leaving behind him nothing but an empty space.

Leanne sobbed and, burying her head in her hands, she gazed at her bleak future. *How am I going to manage? Sam's useless and it's like having another kid around most of the time, but at least he's been there and occasionally he came up trumps, but now ... now I've no one.*

CHAPTER NINE

Leanne was still sitting in the same place a half hour later when the police arrived.

When Detective Sanderson knocked, waited and knocked again and still received no answer, he tried the door. He knew someone was up and awake; the lights were still on.

'Hello, anyone there?' He poked his head round the corner and spotted Leanne. 'You alright love?' he asked, stepping into the kitchen and moving towards her when she ignored him. Sanderson could see she'd been crying and his suspicions were aroused. 'We're looking for your brother, love. Has he been home tonight at all?'

Leanne hesitated, her stomach churning with dread, her throat dry. *Dear God, what's he done?*

Looking up at Sanderson, she shook her head. 'No no … Haven't seen him since tea time at the least. Why, what do you want him for, like?'

'There's been an accident with his friends.'

Leanne groaned, her worst fears materialising in front of her. 'Oh, God. Are they all right?'

'I'm afraid not, love,' Sanderson shook his head.

What do you mean?' Her heart was pounding so hard against her ribs she thought her chest would burst. She prayed that Sam was not responsible, that he had not done anything stupid, even though deep inside she knew that he had. *Why would he run if he was innocent?*

'Well,' Sanderson sighed deeply, 'I'm sorry to have to tell you this, pet, but, Randy McCade died tonight.' He paused a moment, gauging her reaction: innocence and fear in her large, luminous eyes. Sanderson went on, 'His head collided with a windscreen when he was hit by a Jeep, by all accounts he was on the wrong side of the road.'

The colour drained from Leanne's face and she felt sick. 'De ... Dead?' she managed a moment later, in a tiny voice. *Please, please God, please don't let Sam be responsible for this.*

'Sorry, but yes, love ... Jacko Musgrove is in intensive care, the poor bugger has lost an eye, and there might be internal injuries, they're checking it out now. Lorraine Hunt and Dave Ridley are what you might call the walking wounded. Your brother is the only one not accounted for.'

Even though she feared that in some way he might be responsible because that terrible temper he possessed had always been his downfall, she knew what others might not – that deep down inside he always deeply regretted later whatever he had done. Her instinct to defend every member of her family at all costs won through and she faced up to Sanderson.

'But how do you know that Sam was there? He, he could have been off on a ride of his own. He do you know? Sometimes ... sometimes he just likes to ride the damn thing.'

'He's always with them love, you know this, that lot's been glued together since they were tots. Plus his bike's there.'

Leanne dropped her eyes. *Shit, forgot about the bike.* She fidgeted a moment with the sleeves of her blouse. Swallowing hard, she muttered, 'I don't, er, I don't know where he is. Haven't seen him in ...' she shrugged, 'ages.'

Sanderson sighed. 'He's not wanted for anything pet, the walking wounded insist that it was an accident, though the lady in the Jeep seems to think someone was doing some pretty aggressive bike riding along a not-so-well-lit road.'

'Did she say it was our Sam?'

'She doesn't know who was riding that bike and it all happened so fast she's not actually certain how many bikes there really were.'

Leanne stood up, took a deep breath and said, 'Well, I still haven't seen him.'

Taking the hint, Sanderson turned to the door. 'OK, if he turns up tell him to give us a ring. A young man lost his life tonight and we need to clarify a few things. Goodnight then, I'll be back in the morning.'

Sanderson did not mention Sara Layton's murder, which had been discovered in the field that Lorraine had been thrown into. For the moment that was under wraps, but if it turned out young Sam had done a runner for whatever reason, then the lad was leaving himself wide open to suspicion.

Leanne nodded, and, replying to Sanderson's goodnight with one of her own, she locked the door behind him. Dragging her feet as if she were fifty years older than her true age, she made her way up to bed.

Five minutes after putting her head on the pillow she was up and frantically burning the clothes Sam had worn that night.

Later she poked the dying embers, wondering why she was doing this. *The copper said it was an accident, but our Sam didn't act like it was an accident. He's guilty as hell of something.*

CHAPTER TEN

'Cheers mate,' Sam said, jumping down from the lorry, doing his best not to wince when the shockwave ran up his legs. The driver, an ex-army man in his early forties, nodded and gave him a salute.

Sam couldn't help but smile even though he felt less like smiling than he had at any time in his life. The driver was a friendly bloke named Max who was at least ten stone overweight. He had picked him up at Durham and dropped him in London, and he now knew everything there was to know, and more, about the Falklands war and life as a squaddie. If the army had once been an option, it most certainly wasn't now.

The lorry pulled out into the early morning traffic and Sam smiled again as Max forced his way into the line, laughing at the pips from the other cars. An angry driver of a blue Mini leaned on his horn as Sam turned and walked away. *As if,* Sam thought, glancing back at the driver.

An hour later he'd found a clean, cheap pad in a back street and he liked the name of the place that Max had dropped him: Kilburn. The landlady, a Mrs Duffy, was a tiny woman with a pink rinse on her tight perm. She spoke with a thick Irish accent and looked about a hundred years old. She walked with a stoop, a cigarette trembled precariously on her bottom lip and as Sam paid a week in advance he waited for the ash to drop off. When he pocketed his receipt and signed in, the ash was a good half inch longer and still clinging to the cigarette.

A bed, a wardrobe and a set of drawers with cigarette burns on the top. In the corner was a tiny sink. Red walls that were claustrophobic to say the least, and red covers on the bed. On top of the gaudy red bedspread was a lemon bath towel (well, he supposed it was once lemon) and a small green hand towel. Shabby but clean, and at least the room didn't smell too bad. It would do for the time being. He didn't intend to be there for very long: if those streets had any gold in them at all, he planned to find it.

And he would start looking tonight.

Opening the top drawer, he took three T-shirts out of his backpack, two blue, one white, a pair of jeans, four pairs of y-fronts and three pairs of socks. He had nothing to hang in the wardrobe as everything else he possessed was on his back.

Worn out, his legs and his arms giving him hell, he decided to go have a shower in the shared bathroom, but first he needed somewhere to stash his cash – all of fifty pounds of his life savings, plus the twenty he'd stolen out of the jar that Leanne kept in the back of the cupboard, where she put money aside each week for emergencies.

He felt a twinge of guilt as he looked at the money, then he tutted. *Fuck it.* Tammy could bloody well wait for shoes. *When I'm rolling in dosh I'll send fucking gold-plated shoes up for the bloody lot of 'em.*

Lighting a cigarette, he looked out the window at the busy street below. 'Guess this is what you'd call an emergency, our young 'un,' he muttered a moment later, his head wreathed in smoke. He noticed a chemist shop across the road and the thought of infection crossed his mind.

Can I afford some TCP or anything?

Can I afford to be ill?

He opted for the TCP.

Nipping the cigarette he put it on the windowsill. Until there was cash coming in he would have to be careful and ease up on the fags, smoke half at a time. He eased his jacket back on, wondering why he'd gone through the pain of taking it off in the first place, and put it down to the heat. Locking the door behind him he tried it and, satisfied that it wouldn't open without a key, headed down the stairs where the front door opened directly on to the street.

In the chemist shop he was served by a young girl with short black hair, and for a moment he was reminded of Leanne, but he shook the guilty thoughts away. He was on his own, a stranger in a strange land, he had to look out for number one.

He smiled at the girl as she handed his change over. 'Any good night life around here, then?'

Her smile had dimples when she replied in an Irish accent, 'Oh for sure, there's a few good clubs.'

He spoke with her a further ten minutes, flirting lightly, getting as much information as he could about the place he would, for the time being, be calling home, then went back to his room. Twenty minutes later, bathed and medicated, he lay stretched out on his bed, hands behind his head and staring at the ceiling.

He hadn't meant to hurt Randy.

Fucking hell ... No way.

Just maybes rough him up a bit, I'm not that fucking stupid, the McCades are an evil bunch and not to be crossed.

Randy'll be alright, sure he will ... Probably just knocked out, that's all.

It was an accident. He's one of me best mates, for Christ's sake.

Wonder if the others are alright?

He started to drift off. 'I'll call Dave tonight,' he sighed as his eyes fluttered, then closed.

Seven hours later, refreshed, dressed and ready to go looking for a job, he used the few coins he had in his pocket to phone Dave from a payphone on the corner.

'Is that you, Dave?'

'Sam!'

'Aye ... what er ... How's everybody?'

Before Dave could answer, Sam hurried on, 'Alright are they? Course they're a tough bunch, aren't they? A spill off a bike wouldn't hurt that fucking lot would it?' he laughed.

There was a deep silence on the line for a moment, and then Dave brought Sam up to date on everything.

Sam, palms sweating, heart rate up, began to panic. He'd suspected that Randy was at the least very badly hurt, or even, though his mind had shied away from the thought, dead. But to actually have it confirmed was like he'd been hit over the head with a six-foot-wide hammer. *And Jacko's in a bad way an' all. Shit.*

'It was an accident, Dave,' he blustered, his heart sinking, knowing that he could never go home again. The McCades would never forget. Not ever.

'They found Sara.'

The last thing Sam wanted to hear was about Sara, who had probably been off in a huff like she usually was. His own skin was on the line with the McCades, for God's sake. Ignoring what Dave had said he hurried on. 'I didn't want for Randy to be dead ... Fucking hell, you gotta believe me. We've been mates for years. I ... I can't ever remember when we weren't mates.' His tears, hot and fast, splashed on the floor of the phone box. 'You gotta believe me Dave,' he pleaded.

'I do,' Dave said quietly.

'It wasn't my fault.'

'I know. *I know.*'

A long-drawn-out silence again, then just before Sam put the phone down he said, 'It was all your fault Dave. You shouldn't have told me where they were.'

CHAPTER ELEVEN

Sam walked into the crowded pub and headed right for the bar, an unstoppable angry force. Feeling his presence, people moved over, wondering who the stranger was.

'Whisky,' he demanded of the barman and was served instantly. He downed the drink in one gulp, put his glass on the bar and nodded to the barman for another. It came as quickly as the first one had and vanished in much the same way.

Sam slowed down after the fourth, the anger subsiding as a mellow haze glazed over the ache and the fate of his friends. The barman caught his eye and raised his eyebrows in a question. Sam shook his head. He needed to set his plan in action. He'd been told that this bar was under the protection of the hardest man in the area, a man that people were so terrified of they used his name to frighten their kids into obedience.

To secure a door job, the only job he could think of that didn't need qualifications – well, some qualifications, and those he had: strong arms and a strong back and a good right hook – he had to prove in here that he could handle himself.

He took time out to survey his surroundings: nothing special, the bar was on the wall facing the door, all the usual optics behind the bar, red carpet that looked clean enough and wasn't sticky to walk on, the brass was highly polished and there was what looked like a small room off to the right. In the left-hand corner a medium-sized pool table held the interest of a couple of youths, one fat with at least three chins and the other as skinny as a beanpole. Four old men, though he had to squint to see them through the haze of smoke, stared at him from a table close to the other side of the bar. He winked at them, then turned back to look at the room through the mirrored bar.

The opportunity he'd been waiting for came within ten minutes: a drunken redhead, wearing the shortest skirt Sam had ever seen. Her large breasts were fighting each other to see which one spilled out of the skimpy black top first. She didn't even look old enough to drink coffee never mind booze and was hanging on to the arm of a tall guy. As they moved towards him she tripped and nearly fell at Sam's feet. Sam picked her up and, squeezing her breast, he laughed in her face.

Silence fell and all eyes turned to the tall guy, who Sam now noticed had what looked like an old knife scar running diagonally from his left temple to the bottom of his right ear.

'Get your fucking hands off my fucking bird,' he shouted, pushing people out of the way and moving quickly towards Sam.

Sam squeezed harder. The girl squealed and lashed out at him with her handbag. 'What do you think you're doing? Get off me you fucking perv.'

Another Irish, he thought, catching the bag and throwing it at Scarface. *Must have crossed the fucking sea to Ireland in me sleep.*

Reaching Sam, the man pulled back his fist. 'Fucking cheeky bastard. Think you can just walk in here off the streets and do what you want, who the fuck are you?'

'Me name's Sam.'

'A fucking Geordie. I might have fucking known.'

'Well … Not quite, but close enough.'

'Yeah, that right? Well fuck off back up north where you belong, you fucking crazy bastard.'

He launched his clenched fist with the speed of an explosion. Ready and waiting, Sam ducked and came in under the man's arm, grabbed hold of his ears, pulled his head down and nutted him. Wearing a stunned expression, Scarface went down immediately. The girl, who had been screaming at an alarming frequency, stopped in mid-scream and the pub fell silent. Two old men, who had been taking bets, stared in amazement as their champion hit the ground.

With a satisfied smirk Sam turned and walked out. He'd done enough for tonight, word would soon spread, and the right people would come looking.

PART TWO

THE MIDDLE YEARS

CHAPTER TWELVE
1996

'OK,' Big Jim Malloy boomed as Skinny Smith walked into the bar, while Sam watched from the shadows at the back of the empty room. 'I've heard it said that you've took a shine to my Missus, that right?' Big Jim thrust his head forward threateningly.

Skinny Smith's skin faded from mottled red to white and grey patches. 'Who, me?' he asked in total amazement, his heart palpitating at an alarming rate.

'Well I'm not fucking talking to the clock on the fucking wall am I, eh?'

Skinny Smith was as tall as Big Jim, but the resemblance ended there. Big Jim was exactly that: big everywhere. Skinny Smith, at six foot two, barely weighed in at eight and a half stone.

'Marie and me? Are you for fucking real? Like she would even look at me,' Skinny managed to say, past the tightness in his throat and the hammering of his heart that was getting louder and louder in his ears. *As if she would dare, for fuck's sake, as if I would dare.*

Big Jim moved forward again and didn't stop this time until the toes of his steel-capped boots were touching the toes of Skinny's shoes. 'That's what I've been told, Skinny. And we all know you like the ladies.' He thrust his large fleshy face into Skinny's until their noses were nearly touching. 'I have it on good authority that you, you skinny bastard, are humping my wife. I learned a long time ago that there's no fucking smoke without fire.'

The punch, not unexpected, but damn fast, came then and snapped one of Skinny's ribs. Skinny clutched his side and groaned, the pain showing on his face.

'It's all lies, tell him, Sam,' Skinny pleaded, backing away. 'Tell him, for fuck's sake, before he fucking kills me!'

Sam stepped forward and shrugged. 'What can I say, mate? I heard the same rumours.'

Skinny gasped. 'But you know it's not true!' He swung his head back to Big Jim. 'You know I wouldn't. For fuck's sake, you know Marie wouldn't.' He wasn't just fighting for his own life now, he was fighting for Marie's. This had happened before, three years ago, with Big Jim's second wife, Amy. Someone had spread malicious rumours about Amy and the head bouncer on the night club door, and within an hour of Big Jim hearing, both of them were dead.

'Sam!' Skinny pleaded. But Sam was in the shadows again, a sly smirk on his face.

Oh, God. Swiftly, Skinny put it together. *The sly bastard, he took over as head bouncer, and now he's after my job. The bastard, the devious, fucking traitor ... The bastard!*

'It ...' Eyes wide with sheer terror, his finger was ready to point at Sam, but too late. Big Jim whipped the gun out of his pocket with practised ease, pulled the trigger, and Skinny slid down the wall, leaving a trail of blood and matter behind him, dead the moment the bullet entered his heart.

'Clear it up, Sam,' Big Jim said, walking past his new second.

Staring down at the body, Sam flinched slightly when the door slammed shut behind Big Jim. He breathed deeply, controlling himself. You never showed any weakness around Big Jim. Even though he'd gone he could pop back in at any minute and the trembling in his hands would definitely be noticeable.

This was not the first time he'd looked down at a dead body. In Big Jim's employment there had been many of them, and for various reasons, some of them so trivial that he'd reached home still gasping from the effect of watching a man driven crazy with pain hours before he died. Big Jim also had many ways for a woman to wish in her final moments that she had never been born.

Sam shook his head. Big Jim was a psychopath and a fucking big one at that. Half Irish and half Scottish, it seemed at times that he was raging his own war against anyone who was not of Scottish or Irish extraction. If you were, you stood a chance of living and, if you crossed him in any way, you would be permanently damaged.

Sam had figured this out early and invented an Irish grandfather and thrown in a Scottish great grandmother for good measure.

He nudged Skinny with his toe, double-checking that the man was indeed dead, then went to the door. Opening it, he poked his head round the corner, spotted Alf almost at once, and gestured with his head for him to come in.

Alf was a small, stocky man with a bald head and a thick Scottish accent. He peeled his body away from the wall he'd been leaning on and moved towards Sam. A tall gangly youth in a black T-shirt with a grinning skull on the front followed him. No one except perhaps Alf knew the youth's real name, everyone called him Goth. His long, dyed black hair hung past his shoulders, his cold dark eyes were rimmed with black liner and his fingers were covered with skull-head silver rings. No one had ever seen Goth smile, and he rarely spoke. These two were the cleanup crew.

All Alf had been told was that there would be a body to dispose of. He never dreamed it would be Skinny.

'Oh, the nasty bastard. What the fucking hell for? Skinny never did nothing wrong, he was loyal as the day is long, fucking hell. Who'll be next, eh?'

Goth just stared in much the way that Sam had. The floor was now covered in blood, which was leaving the hole in Skinny's body in an ever-slowing stream. Sam shrugged and walked out, leaving them to it.

He collected Skinny's car keys from behind the bar. As Big Jim's second, the Rolls was now his, along with a few other things, but mainly a huge increase in money.

The first thing he did when he got into the Rolls Royce was snap the furry dice air freshener off the mirror. He hated the damn things, made him sneeze like hell, plus they were naff. He threw it out the window and left all the windows open for the fresh air to clear the stink out and let the smell of the leather return.

Wait 'til I pull up at home in this! he thought, smiling to himself as he rummaged through the drawer in the dashboard. A few photos of Skinny's tart, Norrie, and that's all she was – a tart. Skinny had been pimping his own bird for years, the depraved bastard deserved to die. Sam kept Cathy well away from his work. She knew he worked the doors, that's where they had met, but he never told her anything about his extracurricular activities.

He pulled out a couple of chewing gum wrappers, a packet of Jelly Babies, a disabled sticker with Skinny's mother – a sour-faced old bag – glaring out of it.

Yeah, well, she isn't getting any more rides in this beauty. No more will she be able to stick her nose in the air at old Duffy; it's the other way round from now on. Duffy will be tickled pink when I pick her up in this.

Sam had spent his first year in the south at Mrs Duffy's boarding house, and after a few months she became the grandmother he had never had. The old lady idolised Sam, who in her eyes could do no wrong at all. It was mutual.

The word on the street was Do anything at all to upset Mrs Duffy and on your own head be it. No glue-sniffing toe rags congregated on Mrs Duffy's street, joy riders turned at the top of the lane and no rowdy drunks dared disturb Mrs Duffy's rest.

Sam still visited her often and took her out for a bite to eat now and then. Cathy liked having her over for Sunday tea, Mrs Duffy possessed a dry Irish humour and a quick wit that made her good company.

The Rolls started smoothly and Sam drove off. Twenty minutes later he pulled up outside of the house, a medium-sized semi-detached with a large garden, passed down to Cathy by her parents. He could already picture the For Sale sign going up in the garden. Pretty soon they would be able to afford whatever they wanted, wherever they wanted, and it would only take another few years until the whole bloody world was his. He had a plan and it was in action already, it would take time but he had plenty of that. Andrew was part of that plan. Sam wanted his brother here with him to share the empire that was coming, when he was old enough and not in need of babysitting. Leanne would see the light if he had to make her. There was nothing up north for the kid. She'd had him to herself long enough.

Yeah, he thought with a self-satisfied smile on his face, *everything was going according to plan.*

Cathy came to the door, a tall, long-legged, blue-eyed blonde with her hair in a ponytail, the way Sam liked it, and she was carrying their month-old daughter Lorraine in her arms.

CHAPTER THIRTEEN

2000

Cathy looked into Sam's eyes. Nothing that had been the man she married looked back at her. Instead she was looking at a savage, twisted evil that had her pinned against the wall by her throat.

'Please, Sam. Please don't do this. Think of little Lorry. Please, Sam. Please think what you are doing,' she managed to beg in a hoarse, garbled whisper.

She'd been here before, more than once, and knew the score: if she once raised her voice he would probably kill her. She'd done that before and learned her lesson well, having spent three weeks in hospital. Broken ribs, that she'd managed to 'convince' the doctor was from a fall downstairs.

He came back then, back from whatever hell he'd been to, his temper receding slowly, ever so slowly. Keep calm. That's all she had to do, even though every nerve end was screaming for release. *Try to breathe*, she told herself, *small breaths, he will let go, he will.*

Gradually he released his grip and she could breathe properly again. He looked at her for a moment as if he didn't know who she was, then, turning, he walked away from her. She knew he would go upstairs and look in on their daughter. She glared at his back, hating him, wishing him dead, wishing she had the guts to kill him, but not daring to voice her hatred.

Shaking with relief and gently massaging her throat, she went into the kitchen, the super designer kitchen bought out of God knows what. She wasn't stupid, though sometimes it paid to pretend that she was. No way could a doorman's wage pay for this extravagance. She didn't even know which door he was supposed to be on these days, he kept her right out of the loop.

There were phones in the house she didn't dare to answer, the only person she knew was a little man called Alf and she'd only met when he had come to the other house looking deadly worried and a second time the day they had moved in here. This huge, fifteen-roomed house that was not a home. A house she had hated on sight, but a house that Sam loved. On both occasions Alf had seemed to be a nice, kind person, a possible ally.

This latest row, though, had kicked off over a brother she hadn't even known he had until a few hours ago. He never mentioned his family, if there was one, never talked about Sunderland where he came from, then suddenly he tells her that he has a younger brother. A brother that Sam was adamant would be living with them in a few years' time. Whenever she'd asked about any family he'd shrugged, gone quiet for a few minutes, then started talking about something else, all the while staring into her eyes as if daring her to bring the subject up again. She never did unless something triggered the thought off, months or years later.

Cathy's parents were both dead. An only child of an only child and an orphan, she had no one, no one except her daughter Lorraine, and the ghost from Sam's past who shared the bed with her and her husband.

He had always talked in his sleep but usually it was very hard to make out what he was saying. She'd heard Lorry distinctively more than once, then the occasional Lorraine. At first she'd thought he was talking about their daughter, then one drunken night not so long ago the context he had been mentioning their daughter in had been more than explicit. Her blood had practically stopped running in her veins and she'd known if she had moved she would have vomited. Her head ready to explode, and so angry, and to hell with the consequences, she had tried to wake him up, but he had gone on talking and she had realised that it wasn't her Lorraine, their child, but another woman named Lorraine, a woman from his past from the north, a past and a place she knew absolutely nothing about. He could have been born on Mars for all she knew and for all she dare ask.

The kettle boiled and automatically, like one of the many labour-saving devices in the house, she moved and made tea in the pot. If she had even suggested dropping a bag in a cup he would have a fit. She sighed as she sat down and cuddled the cup in her hands. Tonight she had managed to escape pretty much unscathed, but tomorrow and all the tomorrows after that ... she shook her head as a silent tear fell into her cup.

Sam stood at the bedroom door watching his sleeping daughter. He regretted what he'd done to Cathy, he always did. 'But for fuck's sake, when is she ever gonna learn?' he muttered.

Stupid cow.

Lorraine turned over in her sleep and Sam smiled. So much like his other Lorraine, so much like her at that age that she could have been her. Tomorrow he would plait her hair. He had found on the market a pair of pink bobbles exactly like Lorraine used to wear in her hair when they were kids.

Quietly he closed the door and went downstairs. He found Cathy in the kitchen where he knew she would be. Taking his wallet out of his pocket he sat down, opened it, and took two hundred pounds out. 'Here.' He slid his hand across the table. 'For you and the bairn. Treat yourselves tomorrow, have a good time and get something nice for both of you, OK?'

Cathy stared at the money for as long as she dared. She had known it was coming, it always did.

Is this why I stay? Why I put up with his shit? she wondered as her fingers closed around the crisp notes.

Sam smiled at her. 'I really am sorry. I don't know what came over me.' It sounded lame even to his ears; he'd used the same excuse so many times.

Cathy sighed. The truth was that, yes, he really was sorry, until the next time, or until he figured out a way to lay all the blame on her. And there was always a next time. She knew there always would be, until the day he lost all control and killed her.

'I, er I have to go out ... business. Don't wait up. I'll probably be late back.' He stood, looked down at her for a moment, then shrugged. 'OK?'

And what if it isn't? she thought, but lifting her face and smiling, her fingers squeezing the notes even harder, she said the last thing that was really on her mind, the thing she was expected to say, the words well rehearsed: 'Yeah, sure.'

After he left, Cathy folded the notes and put them in her purse, a hundred for a good time, maybe the zoo so Lorraine could tell him where they had been, the other hundred for her stash, for the day she finally got up the courage to break free.

CHAPTER FOURTEEN

Sam threw his cards across the table and glared at Big Jim.

Alf coughed. Smiling at Big Jim, who was now glowering right back at Sam, he said, 'Anybody want a drink?'

'Fuck off, Alf,' Big Jim snarled.

'Ooooh, boys,' Billy Jean, said, flashing his perfect teeth and waving his waxed arms around, his rings sparkling in the overhead spotlights. 'Ow!' he frowned a moment later when Alf kicked him under the table.

Alf knew he was in the middle of a power play, he'd seen it coming for months. He did not quite know yet which one his money was on. He'd watched Sam come up through the ranks in his own devious way, but he'd known Big Jim a lot longer and in his way he was every bit as nasty and devious as Sam had become.

And he wasn't taken in by Billy Jean's simpering act either, sitting there in his pink suit and frilly shirt, even though for once he'd had to take his jacket off and roll his shirtsleeves up because of the broken air conditioner.

Billy Jean ran the whole of Peckham and was as big a snake in the grass as they come. He would love to muscle in on Big Jim's territory, though Alf knew, mean and sly as Billy Jean was, he was no match for the three men he was playing cards with.

'Coffee, then?' Alf said in a further attempt to break the deadlock. Both of his bosses were tooled up and the last thing he wanted was to be in the middle of a firing range.

'Yeah, I'll have one,' Tarak said as he laid his cards face down on the table. Tarak was a rare Turk with brilliant blue eyes, he had over a hundred girls in his stable and every one of them adored him, except for the ones now lying in the cold dark earth.

Alf got up and went into the small kitchen adjacent to the card room. *At least I'm safe in here, for the moment anyhow*, he thought, waiting for the kettle to boil.

God, all this aggro's no good for my blood pressure. The bloody doctor's warned me twice this year already, and it's only halfway through. He wiped the sweat off his brow, then took the coffees in. He could detect a subtle difference when he reached the table, and looked first at Big Jim, then Sam: both were now looking at their card.

Thank God for that, then. Alf poured the coffees, then looked across the room at Goth, who was sitting by the window, looking bored stiff as usual. *Nothing new there*. Goth hated cards, he gave Alf a small nod, meaning everything was cool, and Alf breathed evenly again as he sat down.

An hour later the card school broke up with Tarak walking out ten grand richer. Billy Jean waltzed out after him flashing his teeth and offering him a lift home.

'No, thanks,' Tarak replied, suspecting an ulterior motive and not a money one. 'One of my girls will be waiting outside to drive me home. See you around.'

Alf took the cups into the kitchen, Goth followed him as Sam, five grand down and his anger building, stood up. Big Jim was counting his winnings, not as substantial as Tarak's but a good portion of Sam's five grand.

'You off, then?' Big Jim snarled, letting Sam know he was still the boss man.

'Aye,' Sam replied as he passed him.

'Ha ha,' Big Jim laughed. 'If you can't take the he ... '

The next moment his head hit the table, scattering money every which way. Calmly, Sam pulled the six-inch blade out of Big Jim's back, wiped it on the dead man's jacket and slid it into the pouch in his own.

This wasn't how he'd planned it. Big Jim was supposed to die in a car crash. He'd already made sure the brakes would be sorted next Tuesday.

Serves the bastard right. If he hadn't been so cocky then he would have lived another week. Another week to stuff his fat fucking face, screw whoever he wanted. Sam shrugged and muttered, 'Oh well.'

Smiling, he scooped the money up off the table, quickly counted it, two grand up, pocketed the lot and headed for the door.

'Alf!' he yelled when he reached the door. 'Job for you.'

CHAPTER FIFTEEN
2003

Cathy squashed the notes as flat as they would go. Fourteen grand. A fortune to some, chicken feed to others and years of scraping it from here and there without Sam finding out. It would last them a while, long enough at least for her and Lorraine to get a fresh start in a place as far from here as they possibly could. She would have to get a job, she knew that, fourteen grand wouldn't last forever, not with a growing child, but she was prepared. She'd had fourteen and a half, but five hundred had secured them both with new identities.

Having checked out a few remote places she'd decided that actually she and Lorraine would stick right out amongst the locals in a small community wherever they went. It was better to get lost in a crowd, so she'd decided on Liverpool, right in the heart of the city, that's where they would go to lie low, and when the heat died down perhaps they would be able to live a normal life.

She sighed, and muttered to the glass of white wine she held, 'As if it ever will.'

She took a sip, then put the glass on the table.

'No,' she told herself sternly. 'I am going, and tomorrow. If I wait any longer, I might never get another chance.'

She snapped off another square of chocolate, then another, and to her dismay the chocolate bar was all gone, the third today, and it was only three o'clock.

'Shit.' She hauled herself to her feet. Time to collect Lorraine from school.

Quickly, she ran a brush through her hair, pulling at the odd early grey strand that had started to appear six months ago, the day after she'd walked in on Sam and Billy Jean. The next day she'd woken up in hospital and pretended she couldn't remember anything.

She didn't look in mirrors much anymore. All she saw was a seventeen-stone stranger looking back at her. Grabbing her bag, she checked that her keys were inside, then slipped into her black jacket. She wore black a lot now, it masked the rolls of fat a little bit, though she couldn't hide her double chin, she was reminded daily of its existence by Sam, who, because he couldn't stand to look at her anymore, now slept in another room. She covered her ear with the quilt most nights, pretending she couldn't hear the sound of more than one pair of high heels tapping their way up the marble staircase. She'd lost count of how many blondes had woven their way through her house.

Which suited her just fine. She knew the only reason she was alive was because Sam adored their daughter and would never do anything to upset her.

One night just before the grey had started to appear he had stood in the doorway of her bedroom, she could smell the whisky clear across the room. He'd said, his face twisted into a scowl, 'You don't look like her anymore. You are nothing but a fat ugly cow and useless to me or any man.'

He'd turned and walked away, slamming the door shut behind him. She had doubly feared for her life after that and had spent agonising nights wondering who this other Lorraine was. It was obvious the woman was from his past and the reason their daughter had been christened Lorraine. She had begged him to let her call her after her dear dead mother, Sophia, but he'd angrily refused and said her name had been chosen before she had even been conceived.

When she'd realised the reason their daughter was called Lorraine it had broken her heart, but out of the heartbreak had come a strength she never knew she possessed, a strength that was getting her out of here tomorrow.

Locking the door behind her she got into the silver Mercedes. On no account would she dare to take the Rolls, not even if the house was on fire.

She pulled up outside of Lorraine's posh school ten minutes later, switched the engine off and sat in the car. This was to be her trial run. She never got out of the car; anyhow, she wasn't allowed to; if she got out of the car she would meet people, perhaps make friends and Sam did not allow friends. Lorraine would come to the car the way she always did, the way she would tomorrow.

Tomorrow her fears would be over. She had finally found someone to help her, and he had been there all along if only she had known. Alf was meeting them at the school and he would have the documents with their new identities. It hadn't been safe to keep them at home. *Thank God. Soon I will be free.*

Sam paced the floor of the new nightclub he had recently opened on the high street, his right fist connecting with the palm of his left hand. Each slapping sound made Alf wince. Goth, however, leaning against the wall and lost in a porn mag, barely even blinked.

Alf looked at Goth. Sometimes, even though he was used to him, Goth gave Alf the jitters. Like now, Sam could turn on either one of them, and not for the first time. He'd beaten Goth seriously just a couple of months ago, and Goth had actually smiled as if he was bloody well enjoying it. In his own way Goth was as much an enigma as Sam.

Suddenly Sam stopped pacing and Alf felt his heart lurch as his boss spun round and glared at him. 'Did you honestly think for one minute I wouldn't have found out?'

Alf hesitated. *Found out about what? That his wife was leaving him, or that Tarak was trying to muscle in on the door business? That was the trouble with Sam. Half the time you didn't know if you were standing on concrete or water.*

Alf took a chance, praying he was right, because the other was unthinkable. 'Oh, he's a cheeky bastard alright.'

He heaved a silent sigh of relief when Sam went off on one again. If words could kill, Tarak would have died an hour ago. Alf knew the best thing to do was let Sam rant and rave as much as he wanted. As his heart slowed to normal he regretted again having become involved with Cathy.

Why the hell have I promised to help her?

What quirk of fate had made him drive down that bloody road, a road he hardly used anyhow, a bloody road that Cathy had broken down on? Then when he'd fixed her tyre, she'd broken down again, only this time in a more personal way, the poor bugger had bent his ear for over an hour. And what a tale. If ever there was a woman on the edge it was Cathy.

And so he'd put his own life on the line. He wanted out anyhow, sick up to his eye teeth with the murdering bastards. Even though he'd known twenty-odd years ago what he was getting himself into. It had been exciting then, cleanup crew for the guv, the hardest man around, then he'd started to lose the plot, now Sam was heading the same way.

He guessed the power went right to their heads after a time. It was amazing how none of them ever realised that nobody was invincible. When he'd first arrived, Vince Freeman had been the man, then three years down the line he'd been buried in concrete, helping to support a new railway bridge. Big Jim had carved Vince's name into the concrete himself, drawn a heart around it and laughed.

Alf shook his head and blew air out of his cheeks. He couldn't wait to get away, pleased that everything was in order. He'd bought new names for his wife and two kids. His oldest daughter, Tracy, who hated the idea of moving to Scotland, had kicked up a fuss, but they would be alright. The name they all knew him by was not his real name anyhow and his wife Eva was at this very moment buying hair dyes for all of them. The false names were a scam, just in case Forger Freddie squealed, either for more money or because Sam tortured what he thought was the truth out of him.

The Ramside hotel near Houghton-le-Spring was booked for tomorrow night, apparently all he had to do was pull off at the Durham roundabout and it was about fifty yards down the road to Sunderland.

Easy. We just have to live through today.

CHAPTER SIXTEEN

Alf hit the M1 at speed and kept it up until they were well past Doncaster, nearly twenty-four hours ahead of schedule. He felt it in his bones that Sam suspected something. He hadn't worked with the guy this long not to understand his ways.

He'd done his best for Cathy, sorting a false passport for her and the kiddie, new name, new driving licence, plus he'd chipped in a few hundred quid. It was all up to her now. He sincerely hoped she'd make it, the poor woman was a good sort: just a shame she'd anchored herself to the likes of Sam, a man who he had never seen show mercy to anyone. And without doubt, if she didn't get away Cathy would end up underneath one of the new housing projects going on around the city, though he was praying for her not to, and for her and the kiddie to end up with a new life away from the manic she called a husband.

They pulled into the services, Alf checking the rear view mirror to see if anything followed them off the road. *Good*, he nodded to himself, *nothing suspicious. Thank God.* The roads had been pretty clear all the way up and he was sure he would have known if they were being followed.

As he was filling up with diesel he gave his wife a tenner to get pop and whatever for the kids. Both had sulked all the way, neither wanting to leave the bright lights for a stinking farm in the back of nowhere, as they so nicely put it. He watched her go into the shop. *She's mighty fit, my wife*, he thought and smiled. She knew that he was, for want of a better word, a gangster, and he supposed that's what he was, but he'd always managed to keep the gory bits from her. She thought he collected money, laid a little heavily on folks now and then. She'd never sleep again if she knew the whole truth.

They had planned their new life together, something they had always dreamed of, a small farm, and they were going to have boarding kennels. They both loved dogs, any breed, even cute mongrels, or ugly ones; perhaps they might even start breeding Labradors as well as boarding.

He put the petrol cap on, then slapped his neck. 'Bastard insects,' he muttered, taking a step, not really noticing when the second step was slower than the first, noticing, though, how the third step was like walking on a sponge. He lifted his foot for a fourth step and came crashing to his knees. His face hit the concrete a second later, and the last sound he heard was his wife screaming.

Cathy waited outside the school, her neck craning as she looked for her daughter.

'Where is she?' she muttered. Feeling anxious, she tapped her fingers impatiently on the steering wheel.

Lorraine was usually one of the first ones out, running as fast as she could to the car, but now the rush was down to a trickle, and the noise level down to bearable.

She decided to get out of the car and look for Lorraine, whose new name was going to be Sophia. Her head snapping quickly around this way, that way, she walked up to the gates. Now there were only two kids left in the yard and neither of them was Lorraine.

Feeling an anxiety attack coming on, she tried to control her breathing, slowly in and out, in and out, thinking calm, breathing deep, and after a minute or so the attack ebbed away. A year ago she would not have been able to control these attacks and would have collapsed into a gibbering wreck. She'd found some books in the library on the subject and they seemed to help. she was learning yoga as well, but because she was not allowed to go to classes she wasn't sure if she was doing everything right.

Go to Lorraine's classroom and stay calm, she told herself. Slowly, her legs obeyed, and she reached the classroom just as the teacher, Miss Stavis, a small blonde woman with large glasses, came out of the door laden down with exercise books.

'Ah,' Miss Stavis said, smiling. 'Lorraine's mum. How can I help you?'

Cathy swallowed hard and said quickly, 'Lorraine, I … I can't seem to find her, she's not come to the car.'

Miss Stavis looked at her oddly, 'Well she wouldn't, would she? Her father picked her up about an hour ago, he said she had a dentist appointment.'

Cathy was stunned and it showed in her face as she stared with mounting horror at Miss Stavis.

'Are you alright?' Miss Stavis asked, looking up at Cathy with concern.

'Yes, yes, I'm fine.'

Get a grip, Cathy told herself. 'Oh, yes. I'd forgotten, that's all.' She gave a little half smile, the most she could manage. 'It was just a shock when she wasn't there … I've had a busy day and completely forgot. It's a good job her father remembered … Oh, well. OK then … Thank you, thank you …'

She turned and practically ran out of the school, her heart pounding.

He knows. He knows. Her thoughts were in rhythm with her heart.

Running through her head over and over, crashing against her skull. *HE KNOWS* ... It was all she could do to stop herself from screaming her thoughts out loud.

Reaching the car, she jumped in, started the engine, not knowing where she was going, knowing only that she had to get away, and the worst thought of all, that she probably would never see her baby again. Despair tore at her heart; never even at the worst times had she felt like this. Never imagined this could happen. *HE KNOWS.*

Tears clouded her eyes until she could hardly see and had to pull over at the side of the road.

She reached for her bag, there were tissues inside, she would have to sort herself out, figure what to do, where to go, where to hide. *Oh, God*, she shuddered. Was Sam or one of his friends even watching her now?

'Dear God, please help,' she begged like a small child lost in the woods with no hope of finding her way home.

Her trembling hand was closing on her bag when suddenly her wrist was grabbed from behind.

Her heart lurched and she screamed as she felt the bones in her wrist begin to bend. *Please God no, please don't let this be happening.*

'Believe me, he won't help you, you fucking fat, lazy, pathetic, stupid cow.'

'Please, Sam, please!' she begged between sobs, her terror mounting by the moment and reaching heights she had never in her worst thoughts imagined. Her fear was an actual pain that started in the small of her back and overwhelmed her body.

'Please, *please!* he mimicked sarcastically. 'How dare you? You were gonna run off with the bairn, *my* Lorraine, and you fucking dare to say please?'

He squeezed harder and Cathy let out a gasp of pain. 'Don't, Sam, please don't,' she begged, knowing that she dare not shout or scream again.

'I have a knife here. Give me one good reason why I shouldn't use it, why I shouldn't cut your throat wide open, rip your guts out and leave you somewhere for the fucking crows to peck at, you scheming bitch? You fucking kidnapping bastard ... You were gonna steal her from right under my fucking nose.'

'Oh no, oh no.'

'Cut the fucking whingeing and drive.'

'Wh ... Where to?' Her mouth was so dry she could barely talk. She ran her tongue over her dry lips.

'Down on to the motorway, then keep going. I'll say when to stop.'

He slid the sharp blade over the back of her hand, cutting into her flesh, not deep, but enough to draw blood. Cathy shuddered and did as she was told, knowing she had no other option; she could feel the blade on her skin and the thought of what he was going to do drained any fight from her.

'OK, pull up here,' Sam said fifteen horrendous minutes later. Cathy pulled into the lay-by and brought the car to a slow and shaky stop. As traffic rushed past her, she hoped someone would notice, but not one person looked out at her.

Can't they see the blood on the steering wheel? Surely someone must be able to see.

Help me, God.

She was dead though, and she knew it. God was too busy to look down on her. Sam would most probably stab her and push her body out of the car, drive away and get on with his life.

He jumped out of the back and into the passenger seat before Cathy had time to even register that he had moved. He still had the knife in his hand.

'Now isn't this cosy. Just me and you.' He smiled at her, a cold, cruel smile.

'What are you going to do?'

For a long time he didn't answer and Cathy, thinking she had been frightened before, knew now the true cell-deep terror felt by cornered prey that knows death is imminent.

Finally he said, 'What should I do? What would be an apt punishment for someone who was gonna take my Lorraine away from me? After all, it's not the first time ... Is it?'

Not the first time?

What does he mean?

She looked at him in terror, not knowing what to say, knowing whatever she said might be the catalyst which tipped him over the edge and caused her death.

Then from somewhere deep inside, from a place she had never found before, and surprising even herself, she said calmly, 'She's my child as well.'

Sam raised an eyebrow. 'Yes, I suppose she is ... And for that reason and that reason only I'm going to let you live.'

Cathy blinked rapidly, not sure exactly what he had said, but hoping she'd heard right. 'What?'

'Yes.' He leaned over her and she froze. Never mind what he had said. Sam was a liar, and a cruel one. She felt her skin contract as if it had a mind of its own and was trying to get away from him.

He opened the car door, 'Goodbye,' he leaned over and with both hands shoved her out. She fell heavily, on her hands and knees.

Her face twisted in pain, tears flooding her eyes, she looked up at him. 'Can I have my bag?' she pleaded.

He laughed. 'Don't push it, fatso, think yourself lucky you have your life. I'll tell Lorraine when she grows up that her mother loved her very much once upon a time, even though she ran away and left her. I really don't want to be telling lies to the bairn now, do I?' He sniggered, but a moment later his voice turned deadly serious.

'If you ever, *ever* come looking, I'll kill you, and that ain't no threat, fatso, that's a promise.'

Knowing this was finally the end, Cathy glared at him. But inside she swore that one day she would be back to claim her child.

He drove off. Two miles down the road he left the motorway and opening the window threw Cathy's bag into a field. It was found four months later by an old tramp who had the best winter of his life on the road.

PART THREE

PRESENT DAY

CHAPTER SEVENTEEN

Lorraine pored over at the pictures. Her head felt as if it was splitting in half. She hadn't slept a wink all night, she had seen as she'd tossed and turned those very same images captured on the board. It wasn't until Sanderson coughed behind her that she turned and realised that all of her officers were in the room.

She straightened her shoulders took a deep breath before saying, 'Alright, here's what we do know. The farmer was out checking his fences. It was his dog that raised the alarm. We also know that the vict ...' Lorraine swallowed past a lump in her throat as a fleeting picture of Amy laughing on her bike flashed through her mind.

'Forensics haven't come through yet.' She shook her head.

'No footprints?' Dinwall asked.

'The ground was rock solid, nothing to lift.'

'Anything found on her?' Dinwall shrugged. 'Anything to give a clue as to why?'

Lorraine shook her head. 'No.'

'What?' Peters poked Dinwall's back. 'You think this sicko wrote the reason down and put it in her pocket, like a game or something?'

There was muted laughter in the room that was quickly silenced by a look from Lorraine. Her headache was fast becoming the mother of all and she felt sick, but she had to go on. *I'll do everything I can to nail this bastard, and when we catch him there's going be no way on earth for this weasel to wriggle free.* Taking a deep breath, she went on. 'Death was caused by strangulation ... After she'd been bitten and raped.'

She turned to the pictures and looked at them for a moment, knowing her team would be looking at the close up of Amy's horrendous bite marks, before turning back and carrying on. 'The grazes on her wrist proved she'd been tied up ... The bastard was free to do just about anything he wanted. Nothing in her finger nails to say she'd even put up a fight.'

'Do you think she might have been drugged?' Peters asked.

'We're waiting for her blood tests to come back later this morning.' Hearing the door open, she frowned and turned to see Clark standing there.

'Could I see you in my office, DI Hunt?'

'But sir ...'

'Now, please.' Clark's tone held a hint of warning.

Gritting her teeth, Lorraine gestured for Luke to come up and take over, then she followed Clark out of the door and along to his office. Clark didn't even wait until Lorraine was seated before he said, 'I'm taking you off the case, Lorraine.'

Lorraine was stunned. 'You're what? But why?'

'I think you know why.'

'But, sir!'

'No buts, Lorraine, it's far too personal. Officially, you're off the case. DS Daniels will take over, he'll keep you in the loop seeing as you work so well off one another, and use your knowledge. But he's in charge.'

She looked at him for a moment. Inside she knew he was right, but she wanted this case, she wanted to catch whoever the sick bastard was, she wanted it so much the longing was an actual ache. She stood up. 'That's your final word?'

He nodded. 'Have you told DS Daniels what happened that night?'

Lorraine shook her head.

'Don't you think he needs to know?'

'I'll get to it.' She rose from her seat. 'Is that all, sir?'

'For the moment.'

Lorraine resisted slamming the door though she sorely wanted to. *Prick*, she was thinking as she marched back to the incident room, in time to see the backs of most of her officers heading in the other direction, towards the canteen.

She went into the incident room where Luke was standing holding the case notes and staring into the middle distance.

'All done?' Lorraine asked.

'Oh, oh yes. Here.' He held the notes out to her.

'Keep them. It's your case,' she snapped, then instantly regretted it. 'Sorry. It's not you ...'

'What do you mean it's my case?'

'You're starting to sound as dopey as Carter, for God's sake, how explicit do I have to be? Clark has taken me off the case, so it's yours.'

'Why?'

'Too close ... Amy was once one of my best friends.' She shrugged and looked him in the eyes.

'But that was years ago.'

'Makes no difference. What's so maddening is that he's possibly right. Come on, I'm dying of thirst here and this bloody heat is absolutely killing me. Can you ever in your life remember it being so hot before?'

Luke followed her out of the office to the canteen, wondering if there was something she wasn't telling him. For one thing, no way would Lorraine hand a case over without a fight, and ever since last night she'd been so preoccupied.

OK, so Amy had been an old friend. He sighed inwardly, his mind made up. *I know there's something you're not telling me, girl.*

Leaving Luke to get the drinks, Lorraine pulled up a chair at Sergeants Dinwall and Sanderson's table, who were sat nursing coffees. The place had recently had a makeover: Superintendent Clark had insisted they move into the twenty-first century, only his idea of the twenty-first century looked more like an American diner out of the sixties, all highly polished chrome and bright red plastic seating.

Eying the coffees up, Lorraine tutted before saying 'How the hell you can drink that stuff in this heat beats me. You must all have bell metal stomachs.' She smiled up at Luke as he placed an ice-cold can of Diet Coke in front of her.

'Well, bloody hell, that stuff's really, really good for you, isn't it?' Dinwall, whose dark pony tail was now nearly as long as Lorraine's, sneered.

'Love it,' Lorraine answered.

Sanderson, a small, wiry and intensely loyal man who had worked with Lorraine from the day she had first started, yawned loudly and said, 'Do we have to have this same conversation nearly every day?'

Lorraine shrugged and tapped her fingernail against the side of her can. 'Got something else on your mind? 'Cos I agree we've done this flaming heat to death.'

Dinwall laughed as he put his coffee cup back on the table. 'You know he has, boss.'

'What is it, women problems?' She nodded in Dinwall's direction, 'He's your man for that one.'

Dinwall was left open-mouthed, poised to speak, but Lorraine continued, 'So what then, excited about X Factor, troubled by Eastenders?'

'Actually, it's the erm... air show.'

Everyone grinned.

'No ... really? You don't have to fly the bloody things, you know

Sanderson.'

'Yeah,' Luke put in quickly, in case Lorraine let Sanderson off the hook. The last thing Luke wanted was to get sent to police the show instead of him. 'It'll be ... really fun ... planes, loads of people ... honest.' Luke nodded and smiled at Sanderson, ignoring Dinwall's sniggers.

'Why don't you go then?' Sanderson asked, glaring at Luke.

'Oh, I, er ... I can't. I'm in charge of the case now, far too busy, aren't I, boss?' He sat back in his chair, folding his hands into the nape of his neck, satisfied.

Sanderson snorted. Lorraine peered at Luke over the rim of her can, sighed loudly, then said, 'Forget it ... Dinwall?' she turned her head in his direction. 'I'm looking for a volunteer.'

Dinwall laughed. 'Yeah right, boss. Nice way to put it.' He shrugged, while the other two men looked intently at him. Dinwall milked it for all it was worth, then after a long pause he smiled at Sanderson and Luke. 'OK, why the hell not? Day out at the beach, especially in this heat, just the ticket ...'

Lorraine opened her mouth, but whatever she was going to say was lost as Carter, an aura of urgency surrounding him like a charge of static electricity, came bounding into the canteen and all but jumped over people to reach her.

She watched his progress through the room as he weaved in and out of the tables with a feeling of mounting dread welling up in her stomach. Noticing the emotions flickering across her face, Luke spun round.

'Oh, dear.' As Luke spoke, Dinwall and Sanderson, who were facing Lorraine, turned just as Carter reached them.

'Have you ever had the feeling that you don't really want to know?' Lorraine muttered as Carter opened his mouth.

'It's Dave, boss ... Dave Ridley.'

CHAPTER EIGHTEEN

Lorraine stood perfectly still, staring at the remains of the burned-out bench. 'What the hell happened?' she muttered, shaking her head, 'I can't believe there's no witnesses.'

Knowing she was not talking to him and only thinking out loud, Dinwall remained silent, wondering himself just who the hell Dave Ridley had upset to suffer this.

'OK, Dinwall, if you could just drag your knuckles along to the car and pay Mrs Ridley a visit, seeing as you know her personally, like. You know the routine,' Lorraine said, still unable to take her eyes off the bench.

'Yeah, very funny ... So what do I tell her, that her one and only son poured petrol over himself and then quite casually and calmly struck the bloody match? I would rather wipe me arse with a nettle!'

'Oh, cute.' Lorraine winced at the picture in her head.

'Anyhow, I don't know her that well.'

'She at least knows who you are ... And we all do hope that you'll be a hell of a lot more sensitive than you've just been, you bloody clown.'

Dinwall frowned. 'Send Luke, he's better at this sort of stuff than me ... There's no other family, you know. Ridley's all she's got. What if she gets upset?'

'Of course she's gonna get upset, dickhead ... Anyhow, Luke's taking me to the hospital and everybody else is busy with the tasks he's set them, so you're it. Get going.'

'But can't ...'

'James ...' Lorraine said quietly but with meaning.

'OK, OK. I'm on it.'

As Dinwall was grumbling his way to the car, Lorraine spent a few more minutes beside the burned-out wooden bench remembering a warm, sultry night some fifteen years ago. A night when Dave Ridley's mind had been as free from trouble as the rest of them, a night when he was haunted only by childhood dreams of playing in the sun, and future dreams of what life could be.

She felt tears prick the back of her eyes and found it hard to swallow past the lump in her throat. They should have seen it coming. She should have seen it coming a long time ago, spent more time with him, just a visit now and then. *Does Jacko even bother with Dave now? Although I supposed he does, Jacko's like that, he wouldn't have deserted Dave like I have.* 'Damn, damn, damn,' she whispered, guilt burning in her heart.

Her thoughts were disturbed by a car peeping behind her; guessing rightly that it was Luke she pasted a smile on her face and spun round. She nodded at him, and glanced back at the bench before moving towards the car.

'Alright Lorraine?' Luke asked after she had got in and fastened her seat belt.

She sighed. 'Yeah. I suppose so.' She looked over her shoulder at the bench again as they pulled away and shuddered.

Luke sensed that she was far from alright, but didn't really understand the link between Lorraine and Dave Ridley. He only knew that if ever Ridley's name came up for whatever reason she was always the first to defend him. Likewise with Jacko Musgrove. Luke knew they had all been friends in school.

A lot of people have special friends that they keep in contact with long after newer friends made in adulthood melt away. I still see Stephen Mellows on a regular basis. And that reminded him, he was dying to introduce Lorraine to Stephen. *I must remember to give him a ring.* Figuring that Lorraine was not in the mood for small talk, and knowing that when she was ready she would tell him the full story, at least he hoped she would, Luke headed for Houghton Cut and the road to Sunderland.

CHAPTER NINETEEN

Dinwall parked his car, got out and noticed the throng of neighbours hanging around. *Obviously*, he thought as he closed the car door, *word has spread.* Clustered up and down the street in bunches of threes and fours, they all stared at Dinwall.

'Hope no one's gone in like a bull in a china shop already,' he muttered as he walked up the path.

The sweet smell of honeysuckle that climbed around the red door and halfway up the wall of the council semi-detached was overwhelming, and so was the buzzing of bees.

'Shit,' Dinwall muttered as he raised his hand to knock, keeping a wary eye on the blossoms for any stray kamikaze bees distracted from their pollen hunt.

'Round the back,' came a thin reedy voice from within, after his third knock.

'Thank God for that.' Relieved that he didn't have to step under the heavy swell of honeysuckle and gorging bees, Dinwall made his way round to the back yard.

The back door was open, a thin net curtain hanging in front of it. 'Hello, Mrs Ridley?' Dinwall said as he pulled the curtain to one side and stepped through.

The door led into a small, lemon-painted kitchen that had two brown cupboards on the wall and a matching set underneath the chrome sink. Three and a half feet from the sink was a small dropped-leaf table with a chair at either side. On the far side sat a grim-faced Mrs Ridley.

Sarah Ridley had been old all her life, at sixty with her iron-grey perm and deep wrinkles she could pass for over seventy-five. No one had ever seen a Mr Ridley, nor did anyone know if he ever really existed. Sarah had arrived in Houghton-le-Spring over thirty years ago wearing a wedding ring and carrying a year-old baby boy. She had mostly kept to herself. Her North London accent was still as strong as it had been in the beginning. She had taken odd jobs to pay the rent and feed them both when Dave was old enough to go to school. Her son was her life: she lived with his madness on a day-to-day basis.

Her eyes were dry, dry and very bright, behind her large dark-framed glasses. It was only four steps from the door to the table and he had barely taken the second step when she said, 'I know.'

Dinwall paused as she went on. 'I know what you've come to tell me. A friend came this morning, she's taking me to the hospital later today ... They say, they say he's holding on.'

'Oh, right, that's good.'

'Would you like a cup of tea?'

'Yeah, oh, would I.' Dinwall pulled the vacant chair out and sat down as Mrs Ridley stood up.

Thank God. She seems to be taking it alright, he thought, but asked, 'Any biccies, love?'

'Of course, ginger snaps or chocolate cookies?'

'Hmm, a chocolate cookie would hit the spot, Mrs Ridley ... Thank you.'

She placed the cup of tea in front of him and took the lid off the biscuit tin. 'Help yourself.'

Dinwall needed no urging. A few moments later, having used supreme willpower to stop himself from giving into the urge to dunk his biscuits, he said, 'Did Dave have any enemies, Mrs Ridley?'

It was obvious that the question had not been expected. Mrs Ridley's arm froze in mid-air, holding the teapot that she was about to refresh her tea with.

Slowly, what bit of colour she had draining from her already pale face, she put the teapot on the table, totally missing the stand, her nervous hands coming to rest on the table. 'What do you mean, enemies? Are you suggesting that someone tried to murder my Dave?'

She was totally amazed at the concept, even though Dave had been telling her all sorts of tales for the past year or two. She was used to waking up on a morning to find that yesterday's imaginary arch enemy was now a friend and the battle lines had moved.

Dinwall reached over and put the teapot on its stand before saying, 'Well, we don't really know much at the moment, that's why I would like to look at his room ... You know, it's pretty hard to accept that someone would willingly do that to themselves no matter how ...'

'Mad?' she finished his sentence for him.

Dinwall squirmed. 'Well ...'

Mrs Ridley sighed. The silence stretched between them, leaving Dinwall wondering what to say next. Then looking into her tea she said quietly, 'Upstairs, first room on your right.'

Nodding and pleased to get away from her for the moment, Dinwall rose and went upstairs. Opening the door he was surprised by the polished neatness of everything, and the room smelled of lavender. The TV resting on a stand on the wall gleamed, there was not a speck of dust in sight, the bed was made, the pillows plumped up, the green duvet fresh.

'Hmm,' Dinwall muttered. 'Tidier than me and that's a bloody fact.'

'My son developed a cleanliness compulsion a couple of years ago,' Mrs Ridley said from behind Dinwall's back. 'To add to his other complaints.'

'Christ, you frightened the fu ... sorry, life outta me.'

'Sorry,' she murmured.

Dinwall nodded and gave her a quick smile before moving over to the set of drawers under the window. There were two pictures on top of the chest of drawers: one was obviously Dave's mother, the other a bunch of teenagers. He glanced at the photo, a group of four boys and three girls, and in the background another boy who was staring at the group. He frowned. A couple of them looked familiar but he couldn't quite place them exactly. Shrugging, he got on with the job.

A few minutes later, after diligently searching every corner of the room, under the eagle eye of Mrs Ridley, he followed her downstairs.

When they were back in the tiny kitchen Dinwall said, 'Well, I can't find any evidence at all that says he planned to kill himself, Mrs Ridley.'

'That means nothing officer ... My son is mentally ill, has been for a long time now. He is riddled with guilt over something he had no control over, something that wasn't his fault.'

This was a new slant that Dinwall had never heard before, but she was Ridley's mother and bound to make excuses for him, that was only natural. 'Oh ... I er, I thought it was the, er, booze, you know and the, er, the drugs.'

'The booze and the drugs were used to make life easier, officer, to mask the pain. He was not to know that he was on the road and heading for his own private hell ... But the others know.'

Dinwall was intrigued. 'What others?'

'The ones that were there that night.'

I wish to God she'd stop talking in riddles Dinwall thought with exasperation that he tried to hide. 'What night, Mrs Ridley?'

Her next words fairly had Dinwall's mouth hanging open. 'You should ask your boss. She was there ... She knows. She knows everything that happened that dreadful night when a stranger wearing my son's skin came home.'

'What?' Dinwall felt his own skin crawl. Mrs Ridley's choice of words was creepy, he wondered briefly if living with her son's madness had slightly unhinged her.

'Yes, Ms Lorraine Hunt ... Isn't that what they call themselves these days when they aren't married at a certain age, Mzz?' Mrs Ridley gave a small high-pitched laugh before adding, 'She knows. She was there.'

'But ... What?'

Goodbye, officer.' She closed the door, leaving Dinwall staring at the scratches on the red paint.

CHAPTER TWENTY

Doris Musgrove, Dolly Smith and Mr Skillings were standing at Doris's gate when seventeen-year-old Andrew Knightly sauntered past them.

'Hi oldies,' he grinned at them as he crossed the road to his house.

'Cheeky puppy,' Doris said, her chins wobbling, but smiled as Andrew, now grown into a tall, slim and darkly handsome young man, waved without looking back at them.

'Turned out alright that one has,' Mr Skillings observed, nodding in Andrew's direction as his gnarled hands gripped his walking stick. The sleeves of his blue shirt were rolled up to the top of his thin arms. Mr Skillings was always cold no matter what time of year it was, and rarely seen without a jacket. That he was outside with no jacket today was testimony to the heat that the north east was basking in this summer.

Dolly matched his nod. 'Yes, he has that, but it's all down to Leanne though, not that other bugger, she's done a fine job with the three of them … Though, don't know if you've noticed, but I think there's something odd about Andrew lately. One day he speaks, the next he passes you with his head down.'

'Aye,' Dolly agreed, 'but that's just typical of teenagers now isn't it? No damn respect for anybody, a good clout round the ear hole wouldn't do them any harm … Anyhow, what time are we going to the town tomorrow? I'll start dipping into that money I've got put away if we don't go soon. The bingo's calling, we could even double it you know, it's ages and ages since we had a good win.' Dolly rubbed her hands together.

'Aye, and we could blow the bloody lot …' Before she could say more, Doris started sneezing.

'Bless you,' Mr Skillings said, and was echoed by Dolly.

'It's that bloody damn grass, the council's been round cutting it again, always sets me off,' Doris complained after three more sneezes. 'I hate when they cut the bloody stuff.'

Dolly nodded. 'OK, tomorrow it is then, don't suppose you'll be changing your mind about wearing blue, will you?' Doris changed her mind so often lately – or forgot things – that Dolly was praying she'd forget she wanted to wear blue for Jacko's wedding.

'No chance.' Doris turned and headed down her path. 'See youse both later.'

Dolly sighed as she watched her old friend enter her house.

'So what's so special about a blue wedding outfit?' Mr Skillings asked Dolly as Doris closed her door.

'I've already got a blue suit I've only worn once, for me cousin Steve's wedding to that tart Jackie, could have saved meself a couple of quid, and saved him a divorce if he'd bloody well listened, the idiot.'

'Oh well, Doris is the mother of the groom.'

'Yeah,' Dolly agreed. 'Who would have thought Jacko and Christina would be tying the knot in a few months' time, eh?' she shook her head. 'They'll make a lovely couple, and Melanie gets on really well with Christina … That's the main thing.'

'Aye, so they do, Melanie's a good kid and I'm pleased for them all … And it's true what they say, you never know what's round the corner,' Mr Skillings nodded wisely.

'That's true. See you later on.'

Mr Skillings nodded again before heading off towards Stanhill's shop, and as Dolly crossed the road and made her way to her own house she wondered, not for the first time, where she had gone wrong with her son, Jason, who was finishing a two-year stretch in Durham prison. With time off for good behaviour he would be out soon. She also wondered if she would ever in this life get to be the mother of the groom.

Dolly was nearly at her door when Sandra Gilbride, high heels clicking a quick tattoo on the path, her long brown plait swinging from side to side, came hurrying along the street, waving her arms frantically. Dolly, sensing some juicy bit of news, stopped at her gate and waited for Sandra.

'Have you heard?' Sandra gasped, quite out of breath when she reached Dolly.

'Heard what?' Dolly was burning up with curiosity.

'Thought you didn't know nowt about it. Well,' she paused for effect, 'somebody's just gone and poured petrol over poor Dave Ridley and set him on fire.'

Dolly gasped. 'Who would do that? Dave Ridley's bloody harmless, everybody knows that. I can't believe it. No.' She shook her head in disbelief. 'Are you absolutely sure?'

'Well, actually, I also got told that he did it to himself, so you don't really know what to believe. It's buzzing up Houghton with different rumours.'

'Eee, my God, poor Dave … I'll just pop along and tell Doris. Jacko'll be shocked.'

Dolly had already turned and was heading back to Doris's house when Sandra fell into step beside her. She smiled at Dolly. 'I'll, er, just come with you, love.'

Walking into the kitchen via the back door Andrew pulled his green T-shirt over his head and mopped his brow.

'That you, Andrew?' Leanne called from the sitting room.

'Yeah,' he mumbled, throwing the T-shirt at the laundry basket and scowling when he missed.

'There's a salad in the fridge Andrew, love.'

'Not hungry.' He was staring intensely at his T-shirt, studying the pattern the material made as it folded in on itself. He smiled. A moment later he turned and went up to his room.

As little as a month ago he would have picked the T-shirt up, but not now. Now he was totally indifferent to a lot of things that would have bothered him before.

Now he had other things to concern himself with, better things, great places to hang out, cool exciting things to do with cool exciting people, not boring Leanne.

In the sitting room Leanne frowned. Her thick dark hair was still cut very short in an urchin style that suited her fine elfin features. She would be thirty-four in September and had spent the last fifteen years looking after her brother and sisters. Apart from a spot of shoplifting when Tammy was fifteen and a couple of fights at school, which Tammy had got into defending Stacey, both girls had been very little bother to her. They'd had some hard times, but over the past few years things had definitely started to look up. Tammy worked in the travel agents at Houghton, where she had just been promoted. Stacey was doing really well for herself as well, working as a dental receptionist in Newcastle.

She hugged herself. She was so proud of the girls, Stacey was actually engaged to one of the dentists at the practice and there was talk of a really huge posh wedding next year. *God, I can't wait for that, wait until everybody on the Seahills sees my Stacey, all decked out in white.* Already they had visited half a dozen wedding shops in the area and had a great time.

She nodded her head, a soft smile on her face. *There's another wedding first though, Jacko and Christina, bloody hell, who'd've thought?*

Her mind wandered to a night long ago, and as her older brother's face drifted into her mind the warm glow she'd had thinking of Stacey's wedding disappeared. She had a contact number for Sam that she never used. He sent money now and then, when he remembered them, which wasn't that often. She never answered the odd letter, why should she? He'd left them to fend for themselves for three whole years before he actually got in touch. He could have been dead for all they had known. She wasn't stupid: she'd figured that the money was dirty, but it came in handy. Three growing kids needed a hell of a lot more than she could ever have afforded on the dole.

At first she'd been tempted to send it back, but Sam owed her big time, and if he kept on sending money until hell froze over he would still not pay the debt off.

She sighed, and her thoughts turned back to Andrew. Secretly she was worried about Andrew, really worried. He'd been acting very strangely lately and she didn't quite know what to make of it. Not long ago he would have brought his tea in and sat with her, they would have watched a video together, or one of the sci-fi channels on Sky that he loved, which Stacey kindly paid for, but now, these last few weeks it was as if he was trying his best to avoid her, staying out most of the time, coming in and going straight up to his room, missing meals. That was not Andrew.

Was it just his age? she'd asked herself over and over, and she was yet to come up with a satisfactory answer. She'd thought about following him, but knew that wouldn't be any good: he could travel twice as fast as she could. So she had kept her fears to herself and prayed hard that she was wrong.

'God, it's so hot,' she muttered just as the front door banged open and Tammy bounced in.

'Leanne!' Tammy shouted.

Leanne could easily tell by Tammy's voice that she was excited about something. Tammy always expressed her emotions easily. 'In here,' she said, turning her head towards the door, wondering what it was now that her sister was wired up about.

Tammy entered the room like the whirlwind she was. Tall, slim, with the family inheritance of thick black hair which she wore in a long bob, and dark eyes naturally heavily lashed, she demanded and got attention wherever she went.

'Have you heard?' she squealed, her eyes wide. 'The poor bugger. You're not gonna believe it.'

'Heard what?'

'About Dave Ridley.'

CHAPTER TWENTY-ONE

Lorraine's hands clutched the rail at the bottom of Dave Ridley's bed, her knuckles gleaming as white as the bed sheets.

'My God,' Luke whispered beside her.

Dave was unconscious; the whole left side of his body from his throat to his toes was swaddled with thick cream bandages, machines at his side bleeped in rhythmic tones, signalling life.

But how much? Lorraine wondered sadly, feeling tears prick behind her lids.

Her heart ached to see him like this. She kept seeing a younger Dave, remembering when they were kids and time had no meaning. Days when they picnicked on Seaburn beach or in Newbottle woods, from eight o' clock on a morning until eight at night. Then they would troop home sun-kissed and weary to bed, and to wake up the next day ready to do it all again.

She felt a quick rush of anger overwhelm her and her body shook. *Who the hell would even do this?* God she'd seen some fuck ups, and the things they did, but to actually burn another human being. What sort of sick, feeble mind could conjure up such an atrocity? She exhaled deeply, unable to tear her eyes away from Dave's pale face, and wondered, *Has he got the strength to cling on and pull through?*

Dave has never been the strong one.

'I have to know who did this,' she muttered quietly as if to herself, then was slightly surprised when Luke answered her.

'But who would, Lorraine, and why? Anyhow, I'm sorry to have to tell you this, but I've just come off the phone with Dinwall; he says Dave's mother seems to think that Dave did do this to himself. She swears he has no real enemies.'

When Lorraine didn't answer, Luke looked at her oddly. After a moment he said, 'You don't seem surprised.'

Lorraine's fingers were still gripping tightly to the bed as she stared down at Dave.

'Please don't die, Dave,' she whispered, looking at his face. 'Please don't die.'

Luke put his arm around her and held her close. 'I'm sure he'll pull through, love.'

Lorraine shook her head and, past the lump in her throat, said, 'No, Luke, he can't have done this, Jesus Christ, can you just imagine the pain, the agony he must have gone through?'

Luke said nothing. The last thing he wanted was to imagine was the man in front of him in flames.

In a voice so quiet and sad that Luke had to strain to hear it, Lorraine went on, 'Dave was never very tough. He could never run as fast or do anything that the others could do, he was last in everything, fell off his skateboard every night without fail, it's a wonder he has any knees left at all. But one thing about Dave, he was always there if someone fell down, and I don't mean physically, he was always there to pick us up.'

'But who? Why, even?'

'That's what we're gonna find out.'

'But you heard what Dinwall said.'

'I know, *I know*.' She was silent for a moment, dipping into the past again, then, sighing, she went on: 'He is capable of doing it, I suppose, the state his mind's been in ... but ...'

'But deep down inside, you don't want to think he did, do you?'

Lorraine nodded and letting go of her death-like grip on the bed she walked to the window. Luke followed her with his eyes, wondering again just what this was really all about. And what had actually happened to send Dave over the edge.

He was about to ask her outright when the doctor came in. Lorraine spun quickly round. 'Ah, doctor, at last ... Is he going to be alright?'

Luke winced at the pleading, the longing in that last sentence.

'And you are?' the doctor, a tall, thin man, with hair brushed from the right side of his head over his bald scalp, asked with a raised eyebrow and an arrogant lilt to his voice.

In the same tone, Lorraine replied, 'A friend.'

'Oh, well, sorry, we have to talk to a relative first.' With a dismissive flick of his hand, he turned towards the bed.

Bristling, and thinking *pompous bastard*, Lorraine reached the side of Dave's bed before him. 'I am also Detective Inspector Lorraine Hunt, in charge of this case.' She let that sink in for a moment. 'Now I'll ask you one more time, doctor, and I would appreciate a civil answer. How is he?'

'Oh well, yes ...' the doctor tugged on the stethoscope around his neck and peered at Lorraine, realising that she was not going to go away. He said defensively, 'Sorry about that, but if you had introduced yourself first.'

'I am also his friend, OK, and was, long before I became a detective. So, how is he?'

'Hmm.' He picked Dave's notes up from the bottom of the bed, studied them a moment, then put them back before going up to Dave and slowly examining him.

Seething, Lorraine couldn't stand much more. She opened her mouth to speak, but Luke, in a very pleasant voice, beat her to it.

'There are two things we really need to know, doctor, if you don't mind. First off, is he going to be alright, and second, have you any way at all of knowing if he was capable of doing this to himself?'

Then it was Luke's turn to feel a rush of anger inside but, as was usual for Luke, the anger melted before it even had time to solidify. The doctor had looked him up and down with barely concealed contempt, then completely ignored every word he'd said and turned to Lorraine.

'Excuse me?' Luke said.

The doctor swung his head back, a haze came over his eyes, he curled his lip and turned back to Lorraine.

'He'll live. There will be some scaring to his arm and neck and he'll need one or two skin grafts ... As for his state of mind, I am a medical doctor, not a psychiatrist.'

'Yeah, and thank God for that,' Lorraine snapped.

'I beg your pardon?'

Luke couldn't help but give a small laugh at the expression on the doctor's face, which earned him an angry glare. And when Lorraine gestured towards the door with her head, he followed her outside into the corridor.

'Twat,' she stated, as they started walking towards the exit.

Luke grinned. 'Probably having a bad hair day.'

She stopped and took hold of his hand. 'Doesn't it bother you when people behave like that, as if you ... As if you weren't even in the bloody room? And his face, the miserable git. For Christ's sake, he should know better, he's a doctor.'

Lorraine shook her head. 'You're a saint, Luke Daniels. I should have torn his head off. In fact ...' She turned back.

'No, no.' Luke stopped her. 'Just forget it, eh? Besides, I'm much more interested in the real story behind Dave Ridley. And', he glanced at his watch, 'I'm absolutely dying for a cuppa. Fancy a drink?'

'OK,' she answered reluctantly.

Sensing her reluctance made Luke even more determined to get to the bottom of it all. He knew her well enough by now to know when something was eating away at her, he also knew the only way to get it out of her was gently, very, very gently.

Fifteen minutes later they were sitting in a cafe along Seaburn's sea front. The sun was shining and not a cloud was in sight, the waves were crashing up against the pier and covering the lighthouse in a sparkling rainbow spray. Lorraine was looking out the window, into the middle distance. *It's like she's lost in the past* Luke thought as he put the drinks on the small round table.

Sitting down he looked at Lorraine, and knew that she was aware of him staring at her, but she stubbornly continued to look out the window.

'Well?' he finally said.

She turned to look at him. 'Not gonna go away, are you?'

Luke smiled. 'No.'

Lorraine sighed, and for a moment was lost again, in a long dark night when everything spun crazily out of control and seven lives were changed forever.

CHAPTER TWENTY-TWO

'Good grief Lorraine,' Luke said, finishing off his second cup of coffee. 'It must have been bloody awful for the lot of you. Really, you were only kids, the shock of it all must have been pretty bad.'

'Uh huh. That's one or two of the words I would use. When Dave found me I'd been unconscious for five or ten minutes and thank God I'd landed in fresh hay. A cracked rib, a lot of bruising, make that a hell of a lot of bruising, scraped knees and elbows, but pretty much alive and well really, compared to the others.' She finished her Diet Coke before going on. Luke noticed her fingers twitching, reaching for her bag; he knew she would kill for a cigarette at this moment.

'And that's when I came to and found myself staring at my missing friend Sara's dead face. She was naked, blood everywhere. She, she'd been beaten to death, and, oh god Luke, she'd been raped repeatedly she was hardly recognisable.' Lorraine looked deeply into Luke's eyes and the sadness he could see tore at his heart as she whispered, 'But I knew it was her.'

Luke leaned over and patted her arm. 'Good god Lorraine, how come you never told me about this before?'

Lorraine went on as if she'd never heard him. 'Dave and one of the ambulance men came over and that was when Dave, who had apparently been holding it together quite well, broke down. He ... he took one look at Sara and sort of unravelled right there in front of me. He's never been quite the same Dave since.' She held Luke's hand. 'The murderer was never caught. Sometimes I get Sara's file out.' She shook her head. 'But there's nothing, no leads.'

There was quiet between them for a few moments, then Luke said in a gentle voice, 'The petrol ... do you think that's why he, if he did pour it over himself, do you think ... Perhaps in his mind it all links up, he might think he should have already been dead and that's why he ... you know what I mean?'

Lorraine sighed, then nodded. 'Probably, something along the lines of he should have burned to death that night, because really he's blamed himself ever since.' She fell quiet again for a moment, her thoughts grabbed once more by the relentless past that once released into the here and now refused to let go.

She stared out of the window, then gave Luke a wan smile before going on. 'It was the woman, Brenda Sweeny, who told me the next day in the hospital. We had all of us been kept in overnight. Poor Brenda had suffered a mild heart attack ... She told me what had happened and how brave Dave had been. And, and that Jacko was in intensive care and had lost his eye, that his face would probably be scarred for life. And that ... That Randy, Randy had died.' Shaking her head, she stared at the red checked tablecloth.

Luke steadied her hands, which were ripping a napkin to shreds.

She went on, but not before Luke had noted the deep sadness in her eyes. 'The strange thing was that Brenda Sweeny was adamant that a few seconds after the crash another motorbike screeched past. The doctor said it must have been a flashback from the other bikes, her mind playing tricks on her because of the stress ... Anyhow, two years later she died, her family said she never quite got over the accident. They said she hardly ever slept, just wandered round the house at night, the odd times she did sleep she woke up screaming.'

Lorraine flicked a tear away as Luke lifted her other hand and kissed it. 'I'm so sorry.'

She smiled. 'It's a long time ago now.'

Luke's smile became a puzzled frown. 'But what happened to Sam?'

Lorraine shook her head. 'Nobody really knows. Even though we were angry at what had happened, we all knew that it was an accident, no way would he have planned it, so no charges or anything were ever brought. He disappeared that night and he's never been seen nor heard from since. But there's something else ... Sara, she ... she'd been bitten in the same way that Amy had.'

'What?'

Lorraine nodded. 'That's why you're in charge. Too close, too personal to me.' She looked at him through lowered lids.

He held his hands up. 'I know it's only a technicality, for the books, and you're the one who's really in charge.'

She smiled as Luke said gently, 'When were you gonna tell me about it?'

'Last night ... This morning, but then we heard about Dave.'

Luke was quiet for a moment, then he said, his tone changing, 'So what happened? I take it Sara's murderer was never found. Or were you not going to tell me that either?'

Lorraine shook her head. 'I'm sorry Luke, it's all been a bit too much ... Actually, Clark was in charge of the case. Believe it or not he was quite human back then. I'm sorry Luke, I should have explained last night, but I can't bear thinking about it. I thought it was finally behind me when the dreams started to fade a while back ... But now it's all come back.'

'Do you think Dave or what happened to Dave might have something to do with it? That's three of your friends, too much of a coincidence in my mind.'

'I don't know Luke, I really don't know, and to tell you the truth that possibility doesn't bear thinking about, but the bastard's not getting away with it this time. Together we'll sort this.'

Luke nodded. 'The problem is there are no forensics at all to speak of. He's a clever one Lorraine, very, very clever.'

'We'll get him.'

Luke was pleased to hear the steel back in her voice, but disappointed that communications between them seemed to be a bit off. 'But Lorraine, if this is a serial killer, why wait fourteen years between victims?'

'Who says that he has?'

CHAPTER TWENTY-THREE

'Andrew!' Leanne shouted up the stairs. 'Don't you think it's time you got out of bed, you lazy lump?'

She was answered with a muffled grunt that could have meant anything. Shaking her head she bent down and picked the post up off the mat. 'Bloody post's getting later every day, don't know what they're playing at,' she grumbled.

Sorting through the pile of flyers, snorting when she came across a couple of loan offers – 'Bloody idiots, why the hell do they keep sending them and tempting people when they know they can't afford to bloody well pay them back? Sackless sods' – she froze a moment later when she saw a letter at the bottom of the pile and recognised the handwriting.

'Him!'

Going into the sitting room she put the letter on the mantelpiece, where she left all of Sam's letters. Tammy would open it. She was the only one who kept up any sort of communication with their long-lost brother. Sure, the money had helped, even though at first she hadn't wanted to take it, had refused to take it, wanting nothing off him. But she'd soon realised she would be a fool not to. The wound, though, was still open. He'd left her to cope on her own and she strongly doubted if she would ever speak to him again.

She went into the kitchen and put the kettle on to boil. Tammy had left for work an hour ago, but she always filled the kettle before she left. Sometimes Leanne thought Tammy was much like Sam. She had the same fiery temper on her, and was as stubborn and as strong willed as he was. More than once she'd been called up to school because Tammy had been in a fight. But Tammy was full of little kindnesses that Sam didn't have.

Andrew came into the kitchen when Leanne was halfway through her cup of tea. She put the cup down and studied him as he went to the fridge and got milk.

God, he's really losing weight. It means nothing though, he's growing, boys grow like that. One week they're fat the next week they're thin and towering above you.

'You alright, Andrew?'

'Aye, why wouldn't I be, like?' He frowned at her as he put a bowl on the table and quickly filled it with cornflakes, then sloshed milk into the overflowing bowl.

'Just wondering, that's all. If there's anything bothering you, you know you can talk to me any time.'

Andrew was immediately on the defensive. 'What are you getting at, like?' He shoved a spoonful of cornflakes into his mouth.

'Nothing really, just talking, we used to talk a lot, not so long ago, if you can remember back a few months that is.'

'Huh,' he snorted, his eye on an escaped cornflake lying on the table. He snatched it up and dropped it into his bowl.

Watching him, Leanne thought, *When did his cheekbones get so sharp? Why is his skin suddenly looking grey and spotty?*

Icy fingers crawled up from her stomach and wrapped tightly

around her heart. She'd seen this look before, on the streets, more than once.

Mood swings, weight loss. No ... Noooo. Her mind skimmed away from what she was thinking, but it loomed in capitals. *DRUGS.*

Why have I let it go this long, why haven't I noticed something wasn't right?

But I had noticed, she told herself, sinking deeper into despair. *I just didn't want to believe it.* She sighed, and realised that this head in the sand business was doing neither of them any good and could end up with really dire consequences for Andrew if she let it roll on any longer.

'Andrew.'

'What?' he snapped, a spoonful of his breakfast halfway to his mouth.

'Nothing, I, er, I just worry, that's all.' Needing something to do with her hands she picked the clothes up out of the laundry basket and began folding them.

'Shut up. You're always picking on me.'

'No I'm not,' Leanne said indignantly and more sharply than she'd intended to.

'Yes you are.' Andrew's voice was rising with every word. 'Always on me back, wanting to know where I am every minute, don't get any peace at all.'

'Andrew!'

Impatiently he shoved the bowl of cornflakes away, milk slopped over the edges and spilled on the table. 'Now look what you made me do.'

Angry, he jumped up. He towered above her now, having had a huge growing spurt recently. He glowered down at her, sparking memories of another brother. 'Fuck it.'

'What did you just say?' Leanne was amazed and upset, Andrew had never talked to her like this before and never had he swore at her. With a sinking heart she realised that it was like hearing Sam all over again.

'Shut up, just shut up, and leave me alone!' Andrew shouted, sounding even more like his brother, his face now bright red. He was moving quickly to the back door and before Leanne could gather her wits he was gone and the door was banging shut behind him.

CHAPTER TWENTY-FOUR

'So he pulled a knife first?' Lorraine said to the shaven-haired youth with the physique of a body builder sitting at the other side of the desk in the interview room.

'No comment.'

'That's what it says here.' Lorraine flicked her eyes down at the notes then back at the skinhead.

'No comment.'

'Is your name Lee McCade?'

'No comment.'

'Did you stab Warren Mills?'

'No comment.'

Sitting in the corner, Luke fidgeted on his chair. But unfazed, Lorraine stared the youth out, and after a minute or so he dropped his eyes and looked towards the window.

'Why did you stab Warren Mills? Was it a drug deal gone wrong? Was Mills becoming greedy?'

'No comment.'

'Why did you say there was another knife on the premises when none was found?'

'No comm ...'

That was as far as he got, the explosion Luke had been anticipating happened. 'I'll give you no comment, you ugly bastard,' she banged the desk. 'I'll take your no comments and shove them down your fat fucking throat.'

'Whaaat?' he blustered.

'I said ...'

'I want me solicitor,' he squealed in a high-pitched voice that made Luke grin.

'What do you know about Dave Ridley?'

'What? You can't pin that on me. No way.'

'Where were you when Dave Ridley was set on fire?'

'Nowhere near that bloody nutter. And that's a fact.'

'Got a witness, have you?'

'Oh, aye,' he nodded. 'A whole load of them.'

'And who would they be? Warren Mills and Dave Ridley? Oh aye, and your family? All the McCades? Nice bunch of alibi makers that lot, aren't they?'

He glared at her, his mouth twisted in a mean line. 'Think you're so fucking clever, don't you, bitch?'

Luke stiffened in his chair and gritted his teeth, knowing he should never let it become personal and that Lorraine could give as good as she got with any lowlife they brought in. *Chill*, he thought. *Let her handle it.*

'If you must know,' McCade said through gritted teeth, as Lorraine glared at him, 'I was at Washington Galleries.'

'Witness for that, I suppose?'

'A whole fucking bus full,' McCade grinned.

Lorraine wiped the grin off his face with one sentence as she put her elbows on the table and rested her chin on the back of her hands. 'You do have previous,' she said sweetly.

Lee McCade looked puzzled for a moment, before snapping, 'Piss off. I was only fourteen.'

'Yeah.' Lorraine's tone changed. 'And like that's an excuse? We were all once upon a time only fourteen, you bloody prat, but we didn't all go around getting our kicks setting poor helpless dogs on fire. Did we?'

He squirmed under Lorraine's piercing stare. 'It was only two of them.'

'Jesus Christ!' Luke stated angrily. McCade spun round and glared at Luke, who glared right back.

'OK,' Lorraine went on, 'which one are you going to admit to? By the way, whichever one, the pooch story will surface again, I can promise you that.' She smiled at him.

'Bastard,' he spat at her. '*Bastard*. It was self defence, I told you that.'

'What, the little doggies had a can of petrol and a matchbox and were going to set you on fire first, but you beat them to it?' Lorraine raised her eyebrows, exaggerating an amazed expression. 'Clever little buggers, weren't they. I thought my dog Duke was bright, but he doesn't hold a candle to those two.'

Hate glared out of his eyes as he curled his lip and snarled, 'No comment.'

'OK Luke, lock him up 'til his lawyer gets here, then we'll charge him with GBH against Warren Mills.'

'I told you, it was self-defence, and you know as well as I do that Mills carries. He's been done for it before.'

'What's the word on the street about Dave Ridley?'

McCade blinked rapidly, thinking if he talked now, he would pull a deal. 'Huh. Ridley. You want to know the truth? The word is it was somebody with a score to settle. Been getting on a lot of people's nerves lately. Me, I think he did it himself.'

'Hmm. I don't quite know how much I can believe the word of a puppy burner.'

'Oooh,' Luke couldn't help himself. 'Boss!'

McCade curled his lip. 'It's gospel.'

'OK, Luke.'

'No,' McCade blustered. 'I thought we had a deal.'

'Deal? I can't remember making a deal, and the tape hasn't stopped rolling.'

'Bitch!' he spat.

Luke took hold of McCade's elbow, his fingers digging into the soft flesh. Faced with no other choice McCade stood, and Luke took the now silent skinhead away while Lorraine rummaged inside her drawer for a pencil. A moment later she slammed it shut, remembering she'd cleared every damn chewed pencil stub out. She hadn't needed the cigarette substitute for a while now, but this business with Dave had her on edge and unpleasant memories had surfaced that she would rather keep submerged.

Luke came back, rested his palms on the front of her desk, leaned forward and said, 'Puppy burner?'

'Yeah, I know, it made me cringe too.' With an exaggerated sigh she rose and, leaving Luke to finish off the paperwork, went along to the canteen knowing that in this heat most of her team would be there craving a cold drink.

She sat down next to Travis and Peters and had just opened her Diet Coke when Dinwall came in. Spotting her, he walked over. Dinwall had been to the hospital when they got the word that Dave Ridley had woken up.

'How is he?' Lorraine asked when Dinwall reached them.

'As well as can be expected, the doc said when I asked him, and that's all he said.'

'Huh.' Lorraine pulled a face. 'But did you manage to get any information from Dave?'

'Well ...' Dinwall scratched his ear before taking his notebook out. Flicking it open, he said, 'We have three lots of suspects.'

Lorraine frowned. Travis and Peters stopped talking to each other and listened as Dinwall went on. 'Well,' he said again, and paused for a moment before saying theatrically, 'it's either the government, aliens on the far side of the moon, or the fairies at the bottom of Mrs Reardon's garden.'

Travis and Peters burst out laughing, 'No change there then,' Travis said in-between hoots.

Exasperated, Lorraine shook her head, 'And that's it?'

Travis laughed even louder, 'How many more suspects do you want, boss?'

'Yeah, very funny. Didn't that miserable twat of a doctor say anything else?'

Trying to keep as straight a face as possible under the circumstances, Dinwall went on, ignoring the strangled laughter from his colleagues. 'He says Dave needs specialist help.'

CHAPTER TWENTY-FIVE

Six hours later Lorraine was hanging Duke's leader on the peg when her mobile rang.

'Sanderson, what's up?'

'Just picked up a phone call from Leanne Knightly. Apparently the youngest Knightly's gone missing.'

Lorraine looked at her watch. 'It's only bloody ten o' clock – he'll be where other seventeen year olds are at this time of night, for God's sake.'

'She's very worried boss, seems they've had a blazing row, and she's worried sick. I knew you would want to know.'

'OK, Sanderson, leave it with me.' She looked at Duke, 'Fancy another walk, mate?'

Duke wagged his tail as Lorraine took his leader down off the peg and clipped it back on to his collar.

The Seahills was only a five-minute walk from the cottage that Lorraine lived in with her mother and godmother since her divorce.

When she reached Leanne's house she could see Tammy looking out the window.

Tammy waved when she recognised Lorraine coming up the path. Knowing that Tammy had always been allergic to animal hair Lorraine tied Duke up to the gate post, where, seeing as it was such a warm night and with plenty of new smells in this strange place, Duke was very happy to be and soon had his nose in a patch of dandelions.

'So what's the matter, Leanne?' Lorraine smiled as she came into the sitting room and sat down.

'I've told her she's worrying for nowt,' Tammy answered for her sister. 'He'll come home any minute, full of the gab like the little brat always is.'

'Hasn't he got a mobile?' Lorraine asked.

'Aye he's got a mobile, but the little shit never has any credit on it. Softy there,' Tammy glared at Leanne, 'fills the bugger up for him every week, but he uses it all in a couple of days talking to his daft mates. Anyhow, I don't know what the hell we're all worrying about, he'll be with one of them scumbags.'

'No.' Leanne shook her head adamantly. 'He ... Things haven't been right for a month or two, Tammy ...' Leanne held up her hand, as Tammy was about to interrupt. 'I'm sorry, but you only see him for a few minutes each day if that.' She turned back to Lorraine and blurted quickly, because if she didn't say it now she never would, 'I ... I think he's on drugs.'

'What!' Tammy exploded. 'Why didn't you say something? I'll cave his bloody head in if he is, the stupid ...' She paced the length of the small sitting room and spun round at the window. 'He knows what can happen, he's been told plenty of times. Jesus, you only have to look around you these days, it's like the bloody flu, it's every bloody where. And you lot' – she glared at Lorraine – 'do fuck all about it.'

'We do everything we can Tammy, but half the time our hands are tied. We catch them, twenty-four hours later they're back out on the streets.'

'Aye, peddling their poison while the politically correct tits are banging on about how bad fags are for you. Huh. They haven't got a clue. Christ, they're practically giving the green light for fucking dope, they should visit the mental wards, see the kids in there climbing the fucking walls ... I mean it, when the idiot gets in here I'm gonna kill him.'

Stacey arrived in time to hear most of what had just been said. Going up to Leanne she put her hand on her shoulder. 'Why do you think that? Why would he be on drugs, Leanne?'

Leanne was staring at the fireplace and didn't lift her head. 'I just know.'

Lorraine sighed. 'Technically we can't really do anything until he's been missing for twenty-four hours ...'

'He's just a kid, for God's sake,' Tammy shouted.

'He's seventeen, Tammy,' Lorraine replied calmly, knowing Tammy was just getting her vent out. 'Of course I'll send a report out to all the patrol cars, and if any of them see him they'll bring him right back home.'

'Thanks Lorraine,' Leanne said with a wan smile of gratitude.

'Aye, thanks for nothing,' Tammy added as Lorraine stood up to go home.

'Tammy, have you any idea how many kids run off because they've had a row at home and come home a few hours later with their tails between their legs?'

'No, I haven't,' Tammy retorted. 'But I bet you anything you like there's as many that don't come home at all.'

Lorraine had no answer to that. Tammy was right, thousands went missing each year never to be seen or heard of again. Instead she turned to Leanne, squeezed her shoulder and said, 'I'll do my best, love.'

Leanne patted the back of Lorraine's hand. 'I know, Lorraine.'

A few minutes later Lorraine left the Knightly girls and headed for home. As she walked out of Daffodil Close and entered Tulip Crescent, her thoughts were with Leanne and the job she had been handed fifteen years ago, a job she had done exceptionally well on her own since that rat Sam had run out on her.

Sam had been selfish all of his life, no one knew that better than her, but back then Sam had not been a murderer. He'd been angry and wanted to frighten Randy. He didn't want to kill him. The whole business had been a terrible accident. She'd known that Sam was already nearly at the end of his tether with the responsibility of the kids, and that was one of the reasons why he'd run. He'd have guessed rightly that the McCades would never rest until they made him pay one way or another.

She shivered, remembering just how absolutely terrified she'd been herself. Helpless, unable to do anything but cling on to Randy and scream until her throat was raw. The unwanted image of her friend Sara's dead eyes staring at her, the stuff of nightmares that crept up in the middle of the night when she least expected it.

She tried to focus on Andrew. *He'll be alright*, she told herself. *Of course he will, just another teenage thing. He'll turn up.*

Praying that he would, she crossed the road and spotted Doris Musgrove, Dolly Smith and Mr Skillings standing at Doris's gate.

At the house opposite a group of youths were sitting in the garden drinking cans of lager. One of them shouted something across the road to Dolly and the rest laughed. Dolly shook her fist at them, but she was smiling.

'Are they bothering you at all?' Lorraine asked when she reached the trio.

'Why no, don't worry Lorraine love, we can handle that bloody daft lot.' Doris smiled at her. 'They've had a barbie for the bairn's birthday, but it's winding down now ... Not like that other lot round the corner. Blast music to all hours, they do.'

'Haven't you complained to the council, or phoned us?'

'Aye once or twice, it shuts them up for a few days then they start all over again.'

Lorraine had no doubt at all that Doris and her friends could handle the gang across the road, who had lived there as long as Doris had, and who now, recognising Lorraine, were nudging each other and whispering. But Lorraine knew who it was that Doris meant by 'that lot round the corner' ... The McCades.

'I'll send a patrol car round until they finally get the message. Dinwall hates them, he'll only be too glad to pay them a frequent visit. Getting a bit too big for their boots lately. So, Jacko and Christina all set for the big day then?'

'You betcha, can't wait, and our little Melanie's gonna sing in the church an' all. What d'you think of that?' Doris said, sticking her chest out with pride for her granddaughter while her friends nodded their heads in unison.

'Looking forward to it Doris, Melanie has a fantastic voice, and Mam and Peggy are fighting already about which colours they'll be wearing.'

Mr Skillings nodded wisely at Dolly, who controlled the urge to stand on his toes.

'Er, er, how's Dave Ridley, then?' Doris asked.

'He's doing as well as can be expected, Doris.'

'So he is still alive?'

'Yes, did you think ...?'

'You know what the rumours are like round here,' Mr Skillings put in. 'Sandra was about to start a collection for funeral flowers.'

'Oh, dear,' Lorraine said. 'Well, he's not gonna die, thank god, so tell Sandra she needn't bother, OK?'

They all nodded together.

'Goodnight then ... And I'll make sure a patrol car comes round tonight, and at other times when they least expect it.'

'I told you all to wait until it was in the *Echo*, didn't I?' Mr Skillings nodded his head, agreeing with himself. 'Nowt should be took as gospel 'til you read it in the *Sunderland Echo*.'

'Cheers love,' Doris and Dolly chimed together, ignoring Mr Skillings, who was still nodding at Lorraine.

'Hot, isn't it?' Dolly said. 'There'll not be much sleep tonight I'll bet.'

'Aye,' Mr Skillings agreed, 'you can't leave your windows open like you used to in the old days, that's a bloody fact an' all.'

Lorraine smiled and, after assuring them that they were safe in their beds, left them and headed home, her thoughts heavy with everything that had led up to now.

Were the McCades responsible for setting Dave on fire? They were certainly capable. The only decent one out of the whole bunch had been Randy, and they had sworn that one day they would get even: they swore as they threw soil on Randy's grave.

She passed the McCade house but it was in darkness. This branch was one of the sons, Randy's uncle, Pete McCade, brother of the skinhead who was still festering in the cells. He and his two sons were as evil as the rest of them.

Looks like they've upset someone recently though, judging by that boarded-up window.

'Come on,' she said to Duke as he stopped to sniff at the weeds growing through the holes in the fence.

She reached home and five minutes later she was sitting with Mavis and Peggy.

'So do you think she's worrying unnecessarily?' Mavis asked.

'Well, I certainly hope so. Andrew has never been in any kind of trouble before, he was such a sweetie when he was little.'

'That's true. Leanne's done a hell of a job with them kids, she should start enjoying herself now, not be worrying what the hell he's up to. If I know that Tammy, she'll give him what for when he does get in. Same paddy on her as was on Sam, like two bloody peas.'

'Oh, the lad'll turn up,' Peggy sniffed. 'Don't know what she's doing bothering the police about a seventeen year old, it's just gone eleven now.'

'Still worrying though, Peg, if he's not usually out this late.'

'Give the kid a break for God's sake, will you? I bet it's like living with a bunch of battery hens living with them three,' Mavis stated.

Lorraine laughed at the mental picture she had of Leanne, Tammy and Stacey sitting on top of Andre

'Yeah, I bet,' Peggy said, joining in Lorraine's laughter.

Lorraine stroked Duke's ears while she finished filling Mavis and Peggy in on the missing Andrew Knightly business.

'Oh, dear,' Mavis said when Lorraine had finished. 'Poor Leanne will be in a right state.'

'He'll turn up tomorrow, don't fret, you know what the bloody teenagers are like these days,' Peggy said as she nodded her head knowingly.

'And we were saints?' Mavis looked at her with a wry expression.

'Well, you certainly weren't.'

'Oh my God, and you were?'

Peggy shrugged and said with a smug smile, 'Whatever. I'm off to bed.' And with a flourish she wrapped her pink fluffy dressing gown around her body and left them.

'Oh, sometimes!' Mavis said, shaking her fist at Peggy's back.

Lorraine shook her head and couldn't help but smile as she said, 'How the hell you two have stayed friends all these years beats me.'

'Because, Lorry, she knows everything there is to know about me, and I know everything there is to know about her ... And aggravating bitch that she can be at times, she has the kindest heart in the world, as you well know.'

'OK, you're right, I love her to bits, even though she is, as you say, a bloody aggravating bitch when she wants to be. Anyhow, I'm going up.'

'See you in the morning then ... And don't worry Lorry, Peggy's probably right.'

'Yeah,' Lorraine replied as she gently pushed Duke's head away. 'Bedtime, boy.'

Once upstairs Lorraine started to pack her small suitcase ready take to work with her tomorrow. She stayed over at Luke's on weekends, and Friday nights they usually cuddled up with a pizza shared with Luke's daughter Selina and her boyfriend Mickey. It was good to see how Luke and Selina got along now, well, most of the time, and Luke actually went out of his way, sometimes, to get along with Mickey, which truthfully wasn't really hard. The kid was so hapless you couldn't help but like him and he fell over himself time and again to please Luke.

She packed a lemon T-shirt on top of her jeans. This was supposed to be their full weekend off and they had planned to go hiking in the Lake District.

Suddenly Lorraine folded in the middle and sat on the edge of her bed. She used to go to the Lake District with the guys on the motorbikes. The last trip had been a week before the accident and she'd worn a very similar T-shirt.

'Oh, God,' she murmured.

For a long time after the accident she'd tortured herself with thoughts like *Was it my fault? Did I knowingly tease Randy? Did I lead him on in any way at all? Was I trying to make Sam jealous?*

But the worst thought by far was *Would Randy still be alive today if I hadn't gone for that terrible ride? What if it had all been down to me?*

All our lives changed that night. Poor Randy and Sara lost theirs, eighteen years old, and to die in such a terrible way. Jacko lost an eye, Dave lost his mind, and Brenda Sweeny died as a direct result even if it had been a few years later. And Sam – what had really happened to Sam?

She had wondered more than once if Leanne ever heard from Sam, but she had never asked, and Leanne had never said. The times she bumped into her, or visited now and again, neither Sam nor the events of that night had ever come up. Forensics had found no link to Sam and both she and Leanne had skirted around it, neither wanting to be the first to mention it, and so it had stayed under the carpet.

She hung her head in her hands.

No, no, she'd told herself down the years.

And *No, no,* she told herself now.

Because really she had not been remotely interested in either one of them. They were mates, best friends, that's all.

There was only one of them that she had truly loved, but other than being a good friend he had shown no interest at all. And when she'd come back from university he was with someone else: the mother of his daughter, Melanie.

CHAPTER TWENTY-SIX

'Come on Jacko. It's easy money, for God's sake, and don't tell me you don't need it, what with the wedding an' all,' Danny Jordon said, resting his arm on the bar, his cousin Len nodding behind him as they finished their pints off in the Beehive pub. 'I ask you, who the hell doesn't need a few extra bob these days?'

'It's keeping up with all these electric gadgets nowadays, isn't it? One kid gets something new, next day they all want it, it's like a bloody plague. What beats me though is where it's all coming from, all these inventions. Makes you wonder, doesn't it?'

Both Danny and Jacko looked at Len, then Danny went on as if Len hadn't spoken. 'Like I was saying, it's easy money, a few extra bob that we all need ...'

'Hmm.' Jacko thought it through for a moment then, looking at Danny, said, 'Aye, you're right, it would come in handy. You've come up with some hare-brained schemes before Danny, but I think this one beats the lot.'

'Why no, man, it'll be a doddle, money for old rope, four-way split. I'll just want the diesel money off everybody, equal parts, the rest we share.'

'So who's the other man, then?'

'Adam Glaiser.'

Len put in with a scowl. Jacko chuckled. Len couldn't stand Adam Glassier, but then Len could barely stand himself at the best of times.

'Adam's alright, man.'

'Aye, if you say so. His bloody jokes stink though. I swear he makes them up as he goes along.'

'And yours are great, are they?' Danny said as they made their way to the door, waving at Jimmy Foley, the barman, as they left.

'Goodnight lads,' Jimmy shouted after them before turning to the rest of his clientele and giving his nightly sermon. 'Ladies and Gentlemen, this is not a request, it is a requirement of the law, see your drinks off please and fu ... fu ... fu ... find your way home!'

Jacko and Danny waved again as Len turned and said goodnight. Catching up with the other two at the outside door, he said, 'I don't tell jokes.'

'You can say that again,' Danny smiled at Jacko.

'I don ...'

'Yeah, yeah.' Danny refrained from slapping his hand over his cousin's mouth, though he sometimes ached to do so. 'So what do you reckon, Jacko? It'll be like old times, us lot together. You know we make a good team and if you thought you needed money before, trust me, with a wife you're **gonna** need a whole lot more ... And what about kids?'

'Kids!'

'Yeah, you know, them little buggers that cost you an arm and a leg ... Don't say that you never thought Christina might want a few of her own?'

Jacko licked his suddenly dry lips; he hadn't actually given it a thought. He shoved it to the back of his mind to dwell on later. 'Aye, but look what bother the last little escapade you dreamed up got us into.'

Danny brushed being mistaken for drug dealers, then being chased up the motorway by said drug dealers with guns, losing all the cigarettes and booze from the haul, aside. They had, after all, got everything back. 'But this'll be cool.'

They had reached the street where they went their separate ways, Jacko and Len into Tulip Crescent while Danny moved on to Hyacinth Road.

'I'll have to think about it,' Jacko said, not sounding sure at all. 'The old girl won't be too pleased, me going off with you lot again. I still haven't heard the last of the fag fiasco, and now she has Christina to back her up.'

'But what's there to think about? Piece of cake if you ask me, and damn good money to boot.'

'Aye, but ...' Jacko sighed. Melanie had her heart set on a new dress. He shook his head and looked Danny in the eye. 'Who's gonna do the killing, then?'

Len stopped walking, sucked air in through his teeth, blew it out, then said, 'Now, there's the rub!

CHAPTER TWENTY-SEVEN

'I still say you're far too bloody soft with him,' Tammy snapped, pacing the floor with one eye on the clock. 'It's half past twelve! I tell you, I'm gonna kill him when he gets in.'

'Calm down,' Stacey said, coming in from the kitchen with a tray full of coffees.

Tammy snatched one of the cups off the tray, nearly capsizing the lot. 'You do realise this is the fourth coffee in a couple of hours? If the brat does come home soon we still won't be able to get to sleep.'

'He'll be fine.' Stacey handed a cup to Leanne, it had Leanne's name on it, a present from Andrew's last school trip. Stacey had been hesitant to use it, even though she was convinced that nothing bad had happened to Andrew.

Leanne controlled a sob before taking a sip of the hot coffee. 'I really don't think he will, Stacey.'

'Christ almighty, have the pair of you got bloody crystal balls now?'

Leanne sighed and shook her head. 'What are we going to do?' she asked again.

'I've told you what I'm gonna do. The minute he walks in that door, the little shit is gonna get the hiding of his life. You should have told me he was getting out of control.'

Stacey sat down next to Leanne while Tammy continued her pacing, this time stopping at the window and looking out into the dark night. There were two lights on in the whole street apart from theirs, Len Jordan's at the far end and Jacko Musgrove's just across the street. Jacko's light snapped off as she watched.

Stacey put her coffee on the table; she didn't really know why she'd made more, just something to do, she supposed. 'So how many bridesmaids are Jacko and Christina having?' she asked in an attempt to take Leanne's mind off things and ease the tension.

Shrugging, Leanne replied, 'Dunno. Definitely Melanie, she told me the other day that her dress'll be pink.'

'She's a cutie, bet she'll look gorgeous, all that auburn hair ... Any invitations sent out yet?'

Leanne knew Stacey was fishing to find out if they had got an invitation that she had forgotten to tell her about. 'Don't fret, you know we'll be going.'

Stacey grinned, knowing her sister had sussed her out. She squeezed Leanne's hand and, smiling for a moment, Leanne returned the gesture.

Tammy turned from the window and looked at the clock again, her dark eyes angry. Twelve forty-five. 'That's it. I'm going looking for the little toe rag and trust me I will be dragging him back by his bloody ears.'

'Should we come?' Stacey asked as Tammy swept past them.

'No, wait here.' She went into the hallway and shrugged her jacket on, opened the front door then came back for her cigarettes. 'Don't worry, I'll be alright. I've got the mobile. I'll phone you every fifteen minutes, OK?'

Stacey nodded as she and Leanne watched their sister go out into the night. They both knew it was no good arguing with her, Tammy was like Sam in some ways – she would do what she wanted to do and no amount of arguing would stop her.

Tammy walked to the end of the empty street. Every house was in darkness. The streetlamps provided adequate lighting though, and Tammy's night vision was good.

Reaching the last street in the Seahills, she stood underneath the palm trees on the corner beside the Beehive and looked up the lane towards Newbottle, deserted, not even a car moving down the road. Then she swung her head to the right towards Fencehouses, equally deserted. Crossing the road she entered the Homelands and noticed the odd house light on here and there, but the streets were as devoid of people as the Seahills had been. Some of the boarded-up houses gave the place a really creepy feeling: the Homelands was dying and in its death throes nothing of the community spirit of not so long ago shone through. As for many other housing estates up and down the country, the bell had tolled.

'Where the hell to start looking?' she muttered, feeling helpless and a little angry at herself for not knowing who her brother hung out with. She knew the friends he'd had in school and realised now that none of them came around anymore.

So who the hell does he hang with?

Taking out her mobile she phoned Stacey, she talked for a minute letting them know she was fine. 'OK, OK,' she said to Stacey, who urged her to be careful. She switched off and put the phone in her pocket, all the while her frown deepening. It seemed no one knew who their little brother was out and about with.

How the fuck?

'Are you lost, love?' The deep voice from behind startled her for a moment. Ready to fight or run, she was well capable of either, and she quickly spun round.

'Oh, Mr Stevens. You frightened the life out of me,' Tammy said, relived to see the old man and his Jack Russell dog, who sniffed at her shoes.

'Sorry pet, it's Phoebe, she's getting old now and if she doesn't get out this late on a night to clean herself, it's all over the house in the morning, a right old mess she makes bless her, you wouldn't believe the places she manages to get into. You looking for somebody, pet?'

'Actually yes, do you know if the Stamfords still live round here?' She was pleased that she'd suddenly remembered the name of one of the boys Andrew used to knock around with not so long ago. 'Simon, Simon Stamford.'

'Oh aye, know them well, and you're in luck, pet, top of the street, see, the light's still on.'

'Oh great.' She started to walk away. 'Thanks, and look after Phoebe.'

He laughed. 'That's alright, bonny lass.'

Tammy hurried up the street, frightened in case the lights went out just before she got there. But her luck held and as she drew closer she could hear music, it wasn't too loud but by god if her neighbours were playing music this time of night she'd have the gloves on alright.

Walking up the path she noticed the curtain move, she knew she'd been seen and wasn't surprised when, her hand poised to knock, the door opened, and the music had been turned down a good few notches as well.

'I've turned it down,' Simon Stamford squeaked in the high-pitched voice that Tammy remembered. Obviously he thought she had come to complain about the noise.

'Don't you remember me, Simon?'

Poking his head further out the door and peering at her, he said, 'Tammy?'

'Got it in one, Simon. Is our Andrew in there?'

'Your Andrew?'

'You were never that bloody thick before, Simon Stamford. who the hell else would I be looking for at this time of night?'

Simon screwed his face up. 'Never seen your Andrew for ages ... Months, even.'

'Why?'

He shrugged. "Cos he knocks around with somebody else now, that's why.' He tutted and looked at Tammy as if she should have realised the obvious.

For a moment Tammy was silent, then she asked the same question again.

'I just told you, it's months since I seen him,' he replied sullenly.

'Don't get arsey with me kid, alright, I'm just fucking asking.'

Simon pulled his head back. He'd had a slap off Tammy before and his father didn't hit as hard.

'Is your mother in?'

'Em ... I, er ...' he blustered.

'Thought not. I know she wouldn't put up with this racket. Right, what do you know about our Andrew? And I mean everything you know about Andrew. What's the word, is he in any kind of trouble that we should know about?'

Looking more awkward than ever, he shuffled his feet for a moment, and Tammy could practically see his brainwaves thanking god when he was saved from answering by a teenage girl in a black Mini and far too much makeup coming to the door.

'What's up?' she asked scowling at Tammy. 'You complaining, or what?'

'Shh ... Debs, leave it,' Simon said, panicking, knowing full well that Tammy was quite capable of giving a clout first, then asking questions later.

'Why, what's she gonna do?' the girl named Debs asked, sneering at Tammy.

Stepping forward and with a menacing tone Tammy said, 'Trust me kid, you don't want to know.' She turned back to Simon. 'Now, you ugly scrotum ... Tell me whatever you know about our Andrew.'

'Don't know nothing.'

It was obvious though, the way the kid was practically shaking in his shoes, that he did know something, and whatever it was terrified the life out of him.

The girl tried to shut the door. 'He's told you he knows nowt, now piss off.'

Tammy put her hand against the door. She proved to be much stronger than the girl when the door slammed up hard against the wall, sending a shower of plaster all over the girl and Simon's hair.

Tammy didn't attempt to hide her smile, then, a moment later, yelled in the girl's face: 'Do you think I'm stupid, you daft twat? Of course you know something, it's written all over your face ... Both of your fucking faces.'

'He's said already, he ain't seen him in months, and neither have I. Nobody's seen him. Are you deaf or what?'

Ignoring her, Tammy glared at Simon. 'I'm warning you. If I find out you're lying, I'll skin you alive.'

Simon put his head down and slowly began to close the door. She knew she was going to get nothing out of these two at this time, which didn't mean they wouldn't get another visit in the morning if the brat hadn't turned up by then. Tammy headed for home.

'So that's about it.' Tammy sighed and looked at Leanne, whose face had turned a very pale shade of grey, then to Stacey, who was staring at the fireplace.

'Why would Simon tell lies?' Stacey asked, nibbling away at her fingernail. 'If he hasn't seen him it doesn't mean he's up to other things, nasty things.'

'Why would he, Stacey? For God's sake grow up. Andrew certainly has, right under our noses an' all.'

'I swore he wouldn't turn out like our Sam, I promised our mam I would look after him,' Leanne sobbed.

'Oh, Leanne. You've looked after him, you've looked after all of us, please don't cry, it's not your fault, we all should have seen the change in him. I thought he was just, well, you know, being a typical moody teenager, so it's not just down to you, OK? You did your best, you always did.'

Stacey took hold of Leanne's hand. 'You know, we're probably worrying for nothing. It'll just be a stage he's going through, a teenage thing.'

'No.' Leanne shook her head, 'I'm telling you, he's not the same kid he was a few months ago.'

'Oh for God's sake. Who the fuck is?' Tammy exploded. 'Where's the evidence, huh? Does he come in stinking of glue? Are his fucking eyes on stalks? Is he stealing from your purse? Come on Leanne, you've seen what goes on with the kids.'

'I know something's wrong, don't ask me how, but I know. He's acting differently, and more than once he's come in and practically ran up the stairs before I've had a chance to look at him and he's eating anything he can get his hands on, and the bloody weight's dropping right off him. He's on something, I don't care what you say,' Leanne stated adamantly.

'Oh, fuck this for a lark, I'm going to bed. The kid's most probably drunk somewhere.' Angry, Tammy stormed out of the room, but inside she had her own nagging doubt that Leanne might be right and something terrible had happened to Andrew.

As she undressed her anger was replaced by a feeling of helplessness.

In the middle of the night there was nothing she could do, nothing at all.

CHAPTER TWENTY-EIGHT

Lorraine had left for work early to make a detour past the Knightlys' house. It looked silent and still as she walked up the path. Trying the door, she found it open and walked in. Leanne was sitting in the chair she had been sitting in last night still wearing the clothes she'd had on the night before. Lorraine's heart sank.

'Obviously you haven't been to bed, which means he didn't come home, then?'

Leanne took a deep breath, and shaking her head she let the air out of her lungs and looked up at Lorraine, fear and misery evident in her weary eyes. 'Something's happened, Lorraine. I know it, I can feel it,' she said with conviction.

Lorraine was at a loss as to what to say for the moment. She had learned a long time ago to trust people's instincts. Sometimes they were wrong, their brains and bodies running on fear and conjuring up God knows what sorts of horrors. But sometimes they were right, especially mothers, and to all intents and purposes Leanne was Andrew's mother, even if she had not given birth to him.

'Right then, we'll go to full scale. The night patrol haven't seen him, I phoned in before I got here. All in all it's been a pretty quiet night all round.' She put her hand to Leanne's shoulder. 'You know we'll do our best to find him.'

Twenty minutes later she had the whole crew in the incident room. Perched on the corner of the table, her favourite place, she gave everyone a full run down on Andrew Knightly. Pictures of him had been photocopied and handed out to each officer.

'Boss?'

'Yes, Dinwall.'

'This lad's seventeen years old, he's only been missing a day. He's probably lying on his mate's settee either drunk or stoned out of his skull.'

'That's what we're hoping for Dinwall, but the problem is no one knows who these mates of his are, apparently the lads he used to knock about with haven't seen him in months. It happens. You leave school and find new mates.'

'Aye, but I bet you anything you like the old lot will know who he hangs with.'

'Oh yes, they'll know alright. Tammy Knightly went looking last night. She swears the kid she was talking to was hiding something.'

'Aye, that'll be right. Devious little bastards these days. When I was a kid, a copper would give you a clout if he caught you doing something wrong, and if you went home and told your dad, you got another clout off him. End of story. Nowadays the parents make a big thing of defending the brats and wonder why a few years later they're staring at them through bars. So. What's the plan?'

'I was about to reveal all when you interrupted as usual, Dinwall.' Lorraine slammed the file she'd been holding on the desk. Carter winced, Sanderson frowned, while Travis sniggered. Peters and Luke just shook their heads.

'Sorry, boss.'

'I'm not your boss.'

That caused Travis to snigger again and Lorraine glared at him every bit as hard as she had at Dinwall. 'OK, if the pantomime is over we have a young boy missing. And a serial murderer on the loose. I suggest we bloody well get out there and get looking.'

During the next five minutes she hurled instructions at them. When she had finished they all, except Luke, very quietly left the room.

'You seem really worried about this one, Lorraine?' Luke said, walking over to stand beside her.

'It's Sam's brother, Luke.'

Luke held his breath for a moment, then said quietly, 'Oh, I see, I never put the connection together. Hmm.'

'What do you mean, "Hmm"? You sound like a bloody bee.'

'Nothing, nothing at all,' he shrugged. 'I just wondered, that's all.'

'Wondered what? For God's sake, if you have anything to say, spit it out.' But she didn't give him a chance to say anything as she went on, 'You think I'm giving them preferential treatment, don't you? Because I grew up with them, I know them, don't you?'

Luke took a step back. Lorraine's attack had been ferocious, and she still refused to let him get a word in as she stormed on. 'What about a few months ago, eh? When it was your daughter who was missing? Pulled all the stops out then, didn't I?'

'Jesus, Lorraine!' Luke stopped her in mid sentence. 'What on earth is wrong with you?'

She ran her right hand over the top of her head, then held her left hand in front of her, creating a barrier. 'I'm sorry Luke. That was well out of order. I'll talk to you later, OK?'

Sighing heavily, she walked away, leaving a confused Luke wondering what he'd done wrong.

What is it about these Knightlys? Did she tell me everything that went on that night?

Does she in some way feel as guilty as Dave Ridley?

But why?

Vowing to have it out with her that night Luke turned and went out to the front desk. He was in court that morning, that was if he was lucky and it didn't drag on all day. Anna Bentley was up for shoplifting again and he had actually witnessed it himself, being in the corner shop at the actual time of the event. The trouble was Anna Bentley had the gift of the gab and looked like a bloody angel. She'd talked her way out of more than one offence, but having him as a witness, the prosecution service was certain they had her banged to rights this time.

And he was getting nowhere with this murder. He'd sent men up into Houghton asking if any strangers were about, into the pubs, into the shops. Nada. Nothing. Zilch. And Scottie had come up with even less. He'd studied the notes of the first murder fourteen years ago and it was identical, no clues, all he could do was hope that something came back from the blood tests which – he glanced at his watch – should be sometime this afternoon.

He nodded at Peters, who had just relieved one of the young WPCs of desk duty, and left the station to go into the courtroom next door.

Lorraine sank into her chair. 'Shit!'

She put her head in her hands. *What the fuck is happening, after all this time?* She couldn't remember feeling so, so jittery. *But why?*

Why has Dave been set on fire at nearly the same time that Andrew Knightly goes missing? She pictured Dave lying in the hospital bed. *God, the pain he must be in, surely no matter what his mother said he can't have done it himself.* But deep down inside she knew that he was capable, and she was probably wasting valuable time and energy looking for a culprit. Even more puzzling though, Amy turning up after all this time and being murdered in exactly the same place as Sara had been.

Is it connected?

Have the McCades finally woken up?

Feeling her head start to throb, she opened the drawer, claimed a packet of paracetamol from its depths, closed the drawer and went over to the water cooler in the corner. She had just swallowed two of the tablets when Carter came in.

'The photo's gone off to the Sunderland Echo, boss. It'll run in to-day's edition.'

'Right, Carter. Come with me.'

'Where we going, like, boss?'

'Back to Leanne Knightly's. I need to question the girls some more.'

CHAPTER TWENTY-NINE

Jacko stood outside the door. He didn't usually eavesdrop, but sometimes he found it very entertaining when his daughter thought she could get her own way with his mother, Doris, when she thought he wasn't around.

'I'll wash the dishes every day for a week. Honest. I promise, Nana.'

'Melanie, pet, you can promise 'til you're blue in the face, the answer's still no.'

'But ...'

'No buts, we can't afford it and that's that, young madam. Now, where did I put the butter?'

'In the oven.'

'Very funny.'

Jacko's heart dropped. Obviously Melanie wanted something so desperately that she was willing to wash the dishes for a whole week to get it. He hated it when they couldn't afford to get her everything she wanted. *Mam's right though, it isn't good for kids to get every little thing they ask for, or they grow up thinking they have a right.* But still, up until now Melanie had been his life and always would be, even though Christina might want kids. If they came they came, and would be loved for themselves, but in the here and now Melanie was top priority.

'But Nana, that dress is horrible, and I'm not gonna wear it ... So there.'

'It's not horrible, you little minx, it's a perfectly lovely dress, and I'll not have you upsetting our Jacko and Christina by saying it's horrible. And you'd better stop behaving like a brat or you'll be sorry, you mark my words, madam.'

'Huh!' Melanie flounced from the kitchen into the sitting room and threw herself on to the armchair, where she shouted, 'The butter's in the bread bin.'

Jacko thought this was just about the right time to make his entrance.

'OK girls. What's the problem?' he asked walking into the kitchen.

'Dad!' Melanie jumped off the chair and ran to Jacko who scooped her up with one arm.

Kissing her cheek he gave her a big hug, then put her down. 'I'm waiting.'

Doris pulled a just-you-wait-my-girl face at Melanie as she proceeded to tell Jacko all about the horrible dress she was going to have to wear at the wedding.

'And the other one's loads better, Dad,' she finished off.

Jacko frowned at Doris. 'So what's the difference?'

'Well, actually, just about forty-five quid,' Doris said sarcastically, banging the kettle on to the cooker.

Oh Lord, Jacko sighed, *it might as well be forty-five thousand quid.* He looked at Melanie, who gazed up at him with adoring eyes.

'Has Christina seen both dresses?'

'Aye,' Doris answered. 'Of course she has. She is the bloody bride after all ... Right wise girl she is too. She says Melanie has to have the cheaper one, and I agree with her. There's nowt wrong with the bloody dress.'

It's horrible, Dad!' Melanie wailed. 'Dad, it ... it's *so* not me!'

Jacko smiled. 'Is it that bad, petal?'

'It's worse than bad. It's got daisies on it ... How gross. Daises!'

Jacko thought for a moment while, behind her back, Melanie had her fingers crossed.

'OK, there might be a way, love. I'm not promising,' he said quickly as Melanie's face lit up. 'But I might be able to get the one you want.'

'Can you Dad? Really? That's awesome. Dad, I love you,' Melanie grinned and clapped her hands together, bouncing up and down on her tiptoes excitedly before skipping back to the sitting room.

Doris shook her head but felt more like shaking her fist. 'Jacko, what on earth are you thinking about? How the hell can we afford another forty-five quid? The bloody invitations cost double what we budgeted for.'

'But if she hates it that much she's not gonna look good scowling all day, is she?'

'Son, you have a heart of gold, but sometimes you make promises that are nigh on impossible to keep. It's not fair on you and it's certainly not fair on the bairn, or Christina for that matter. She is the bloody bride you know ... And our Melanie, the little minx, wraps you right round her little finger.'

Jacko sighed. 'But I might have a way, Mam.'

'Oh aye, and what way is that?'

'Well, Danny has ...'

Doris held her hand up. 'Say no more. If it involves that crazy crew then the least I know the better. Just be careful, son, that you're not spending the honeymoon in jail, that's all. Anyhow, I knew I had something to tell you. Have you heard about the murder in the field up past the garage?'

'No. Who?'

'Nobody seems to know. I've had the local news on but it just says body found in field. Didn't give a name.'

But Jacko wasn't listening anymore, he was looking out of the window where a police car had pulled up outside of the Knightlys' house. Lorraine Hunt was getting out of it.

'What's going on over there?' he strode quickly to the window.

'What? Where?' Doris spun round like a homing rocket turning tail and followed Jacko to the window. 'Oh dear, I hope there's no trouble. Although now I remember Mr Skillings did say at the post office this morning that he'd heard that Andrew Knightly didn't come home last night. Oh!' she gasped. 'You don't think it could be ...?'

He shook his head as he watched Lorraine walk up the path. She'd hardly changed at all over the years. He wondered briefly if looking as good as she did was a hindrance in her line of work, then smiled softly, thinking *Lorraine wouldn't let anything hinder her in anything she did, she never has.*

He remembered Randy, who would never look a day older than eighteen, and wondered what he would have been doing now if he'd still been alive. Randy had been nothing like his brothers. He supposed that as the saying went there's always one bad apple, but in Randy's family he had been the only good apple.

'Doesn't look good to me. I forgot to tell you, Lorraine Hunt was there last night as well,' Doris said, pulling Jacko out of his reverie.

'I'm sure it's nowt to worry about, Mam.'

'Well I'd be bloody worrying if the coppers were knocking on my door.'

CHAPTER THIRTY

There was more than one pair of eyes trained on Lorraine as she walked up the Knightlys' path. Tammy Knightly was watching her from the bedroom window and Lorraine couldn't miss her glowering face.

Letting the curtain drop, Tammy hurried downstairs and reached the door exactly as Lorraine was about to knock.

'Anything?' she asked yanking the door open so hard that it bounced off the wall.

'No.' Lorraine shook her head as she stepped inside.

'Oh, God. Don't you know there's a bloody murderer on the loose out there for fuck's sake?' Tammy turned and went into the sitting room knowing Lorraine knew her well enough to follow. 'Nowt,' she said to Leanne's eager face, stomping to her usual place by the window, where she turned and stared at Lorraine with her arms folded across her chest.

Lorraine sat down next to Leanne. 'Sorry, love, but we've been out all day, nobody seems to know anything at all about Andrew. Who he hangs with, where he goes, which in itself is mighty suspicious, especially in this town.'

'So what?' Leanne lifted her hands in a helpless gesture.

'We keep on looking, I'm having a few guys that he's been known to hang with, mostly old school friends, pulled in tonight. I just popped over to let you know that we are doing something.'

'Get that Simon pulled in, I'm sure the little squirt knows something and he's not letting on,' Tammy snapped.

'It's OK, his parents are bringing him in tonight, so ...'

'The little grass,' Tammy snorted.

'So what happens now, Lorraine?' Leanne asked, her eyes red rimmed as she looked into Lorraine's.

'We keep on looking, that's all we can do.'

Leanne nodded, then tears spilled over. 'I know there's something wrong, Lorraine. And everybody's talking about that murder now. They say it's a woman's body you found. At first I thought it might have been our Andrew ... It is a woman, isn't it, you wouldn't keep it from me while you did those test things would you?'

Lorraine sighed deep inside as she looked at the despair on Leanne's face, deeply regretting that there was nothing more that she could do at this moment in time. She stood up. 'No Leanne, no way would I put you through that.' She hesitated a moment, she hated telling lies, but Amy's name had not been released yet. 'We don't know who she is ... for sure. I'll have to go now, believe me I'll keep you informed personally.'

As Lorraine passed Leanne her thoughts were bubbling. *Somehow it is all connected to that night, it has to be. First Sara, then Amy ... Now Andrew missing.* 'I'll be back as soon as I find out anything, Leanne.'

Tammy saw Lorraine out of the door then went upstairs. From a side pocket in her handbag she withdrew a slip of paper, for a long moment she stared at the London phone number before picking her mobile up.

'Where now, boss?' Carter asked as Lorraine got into the patrol car.

'Back to the station.' She glanced at her watch. 'Somebody's got to know who the hell this kid was running with and although I have a hunch or two I need confirmation. And that I intend to get off somebody pretty damn soon.'

Reaching the station Lorraine headed towards the canteen for a much-needed cold drink while Carter made his way to the computer room. Ever since an evil cult calling themselves the Blessing Guides had turned up in Houghton-le-Spring last year, if any kids went missing it was Carter's job to check on the whereabouts of the cult. They were last heard of somewhere in Essex.

Lorraine was surprised to see Luke sitting at their usual table with Dinwall.

'Case over, then?' She sat down, opened her can and smiled at Luke.

'Oh, yeah,' he nodded, not looking very happy at all.

'Don't tell me she walked again?'

'Well, yes and no ... She was convicted, but ended up with a measly hundred hours' community service.'

'Shocking. With results like that it makes you wonder if it's all worthwhile. Look, get off home, Dinwall's here, he can help me with tonight's interviews. Should be done by eight o'clock.'

'Me?' Dinwall interjected. 'Don't think so, boss. I'm off duty as of an hour ago.'

'So why haven't you hightailed it home then?'

'I ... er ... I ...' Dinwall blustered.

'And since when have you ever turned overtime down? Look James, it's obvious you're sleeping on the couch again, you've had a face like a slapped arse for days now ... Who was it this time?'

Luke coughed and put his hand over his mouth to hide his smile.

'What do you mean?' Dinwall did his best to sound indignant.

Lorraine laughed. 'Come on. I'm the boss. I know everything.'

'You're not the b ...' Dinwall hesitated. 'OK. But she's just bloody well imagining it again, I swear. I can't even look at a page three girl without her taking the horrors.'

'Like I'm gonna believe that's all it is.'

'OK guys, I'm off,' said Luke before Dinwall could protest his innocence further. 'I'm expecting an email from Scottie. He phoned earlier. Still waiting for one more test, which is due in an hour. He's putting them all down on paper. And I promised to take Selina and her sidekick to McDonald's.'

'Catch you later,' Lorraine smiled up at him.

'OK, and I thought that seeing as it's McDonalds for tea, I might cook us a nice healthy bolognaise for supper for a change.'

Dinwall tried not to lick his lips but failed. Luke's bolognaise was famous.

Luke caught Lorraine's eye and she shrugged.

'You're welcome to come for a bite, James,' Luke said.

'No, no. I couldn't really ... Well, maybes I could.'

Laughing, Luke said, 'OK, see you both around half eight,' and left.

Lorraine and Dinwall made their way to the interview room.

Carter was deep in conversation with a bald-headed man who turned out to be Mr Stamford, his son Simon was sitting on a chair looking like he'd rather be in hell than here.

Lorraine nodded at Mr Stamford and went into the room. Dinwall was busy sorting chairs when Carter came in. 'Mr Stamford's in a bit of a hurry, boss. Asked if you could possibly see him first?'

'I'm afraid that'll have to be a no, Carter, I need his son to simmer for a while, OK? Send the others in first.'

'Right, boss.'

Dinwall grinned as he sat down. 'I take it you hold high hopes for Simon Stamford?'

'He was Andrew's best friend all through school. If anyone knows anything it'll be him. And according to Tammy Knightly, the kid's running scared about something, or somebody.'

CHAPTER THIRTY- ONE

An hour later, after what Lorraine and Dinwall considered time totally wasted, Carter ushered Simon Stamford and his father in.

'Sit down please,' Lorraine smiled at both of them, noting the absolute terror on Simon's face and the undisguised anger on his father's.

'I hope you know I will be making a formal complaint about all of this,' Stamford Senior snapped, as he sat down.

Lorraine ignored him. The way she was feeling lately he could complain to the flaming Pope if he wanted to.

She saw that Simon was smartly dressed in jeans and a check shirt instead of the usual compulsory uniform of joggers and hooded top, which was a statement in itself these days. Obviously his parents still had some influence over him.

'OK, Simon. I want you to tell me in your own words everything you know about Andrew Knightly, who I'm sure you know has been missing for a few days now.'

'Haven't seen him in months,' Simon said after a moment's hesitation.

Lorraine leaned forward. 'And what if I say to you that you're lying, Simon?'

Simon's face blanched while his father glared at her. 'My son does not tell lies.'

'Oh, doesn't he, Mr Stamford?' Lorraine raised a questioning eyebrow at Andrew's father.

'Simon,' he snapped at his son, 'tell her what she wants to know. If you've seen the lad, tell her.'

Simon swallowed hard. *For God's sake*, Lorraine thought, *if he can't see that the little sod knows something!*

'He ... he doesn't knock around with us anymore. He's got some new mates ...'

'And who might they be, Simon?'

He hesitated again. Lorraine wanted to lean over and pull his tongue out.

'The ... The ...'

'Yeah, who?' Dinwall demanded, feeling pretty much the same as Lorraine.

'I daren't tell youse.' Simon shook his head while his father looked at him as if he were a stranger.

'Tell them, boy,' Mr Stamford ordered.

Simon licked his lips and Lorraine could tell he was weighing the consequences up. Finally he blurted, 'The McCades.'

Lorraine sat back in her seat. 'The McCades.' She echoed it so quietly it was almost a whisper. Her thoughts winging back over the years, hearing the threats once again, that the McCades had sworn over their brother's grave.

No. Dear God, not after all this time.

'Are you sure?' she asked.

Simon nodded, his face a mixture of despair and misery.

'Don't worry, son,' his father said. 'I ain't frightened of no McCades.'

Then you're a fool, Lorraine thought, but said, 'Who knows you're here?'

'Them bloody toe rags you had out there. They all clocked us, the lot of them. Which means half of bloody Houghton'll know.'

Lorraine quickly ran through who had been sitting and saw none of them as any kind of real threat, although she could understand where Stamford was coming from. 'We will, of course, never divulge any information given to us.'

'Like that'll stop them from finding out.' Mr Stamford shook his head.

Lorraine looked at father and son for a moment and chewed her lip. 'OK, here's what we'll do. Over the course of the next twenty-four hours we'll be interviewing all of Andrew's old school friends. Word will soon spread, and Simon will just be one of the many. How's that?'

Mr Stamford stood up. 'It's something, I suppose ... Can we go now?'

'Unless Simon knows something else about Andrew.'

'Like what, for God's sake?' Mr Stamford placed a protective hand on his son's shoulder.

Lorraine looked directly at Simon. 'Like was Andrew on drugs, Simon?'

Reluctantly, Simon nodded. 'It was them, the McCades, who got him to use.' Then suddenly, in a flash flood of words, Simon started to talk while his father sat back in amazement at the revelations that were spewing forth from his son's mouth.

'At first he said no, like we all did, but they kept on pestering him. They wouldn't leave him alone; wherever we went one of them would turn up, like they were following us. Then it was like they realised that Andrew was never gonna give in ... So, so one night when we went to the pictures, Mandy McCade came in and sat next to Andrew.' Simon glanced quickly at his father, then put his head down as he said quietly, 'They did things ... You know ... She ...' He glanced at his father again, then the words came out in a rush. 'Mandy was climbing all over him. Then all the next day he was quiet, like he was thinking all the time and kept snapping your head off if you said anything about her, and that night she turned up on the Broadway where we were hanging for a bit and ...' Simon shrugged, 'that was that, he went away with her and we hardly ever saw him anymore after that.'

Lorraine sighed before saying, 'Well Simon, you've been a great help to us, and don't worry I will do my best to keep you out of court, even if it comes down to it I'll insist on a video link. Thank you again for your help, you really have done the right thing, and very bravely too. It could help a lot.'

She looked at Mr Stamford and went on, 'OK you can go, if we need you for anything else we'll get in touch. Thanks again for your help.'

When they had closed the door behind them, Dinwall groaned, 'Twenty-four hours, boss? We gonna get any bolognaise or what?'

'Yup. We go to Luke's, we eat, we come back. Get Carter on it while I sort a few things out in my office.'

Still moaning, Dinwall went to look for Carter.

Back in her office Lorraine opened her drawer, but instead of searching for a pencil stub she sat and stared at the higgledy-piggledy assortment of odds and sods, seeing none of them, seeing only a dark, dark night that ended in flashing lights, loud noise and tragedy.

CHAPTER THIRTY-TWO

'So,' Luke said around a forkful of spaghetti, 'I think it's a coincidence. These things happen.'

Lorraine put her fork down. 'Patrick McCade swore as he threw soil on Randy's coffin that he would get whoever was responsible for his brother's death.'

'That doesn't necessarily mean that the McCades have Andrew. What would be the point? Especially after all this time.'

'Near enough to what I said,' Dinwall agreed. 'Remember, didn't I, boss?'

Ignoring them, Lorraine turned to Mickey. 'Did you know Andrew Knightly at all?'

Mickey shrugged. 'Not really. He was in the year below me at school, saw him a few times when I went to Robbie Lumsdon's house though. He always spoke.' Mickey grinned. 'A couple of years ago the whole street had a snowball fight, Andrew was on our side, lads against lasses, he seemed pretty cool.'

'When was the last time you saw him?'

'Oh, months ago.' Mickey smiled at Selina, who pointed at his mouth where a strand of spaghetti was hanging. 'Oh.' Blushing, he quickly shoved it into his mouth.

Her lips twitching, Lorraine went on, 'So you've heard no rumours about him, nothing?'

'Nope, sorry. But I'll ask around for you.'

'Yeah, you do that Mickey.'

'Eh, Selina, me working for the coppers! Sorry,' he added quickly, 'I mean the police. Does it pay well?'

Lorraine shook her head and smiled at Luke, who was looking at Mickey and frowning. *Mickey is a hapless sod*, she thought, *but extremely likeable.*

'Just kidding,' Mickey added a moment later after a swift kick under the table from Selina.

Supper over, they left Mickey and a scowling Selina in charge of the dishes. Because no word had come from Scottie, Luke surmised that the damn tests still had not come through. Annoying, but he'd known them take a lot longer. He decided to go back and help Lorraine and Dinwall.

Dinwall never shut up on the way there, which suited Lorraine, who let him get away with saying that men were better cooks than women, which she secretly agreed with but would never say out loud, but when the talk turned to football, she tuned out.

Could it be the McCades?

Why, after all these years?

It's like because they can't get their paws on Sam, wherever the bastard is, they've waited for Andrew to grow up.

Jesus Christ!

CHAPTER THIRTY-FOUR

Luke stared up at the ceiling, his hands behind his head, listening to Lorraine snore. To be fair, he thought, smiling to himself, she only snored after too much wine. Snuggled into his chest, she moved slightly, then still asleep lifted her head and dropped it again. Luke blew wisps of her hair off his face.

Why won't she tell me what the hell is bothering her?

The wine-induced sleep had been restless, she'd muttered once or twice but he hadn't been able to make out what it was, and it troubled him a lot that she didn't trust him with whatever it was that seemed to be eating away at her.

Debating whether to try to slide out of bed and grab the shower first, or stay cosy, he was startled a moment later by Dinwall shouting up the stairs.

Shit. He'd forgotten all about Dinwall. They had all arrived back around three in the morning, finished the spaghetti off, drunk too much and Dinwall had crashed out on the settee.

'Boss ... boss ... You've gotta help me here, she's never gonna believe me on this one, you gotta come and tell her where I've been all night ... Boss?'

Lorraine groaned and opened her eyes, blinked and said, 'I've just had the lousiest dream.'

'Let me guess ... Dinwall.'

Lorraine's sleepy eyes opened wide. 'How on earth did you know?'

'Hang on.'

A second later Dinwall's voice floated up the stairs again. 'Boss, ha'way man, wake up! She's gonna kill me!'

'Oh, God,' Lorraine groaned as she put her head in her hands, remembering.

Luke grinned. 'Yeah, well, you were the one who threw the challenge down.'

'Who won?'

'Hmm, I think it was pretty even.'

'BOSS!'

'OK, OK,' Lorraine yelled back, jumping out of bed and instantly regretting it. She winced and put her hands up to her head. 'Ohhh,' she moaned.

'Oh, dear,' Luke laughed. Lorraine grabbed her pillow and threw it at him before heading for the shower.

Fifteen minutes later they were sitting at Luke's breakfast bar, both men drinking coffee, Lorraine with her hands wrapped round a can of Diet Coke.

Dinwall put his cup on the saucer and winced at the clatter. 'I phoned in while I was waiting for youse two to stir, and nothing, he's still AWOL, it all adds up to what we got last night, though none of them mentioned the McCades.'

'So,' Luke frowned, 'we have a kid missing three days now and a murderer on the loose. House to house?' He looked intently at Lorraine, who was deep in thought, eyes on her can.

He sighed. He'd thought that they were now close enough to share everything and that if something was getting to her this badly she would at the very least be able to tell him. It was starting to seriously bug him now.

'Lorraine.'

'Right,' she said quickly, as if Luke had not asked her a second time. 'Here's what we do, the three of us go to the McCades' now. A show of force might shake something loose.'

'Oh but ...'

'It's alright, Dinwall,' Lorraine tutted at him. 'I've already phoned your lovely long-suffering wife before I came downstairs, and everything's cool. I also told her that I was pretty certain that you've been behaving yourself.'

'Oh, thanks boss, she always listens to you.' He heaved a giant sigh of relief. 'Yeah, great.'

'OK, but mind you, if you stray one more time, I promise I'll never help you out again.'

'But I haven ...'

'OK. Enough on the subject. We have a missing kid and we've stepped well into the danger zone, time wise. So we call at the McCades' before we go to the office.'

Selina came in then, wrapped in a huge white terry towelling dressing gown, a white towel wrapped round her head. She walked over and put her arms around Luke's neck. Lorraine smiled; the change in her over these last few months had been fantastic. All Selina had ever really needed was a change of luck and a loving home and Luke had supplied both, even though it had been touch and go for a while.

'Dad.'

Knowing what she was after, Luke winked at Lorraine and said, 'What Selina?'

'You know what, detective, a girl's gotta eat and it wouldn't look good for your image if a copper's daughter was found starving in college, would it now?'

Luke reached for his wallet. 'Got any change?'

'Very funny, Dad.'

Lorraine laughed. 'Feed the girl.'

'Oh, OK,' Luke grinned, and tapped the side of his nose. 'But there's something you all seem to have forgotten. It's Saturday today. No college.'

'Never said there was,' Selina replied, her eyes wide and shining innocence. 'Did I Lorraine? Mr Dinwall?'

'Actually,' Dinwall, always a sucker for a pretty face said, 'it wouldn't be at all good for your image if she was found starving anywhere.'

'OK, OK.' Luke handed Selina a tenner, 'Spend it wisely love, 'cos God only knows what time the cook's back today.'

'Thanks, Dad.' Selina kissed Luke's cheek, and Lorraine felt her heart warm for a moment, then she was back to business.

'Right! Time we were on our way guys, got us some baddies to visit.'

Dolly and Doris were upstairs in Doris's bedroom, which faced out the back and overlooked the rear of the McCades' house. Usually when they were up there together it was on a spying mission, keeping an eye on the McCades and anonymously reporting anything suspicious they heard to the police, via the telephone outside of Houghton's Post Office so it couldn't be traced back to them.

In the high fence at the bottom of the garden there were three spy holes, one each for Doris, Dolly and Mr Skillings, which Mr Skillings had poked out with his screwdriver.

Today though, having thoroughly worn out the topics of the dead woman found in the field and the missing Andrew Knightly, and not a McCade in sight, Doris was busy unwrapping her wedding hat from a mound of tissue paper.

'There. What do you think?'

Dolly looked at the pale blue hat with the large brim. It had a darker blue trailing feather on one side and a huge white daisy on the other. The overall affect was ghastly.

Doris put it on her head, admiring herself in the full-length wardrobe mirror. 'What you think, then?'

Well ...'

'Well what?' Doris spun round to her friend and had to grab hold of the bedpost. She shook the sudden dizziness away and asked again, 'Well what?'

'Nothing, really, it's a wonderful hat.'

'Dolly, don't tell lies. You don't like it, do you?'

'It's not that I don't like it as such ... it's ... Oh for God's sake, lose the bloody daisy.'

'Lose the bloody daisy,' Doris murmured, then burst out laughing. She took the hat off turned it upside down and the daisy fell off. 'Didn't much like it anyhow. I reckon it's too big. It looks much better without, doesn't it?'

Dolly sighed. 'It wasn't even fixed on anyhow, was it? You and your little tricks.'

Doris didn't answer – she was too busy staring out of the window. The front gate of the McCades' was on an angle, so from Doris's back bedroom you could see the McCades' gate and halfway up the path, but not actually the door.

'What's the matter?' Dolly asked, and hurried to the window just in time to see Lorraine, Luke and Dinwall walk up the path. 'Oh oh, wonder what them bloody creeps have done now?'

'Dunno.' Doris was heading for the door. 'But we better go and tell Mr Skillings, he'll be over the moon if that lot's in trouble.'

CHAPTER THIRTY-FIVE

Luke knocked hard on the McCades' door. It was answered by the grandfather of the clan, Seth McCade, who spent so many months at each of his sons' houses and was sent packing to another brother as soon as they could no longer put up with his ways.

'What?' he demanded, lifting up his once-white vest and scratching his huge hairy belly. 'It weren't none of my lot.'

'What wasn't, Mr McCade?' Lorraine said.

'Whatever it is what's brought you lot to this bloody door. That's what.'

'Oh, so they won't want the reward?'

Seth didn't miss a beat. 'Oh aye, they'll have that alright ... Emm ... what's the reward for, like?' His tone actually held a touch of amazement.

'Perhaps we'd better talk inside.'

'Oh, aye They're all in.' Smiling and exposing a mouth full of broken and brown-stained teeth, he stepped to one side, and waving them in as if they were entering a stately home said, 'Come in, *come in*.' He let Lorraine pass him, then, following her, said over his shoulder, 'Shut the door, one of youse.'

Luke and Dinwall grinned at each other as Dinwall closed the door.

'What the ...?' Pete muttered, his jaw hanging open as his father marched into the sitting room with the police in tow.

'Now don't be shy lads, which one of youse is the hero?' Seth beamed at his spawn.

'Fucking hero?' Tony snarled. 'You've finally lost the plot, daft old bastard, haven't you? Jesus.' He turned to Lorraine. 'So what's the old sod rabbiting on about now?'

Wondering why practically the whole clan was gathered this early on a morning, Lorraine answered Tony with a question of her own. 'Who was the last person in your family to see Andrew Knightly?'

'Who?' Tony asked, while the others found interesting points around the sitting room to rest their eyes.

'You aren't deaf Tony, you heard what I said. But just to be sure you get the name right, it's Andrew Knightly. I want to know what you lot know about the kid and I want to know *now*.'

Tony curled his lip. 'You know as much about the Knightlys as we do, I would say, wouldn't you, Mizz Hunt? After all, weren't ...'

'I am not here to be questioned by you,' Lorraine got in before he could say any more. 'Rather the other way around.'

'So, we ain't got no heroes?' Seth looked around. His eyes settling on Lorraine, he shrugged. 'Thought it was too good to be true ... You tricked me, lady. I can remember once over when you were such a sweet child.'

Lorraine sighed. Seth McCade had never been a bad man, never in trouble, just lazy and too fond of the booze, but his laziness and love of the bottle had produced a handful of sons that were allowed to do whatever they wanted and were always in bother. And now his grandsons were following the fast-growing family tradition.

'Seth, we have a missing kid and I'm sure you wouldn't want us to leave any stone unturned if it was one of yours.'

Before Seth could answer, Patrick said, 'We ain't seen him in weeks, he knocked around with my Gary for a bit, but that's all. Our Gary says he was a miserable little twat anyhow. Our Gary's into football.'

'And where's Gary?' Lorraine raised her eyebrows. *Jesus, was that a note of pride in his voice?*

'It's Saturday, for Christ's sake, he's still in bed.'

Obviously Gary and the rest of the younger lot had not been invited to this family pow wow. Lorraine looked at Tony, who was leaning against the radiator with his hands folded across his chest, glowering at everyone in the room. She wondered briefly if Randy would have looked like Tony when he grew up, but Tony had a mean face with a slash for a mouth. He probably would have looked more like Patrick, who had a touch softer face than Tony and the rest of them, though looks were deceiving, because Patrick was the meanest of the lot.

She became aware of Luke giving her a questioning look, and, feeling a need to get out of there, pulled herself together and said, 'OK, two o'clock, I want the whole lot of you down the station. And if I have to send cars it'll be an overnight stay.'

'Fucking can't do that,' Patrick stated adamantly, while Tony just went on staring. 'We've got our rights same as every other law-abiding citizen.'

'Watch me.' Lorraine turned and headed for the door, feeling all the while that the walls were closing in on her.

'Two o'clock,' Luke reminded them before following Lorraine and Dinwall.

'And how long'll youse be keeping our Lee down there for?' Seth shouted after them. 'That's not right either, he's not done nothing.'

'For as long as it takes,' Dinwall answered before he closed the door.

'What's happening?' Mr Skillings asked, hurrying down the garden path, walking stick in one hand, bacon sandwich in the other.

'Shh,' Doris hissed from her spy hole.

Dolly looked round and put her finger to her lips as Mr Skillings reached his post.

It was then that Lorraine and the others came into view. Doris and co watched silently as they got into the car and drove off. Another silent minute passed, then as if on cue the three of them turned and looked at each other.

'Don't know what that's all about, then,' Dolly said.

'We'll find out later though when they start that bloody damned barbie up, a few cans and they'll sing like canaries, just you wait,' Mr Skillings stated, while Doris nodded her head in agreement.

CHAPTER THIRTY-SIX

'Face it, Lorraine. We're stumped,' Luke said as the last McCade closed the door behind him. They had worked on the McCades until eleven the previous night and started again this morning on the last of them, with no joy.

Lorraine had tried tripping them up time and time again, mentioning the dead woman's body, but to no avail: they were either damn good actors or totally innocent.

'Oh,' she gritted her teeth. 'They're guilty of something, I can feel it,' Lorraine snapped.

'That's as may be, but we haven't got a case. Andrew Knightly has probably run away, you know how many teenagers run away every year.'

'No,' Lorraine shook her head. 'There's more to this, I know for sure there is.'

'Like what?' Luke said, exasperation showing on his face. They should have been in the Lake District now for a long-awaited break, not wasting time on some bloody hunch, but a moment later he had to admit to himself that in all honesty Lorraine's hunches were usually spot on. But she was becoming too obsessive with this.

Carter's customary knock sounded on the door, followed by his head peering round it. Grinning, he said, '*Sunderland Echo* on the phone boss, asking to speak to you and nobody else but you.'

'Oh, Christ.'

'It's the editor though boss, not one of the reporters.'

Lorraine picked the phone up. 'Hello?' She listened for a few minutes then said, 'No you have it all wrong, we don't know the name of the murder victim yet, and yes there is a missing teenager who belongs in the area but he isn't the murder victim. And I assure you, it has nothing to do with that Blessing Guides cult that was in the area last year. They're long gone … OK. Yes … bye.'

She put the phone down and glared at Carter, who shrugged and quickly left.

'I nearly forgot, your mother phoned. She wants to know if we'll meet her and Peggy in the Sun Inn for a bite at dinnertime.' Luke looked at his watch. 'Which is just about now, and actually I'm pretty hungry too.'

'God, they love living it up, those two, don't they?' She stood up and grabbed her bag. 'Come on, might as well.'

Jacko walked into Newbottle Club knowing it was where he would find Danny and Len. He smiled on entering the bar. *Yup, there they are, propping it up.* He walked over to them. 'Thought youse'd be here.'

Danny slapped him on the back. 'Does this mean it's on for tonight?'

'Guess so.'

'Great,' Len nodded, before taking a swallow of his pint. Smacking his lips, he said, 'Wanna drink?'

'Yeah, why not. I'll have a lager.'

Len ordered another round while Danny picked his glass up and pointed to an empty table by the window. 'We'll sit over there, too many big ears round here,' he said quietly.

Jacko followed him. They had just sat down when Len arrived and placed the drinks on the table.

'OK, Jacko mate, I'll pick you up at twelve tonight.'

Jacko nodded and leaned back in his seat. *That's the dress sorted, thank God*, he thought, reaching for and taking a long drink from his pint of lager. 'Where we heading for?' he asked, putting his glass back on the table.

'Stanhope Common,' Danny answered him.

Jacko raised his eyebrows. 'Hope you can see in the dark.'

'Don't fret, it's all sorted.'

'Aye,' Len said. 'We've been up twice, got it all sussed out, haven't we mate.' He nodded at Danny.

Jacko hid a smile. Danny was completely ignoring Len, like he did most of the time. He said, 'OK, midnight it is.'

'Is your lot going on the trip to Whitby that Sandra Gilbride and Vanessa Lumsdon are planning?' Len asked.

'Oh, don't bloody mention it,' Danny put in before Jacko could answer. 'I've got a perfectly good minibus that'll take us to Whitby anytime we want, but no, she says, it's better on the trip bus with everybody else.' He let out a huge sigh. 'Can youse think of anything worse than being stuck on a bus in this heat with a bunch of screaming, yelling kids?'

'Don't much fancy it meself, but Sandra's been collecting a pound a week since Christmas, and our Melanie's really looking forward to it.'

'Tell you what though.' Danny smacked his lips. 'That Sandra's a fit bird alright.'

Len snapped his head round, glared at his cousin, and said, 'She's a married woman.'

Jacko grinned, downed his drink, saying to Len as he stood up to go, 'When has that ever stopped him before?'

'Huh,' Danny snorted. 'Anyhow, that husband of hers is always on the road, how many times have any of youse seen him in the last twenty years, eh? Bet you can count on one hand.'

Danny was right, even for a long-distance lorry driver Sandra's bloke was away a hell of a lot. He shrugged, and said, 'Nowt to do with us though, is it?' although he was thinking, *Can't even remember what the hell he looks like.*

Leaving the club, Jacko crossed over the road to head on down to the Seahills. As he was passing the Sun Inn, a car pulled up to the curb. Jacko was surprised when Lorraine got out of the passenger side and Luke the other side. Lorraine, less than a foot away, smiled up at him and for some strange reason actually blushed.

'Hello, Lorraine,' Jacko smiled back, then looked over the top of the car and nodded at Luke, receiving a barely perceptive nod in return.

'Hi, Jacko, everyone alright?' Lorraine said.

'Oh aye ... You?'

'Fine.' Smiling again he sidestepped past her, saying over his shoulder, 'Tell your mam and Peggy I'm asking after them.'

'Yeah, will do.' Lorraine quickly moved towards the doorway of the pub and flinched a moment later when Luke slammed the car door.

CHAPTER THIRTY- SEVEN

Sam had decided to take the train, knowing that if he pulled up in the Seahills in the Rolls the tongues would be wagging like crazy and pretty soon someone would figure out it was him. Plus he had not long been back from the north and didn't fancy another long drive so soon. The message from Tammy had been short and to the point: Come home Sam, Andrew missing.

He had phoned her when he got the message only to find it was worse than he thought: Andrew had been missing for three days and Tammy was convinced something was really wrong.

The train was on time at King's Cross, it would get him into Durham at eleven thirty; a taxi from the station would get him to the Seahills in about ten to fifteen minutes at that time of night with little road traffic. He was dressed casually in jeans and open-necked black shirt. He planned to keep as low a profile as possible. The holdall with changes of clothes was also black. Anything else he needed he could buy. If he could sneak in without being seen to sort this bloody mess out, then sneak away again, so much the better.

By the time the train reached York it was dark. Sam watched a young girl struggle with a twin buggy while people rushed past her to get on the train. A young boy of about fourteen took hold of her bag. The girl gratefully thanked him.

Stupid tart, Sam thought, smirking to himself. *The kid'll be off any second with the bag and he'll score tonight alright.*

But Sam was wrong. The boy helped the girl on to the train and placed her bag on the rack before going to look for his seat.

Sam shrugged. People, they never failed to amaze. As they pulled out of the station and the bright lights disappeared he found himself staring at his reflection in the window. He hadn't changed much, receding a little at the temples, filled out in all the right places, though without doubt the oldies on the estate would recognise him right off and God wouldn't the tongues wag.

'Aren't you coming up to bed, Lorraine?' Luke asked, looking down at Lorraine as she sat on the settee, legs curled underneath her, staring at the blank TV screen. 'Come on, a nice back rub's just what you need.'

'What, sorry?' she frowned slightly then looked up and gave a quick one-sided smile.

'Nothing. I'm off to bed now … OK?' He headed for the door.

'Yeah, fine,' she replied, her eyes returning to the same spot.

Luke watched her for a moment from the door then turned towards the stairs.

What the hell's wrong with her?

Why won't she open up and tell me?

Whatever it is, the Knightlys and the McCades are at the bottom of this.

And today, why did she blush when she saw Jacko?

He kicked his slippers, a present from Selina and the first pair of slippers he'd ever possessed, under the bed, undid his jeans, took them off, folded them over the back of the chair, then stripped everything else off and stepped into bed naked, the way he liked to sleep.

He lay on his right side then a moment later flipped over to his left, finally ending up on his back.

Why did she blush? She's seen him umpteen times and never had that reaction before.

Does she fancy him all of a sudden?

That thought was almost unbearable. Agitated, he turned over on to his stomach, a few minutes later, after lying on his right side and again his left, he was now on his back once more, eyes tight shut, willing himself to sleep.

Downstairs Lorraine had hardly moved, apart from picking up a cushion and cuddling it to her chest.

'I love Luke.' She said the mantra over and over, but a little voice kept adding, *So why did I react like that to Jacko after all these years? It was a stupid schoolgirl crush that he never even knew about, and I'd forgotten all about it.*

She sighed as she muttered into her cushion, 'What the fuck's going on with me?'

Jacko stood at his gate waiting for Danny to arrive in his beloved white van, which he called Elizabeth after his dream girl, Elizabeth Taylor.

He watched across the road as Christina's bedroom light came on. He smiled. He loved Christina to bits and soon they would be married and she would be living on his side of the road, away from that tyrant of a father.

Though, Jacko smiled, the old bastard was no match for Doris.

It looked like for once in his life things were going right for him. He couldn't remember ever feeling so happy, except for the huge rays of sunshine that Melanie had brought into the darkness from the day she'd been born.

Christina's light went out as Danny came round the corner. Jacko noted that the only light left on in the street was the Knightlys'.

Hope to God the lad turns up alright. He well knew the fear of a missing kid. *Nothing in the world more terrifying* he thought, stepping into the minibus to be greeted by Adam.

'Yo, Jacko.'

'Oh, God,' Len groaned. 'Heaven help us all, the idiot thinks he's Rambo now.'

'Who's Rambo?' Adam asked winking at Jacko.

'No change here then,' Jacko grinned as he flopped down on to the only empty seat, noting that the van had been cleared of all the other seats at the back, leaving just one row.

'What's black and white and red all over?' Adam asked.

Before Len could react with his usual moans, Danny, who usually liked Adam's jokes, said, 'A newspaper, you daft twit, everybody knows that one.'

'Just testing,' Adam replied.

None of then gave the taxi or its occupant a second look as it passed them on Blind Lane and turned into the Seahills.

CHAPTER THIRTY-EIGHT

'Go to bed, Leanne,' Tammy said. 'Three bloody nights in a row, you'll end up being ill. Tell her, Stacey.'

Stacey, too tired herself to speak, nodded.

'Thanks for that,' Tammy snapped.

Stacey sighed. 'Look, we're all worn out, why don't we all just go to bed? If he comes home he'll knock on the door for Christ's sake, how long are we gonna go without sleep? He's probably having the time of his life.'

Ignoring them both, Leanne stood up and went into the kitchen.

'Not more coffee,' Tammy shouted after her. 'We're wired up enough already.'

'No, I'm just gonna have a glass of juice.' Leanne opened the fridge and poured herself a glass of orange juice. Too tired to carry it through into the sitting room, she was about to sit down at the kitchen table when the door opened and Sam walked in.

'Oh my God,' she gasped as the glass slipped through her fingers and shattered into a hundred glittering pieces on the floor. 'You!' Feeling as if her feet were on sliding sand, she sat down.

Tammy and Stacey came hurrying in and both stopped dead in the doorway when they saw Sam.

Recovering first, Tammy smiled and moved towards their brother. 'Sam.'

Sam stepped right in and closed the door. 'Ladies. My, how you've all grown.' With a sarcastic flourish, and as if he had just stepped out an hour ago, he bowed.

Finding herself and shaking with anger Leanne snapped, 'Yeah, what? You thought time would stand still 'til you decided to come back? What the fuck do you want?' Not waiting for an answer she turned on Tammy and shouted angrily, 'It's you, isn't it? You brought him here after all this time. How dare you. How dare you bring him back to this house!'

'He had a right to know ... We may need his help. Because actually we haven't really got a fucking clue what we're dealing with here, do we?'

'Rights? He has no fucking rights. Don't you understand? For God's sake. How dare you talk to me about rights? Any of youse.' She spun round to Sam, who, expecting this very reaction from Leanne, had remained silent.

'Get out, go on. We don't need you and we never have. We managed fine without you.' She pounded the table with her fist to emphasise each word.

'Put the kettle on, Stace,' Sam said in a bored voice that incensed Leanne even more.

'You cheeky bastard. Don't you dare put the kettle on, Stacey. I would see you die of thirst before you ever sup in this house.'

Sighing, he pulled a chair out and sat down facing Leanne, whose chest was heaving frantically. 'Simmer down Leanne, or you'll more than likely have a panic attack. You're not a teenager anymore.' He moved his head from side to side, eyeing her up and down. 'Still got your looks though, I'll give you that.'

'Don't tell me what to do. How dare you come here with your posh London voice, saying this and that. You're bad news and you always have been. I want you out of here *now.*'

'Leanne.' Stacey turned from the cooker where she'd been holding the kettle, wondering if she dared put it on. 'Don't be like that, Sam's come back to help.'

'Help? *Help?* Where was his help years ago when we fucking well needed it, eh? Eh?'

Sam eyed her, his mouth in a firm, thin line, saying nothing, knowing she was right, knowing also that no one else in the world other than this sister would ever get away with talking to him like this. Well, perhaps one other, a long-legged blonde from the past.

At last he spoke. 'OK, Leanne. You're right, everything you say, you are right. But I've come to help now.'

'And we do need his help Leanne,' Tammy butted in.

'She's right.' Stacey lit the gas underneath the kettle. 'We do need him. All of us need his help and it's not just your decision. Andrew's our brother an' all.'

Leanne's mouth was as firm and straight as her brother's. After a moment she swallowed, looked up and said, 'OK, tell me this. What can you do? What can you do that the coppers haven't already done?'

Sam laughed, but it was a laugh devoid of humour and totally lacking any emotion. 'Tell me everything there is to know about him, and I mean everything.'

Leanne quietly and calmly proceeded to give Sam a rundown of the last six months, of the changes, some of them only being realised now as she spoke.

When she was finished Sam rocked back on his chair, brought it forwards, dry washed his face, then, shaking his head, said, 'Well it certainly sounds like he's delving into something. Actually, it's a sure fire thing. So, do you know who deals around here? I don't mean the little guys on the street dealing for their next fix, I mean the boss guy, the bastard that's making all the cash?'

'How the hell would I know that? But I will tell you this. The McCades are at the bottom of it,' Leanne said adamantly. 'They swore, they swore on Randy's grave that they would get even. They've killed him. I know it.' She thumped her chest with her fist. 'I know it in here.'

Stacey gasped. 'Don't say that Leanne. Please. *Please*. We don't even know if he … if he's …' She ran out of the room. Tammy followed her.

Leanne had not taken her eyes off Sam. 'He wouldn't run away, I know he wouldn't.'

'But you aren't even sure what sort of shit he was on, Leanne. Drugs, they fuck the mind up and it's only fucked-up idiots that say they don't.' Sam punched his left hand with his fist. 'Fucking stupid kids,' he sighed. 'Look.' He reached towards her but she flinched away from him. Accepting her rejection, he went on, 'I know without asking that you lot probably haven't been to bed. Go now, I'll sit up, wait for him … Think what the fuck to do.'

Leanne knew that she desperately needed to sleep, that Tammy and Stacey were right: if she didn't sleep she would become ill and that would benefit no one. Loath to do it, not wanting Sam to think he could just swan in and take over and start acting like he'd never been away, she slowly though very reluctantly nodded.

Sam watched as, like an old woman, she dragged her body off the chair, manoeuvred around the broken glass and headed for the stairs. Halfway up she started to shake and Sam quickly moved to the bottom of the stairs.

'Need some help?'

'No, not from you.' She stiffened her back and managed to climb to the top, where she turned and looked down at him. 'You owe me big time,' she whispered, just loud enough for him to hear.

Sam gave her a nod, then went into the sitting room and flopped on to the fireside chair. A moment later the kettle whistled. He smiled as he went into the kitchen. 'I knew it,' he murmured. 'Same bloody kettle.'

He made a cup of tea while Tammy and Stacey cleared the spilt juice and broken glass up, then went back to the armchair, took a sip and got his mobile out of his pocket. If the McCades were behind this he was going to need some help, big help. The sort of help that would leave the whole fucking lot of them wishing they had never been born.

CHAPTER THIRTY-NINE

'Wow. Would you look at all the bloody stars?' Adam declared in amazement.

'Yeah, you can see 'em 'cos we're away from all the shite the cities spew out,' Len said.

'And because of the light pollution,' Jacko added, craning his head backwards to look through the side window.

'Aye, that an' all,' Len nodded.

'I can't think of any star jokes, can you Len?' Adam grinned, at Jacko.

'No I bloody can't,' Len retorted.

'So, how much further do you reckon?' Jacko asked Danny. "Cos there's quite a lot around here.'

'We'll just dip a bit further down the valley. I'm gonna switch the lights off now, so I need all eyes on the road, OK guys?'

They all muttered their agreements as Danny switched the lights off and slowed down to a crawl. In complete darkness the winding road, full of sudden dips and sharp turns, was not easy to navigate, but Danny managed to keep them on the road, only twice hitting a rut on the near side.

'Bandit at two o clock,' Adam suddenly yelled, startling them all.

'Bloody idiot,' Len snarled at him, while Danny cursed under his breath.

'But it's just a young 'un and it ran into the road,' Adam said in his defence.

Ignoring him, Danny pulled over, switched the engine off, then turned to the other three. 'Right, you know what you have to do.' He was met with blank stares. 'Yes?'

He leaned over, picked up a heavy wooden mallet and passed it to Adam, then one each to Jacko and Len, followed by a torch for each of them.

'No ...' Adam moaned, 'you never said we had to actually murder the bloody sheep.'

'It's not murder, you pillock, we eat the flaming things don't we? Just don't shout mint sauce when you're chasing, apparently the woolly bastards know what it means.'

'And you call my jokes.' Adam pulled a face.

Jacko shook his head. 'Haven't ever killed an animal. I thought we were gonna take them to the butcher and he was gonna do it. Wasn't that the deal?'

'We'll catch them and you kill them.' Len looked hopefully at Danny.

'No,' Danny replied. 'We're in this together, you're not leaving it all up to me.' Grasping his mallet he jumped out of the van. 'Come on then.'

Reluctantly and giving each other odd glances Jacko, Len and Adam got out of the van. A moment later they were laughing their heads off when Danny made a lunge for a sheep that easily escaped and Danny fell flat on his face.

'Fast little buggers, aren't they?' Adam laughed, chasing after one himself.

'Pick one,' Len said to Jacko as he advanced menacingly on a particular sheep that was standing staring at them. 'Here sheepy sheepy, come to daddy.'

'Oh, God,' Jacko laughed out loud.

It was a further frantic five minutes before Danny caught the first sheep. 'Got ya, woolly bastard,' he yelled, while the others cheered.

Then silence fell as Danny raised his mallet in the air. They all stood perfectly still, holding their breath as they waited for it to fall. After a moment Danny slowly dropped the mallet to his side.

Thinking that Danny had given up and couldn't go through with it, Jacko snapped his fingers. 'Yes,' he breathed.

A moment later the three of them were disappointed when Danny said, 'Len, come and keep hold of the bastard, the bloody thing's wriggling all over the place.'

'So would I if I thought you wanted me for supper,' Adam snapped throwing his mallet down and walking away.

'Soft shite,' Danny yelled after him.

Len took hold of the sheep, straddled it, then held its head up for Danny. Both the sheep and Len stared into Danny's eyes as he raised the mallet above his head. Feeling sick to his stomach, Jacko turned away.

'Look the other way, grass-eating twat.'

'How the hell can she,' Len demanded, 'when I've got hold of her head?'

'Fuck it,' Danny said a moment later, throwing his mallet on the ground.

'Knew you couldn't do it,' Len said with heartfelt relief. 'What we gonna do now?'

'Guess we let them go,' Jacko said.

'No way, we put them in the back of the van, Clive the butcher said he'd finish them off if … if we couldn't go through with it. He'll pay less money though,' Danny sighed. The kids were going through shoes like there was no tomorrow.

'OK,' Jacko said. Relived that they didn't have to actually kill them he turned to help Len with the sheep, which was doing its best to escape. They managed to get it to the van doors when they heard Adam give an almighty scream. 'What the fuck?' Danny stopped dead in his pursuit of another reluctant sheep.

Len and Jacko looked at each other, grabbed the sheep and with a mighty heft managed to get it into the van and close the doors just as Adam screamed again.

Spinning in the direction of his scream they pinpointed him in their collective torchlight. 'What the ...?' Danny moved towards Adam. 'If it's another one of his jokes I swear I'll fucking kill him.'

Adam was bent over and they could see he was being sick, his torch lying on the grass and pointing at the stars. They moved towards him.

'What's the matter?' Jacko said as they reached him. 'Something bit you, or what?'

'Probably a flaming vampire this far away from humanity,' Len said solemnly, before looking quickly around.

In the torchlight Adam's face was a ghastly grey shade. He stood up straight, took a couple of deep breaths, then with a trembling finger pointed at a darker patch of grass less than a yard away. 'It's ... It's a body.'

'What?' The three of them said together in amazement.

'I warn you, if it's a fucking dead sheep you'll be joining it' Danny snarled, waving his torch in Adam's face.

'It ain't no sheep.' Adam nodded, his eyes wide and staring, then his knees gave way and Danny caught him just before he fell.

The hairs crawled on the back of Jacko's neck. 'Who is it? I mean ... what?'

'I don't know, it ... it ... Oh, Jesus. It hasn't got a fucking head.' The others stared at Adam, who was leaning heavily against Danny, in stunned silence for a moment.

'Honestly man, I'm not taking the piss, its neck's all ... all raggy,

like it's been, like it's been ...' he swallowed hard, then went on:
'... hacked off.'

'No way, man.' Jacko shook his head in disbelief. 'You've been on them magic mushrooms again.'

'I swear to God, guys, take a look. Go on, look for yourself, do you honestly think that I'd make something as sick as that up? Jesus.'

Jacko moved cautiously over to the dark shape in the grass and shone his torch. 'Oh, fucking hell. No way.' He looked at the others and nodded.

'Oh my God, what do we do now?' Len asked, turning quickly and looking in the other direction, not wanting to go over to the body. He trusted Jacko's word where he'd not been sure of Adam's.

'We report it,' Jacko said.

'We can't get involved,' Danny panicked. 'They'll want to know what we were doing up here. They'll think it was us and throw the key away, for God's sake.'

'Oh,' Len cried. 'Granny Hazel always used to say to me "Keep away from our Danny, he'll get you into trouble."'

'That's strange, the two-faced old cow used to say the same to me about you,' Danny snapped back, glaring at Len.

'OK,' Jacko butted in. 'Keep family arguments for later. We gotta think of something. That's a body lying there and if we don't report it we're in real trouble.'

'But who's gonna know we were here?' Danny asked, staring at the body for the first time. He moved his torch up the length of the torso. Not prepared for what he saw, he gagged before yelling loudly, 'Shit!'

Len looked this time and a moment later screamed as loudly as Adam and Danny had. He couldn't tear his eyes away from the mutilated corpse. 'Oh, sweet Jesus, the poor bastard. The poor, poor bastard ... What the hell we gonna do?'

'Like I said, we'll think of something.' Jacko looked away knowing he would have nightmares for years to come as an unwanted image of Randy spread across the Jeep entered his mind, an image that still haunted him now and then, and an image that had suddenly been reinforced a hundredfold.

'Why do we need to report it? Don't know if you've noticed or not, but no cameras, OK? No Big Brother watching our every move out here, mate. It's wild it's free.'

Jacko drew himself to his full height and glared at Danny. 'Think we should leave him for the sheep?'

'Oh,' Len shuddered as Adam retched again.

Danny sighed. 'No, not really, I was just thinking of us and what the coppers are gonna think right off.'

'We'll come up with something.'

'OK,' Danny nodded. 'But it better be good.'

Jacko glanced once more in the direction of the body, shivered, then said, 'Phone the coppers Danny, whoever the poor bastard is some-one's missing their company.' He nodded. 'It's the right thing for us to do.'

Knowing Jacko was right, but really wanting to do nothing more than put miles between himself and the headless corpse, Danny took his mobile out. He informed the policewoman on the other end of the line and gave her directions.

'She says we haven't gotta move, might disturb some evidence or something.' Danny snapped his phone shut and put it in his jacket pocket.

'But we gotta move Danny, for one thing there's a bloody sheep in the van,' Jacko reminded them.

'Shit,' Len said.

'OK. Danny, you come with me, Len and Adam stay here, we'll let it out and check the van for any presents the sheep might have left and switch the lights on so the coppers can see us.'

'Why do we have to stay here with ... with that?' Adam wailed.

Ignoring him and still looking away from the body Len asked, 'Then what do we do?'

'Ask him,' Danny replied, gesturing with his head towards Jacko.

'He's the one with all the answers tonight.'

He started to walk towards the van. Jacko understood the reason for his attitude; he was as disappointed as Danny and needed the money as much, but a dead body. He shook his head in disbelief. *Why the hell did we have to find it? Stanhope bloody Common is huge, why the hell did it have to be here of all bloody places?*

If they didn't report the body and the police found out in some way that they had been here, God knows what sort of trouble they would have to talk themselves out of. They would be an easy collar, and everyone knows there's more than one innocent man done hard time for something he didn't do.

He hurried and caught up as Danny reached the van at the same time they heard the sound of sirens and saw the flashing lights dipping in and out of the dark hills.

'Oh, God, hurry up.' Danny yanked the doors open. 'I think sheep rustling still might be a hanging offence.'

'What? You never told me that!'

'Just a stray thought.'

Grabbing hold of the bewildered sheep they lifted her out of the van, Danny gave her a slap on her flank to get rid of her, then they scoured the van for any stray hairs or gifts the sheep may have left them before running back to Adam and Len.

'What we gonna say then, Jacko? Quick, they're nearly here, man,' asked Len frantically.

'Right, er ... OK, we were out for a few drinks in Stanhope, er ... Aye, this is how it goes, right, on the way back Adam wanted a piss, he got out of the van and he fell over the body, nice and simple. And that'll explain if there's any skin flakes or whatever belonging to Adam on the body, OK?'

'Skin flakes?'

'You know what I mean, these forensic-type people, they find all sorts of things. Skin, sweat, that DNA stuff ... Don't you ever watch the telly, man?'

'Aye, but we don't smell of drink, that's the first thing they're gonna notice, and which pubs? They're definitely gonna ask that,' Danny said, chewing on his thumbnail as the police car, now followed by a riot van and behind that an ambulance, drew ever closer.

'I don't know the name of one pub in Stanhope, do any of youse?' Len asked.

'Hang on, hang on. Give us that phone, Danny.' Adam stretched his hand out.

'What for, like?' Danny asked as he reluctantly passed the phone over. 'There's not much credit left on it, mind, so you'll have to be quick.'

Ignoring him Adam dialled, a moment later he spoke. 'Alright mate, look we've got what you might call a spot of bother here … Er, what it is like … Me and a few mates have found a body on the common, can we say we were at yours tonight?'

He was silent for a moment, listening, then excitement building up in his voice he went on, 'No it's not a fucking joke! Like we would, what do you think we are? Look, the truth … we was gonna nick a few sheep, OK? That's all. A few lousy stinking sheep, but the bastards are fast little fuckers alright. I was chasing one and fell over this body, like. What? No, I don't know who the fuck it is, it hasn't got a bloody head with a gob in to tell me who the fuck he is, could be a lad or it could be a bloke. Look, we're in deep shit mate, and the coppers are gonna be here any minute, you gonna help us or what? I swear on me mother's life – that's your fucking sister, remember – we had nothing to do with it. Do you think I'd get you involved if we had? Look, please help mate, you've gotta help us.'

He looked worriedly at the others for a moment, then to all their relief he smiled. 'Thanks mate, we all owe you.'

Closing the phone, he blew air out of his cheeks, then handed the phone back to Danny. 'We were all at me Uncle Paul's in Blanchland, OK?'

Relieved, they all nodded. Danny patted him on his back. 'Well done, mate. Paul, right?'

'Yeah.'

'Didn't know you had posh relations living in Blanchland,' Len said, his eyebrows raised.

'Just goes to show you don't know everything then, doesn't it? Uncle Paul's a vet, he comes over now and again to check the dogs out for me mam.'

'Right, what's he look like then?'

'What do you wanna know that for?'

'Because, dimwit, they might ask us what he looks like.'

'Thicko,' Len said with a smirk, looking at Adam.

'Ah ... Actually, a bit like you. You ugly fucker.'

'OK. So I guess we've all got the picture. We just describe Len.'

They all nodded and Len gave his usual scowl.

'It's supposed to be haunted there in Blanchland, isn't it, the white monk or something?' Jacko asked, knowing he was babbling, but his heart was beating faster by the second as he watched the lights of the police car coming closer and closer.

'Don't know about that.' Danny lit a cigarette up. 'But we went in the pub for a coffee one day when we were passing through and it cost an arm and a leg ... *Shit.*'

All four of them stared at the dark mound on the grass.

'Wonder who he upset?' Jacko muttered.

'Some real nasty bastard by the look of it,' Danny replied shaking his head.

'You know they're gonna find out what we're really doing here, don't you?' Len said with conviction.

'Only if you open your big fat mouth,' Adam snapped at him.

'Well, I'm only saying.'

'Len, do us all a favour and say nowt, OK?' Danny warned him, flicking his cigarette away as the police car came to a halt beside the van.

CHAPTER FORTY

Lorraine got out of her car and slammed the door behind her. She stomped towards the police station entrance, the gravel in the car park crunching under her feet.

'Fucking men,' she muttered under her breath as Carter caught up with her.

'What did you say, boss?'

'Never mind. Let's walk and talk.' She pointed at the brown file he was holding under his arm. 'What's that?'

She couldn't have cared if it was Carter's shopping list, anything to take her mind off Luke.

'Well ...' Carter always took a moment or two to depart news that he thought of great importance. Just as Lorraine was getting ready to throttle him he said quickly, 'It seems that Stanhope police are holding four of our citizens.'

'And?' *I swear I'll bloody well kill him any minute now.*

'They all claim to have been over there visiting with a relative, and believe this if you will … Tripped over a dead body on the common, of all places.'

'Have you any idea at all just how vast Stanhope Common is, Carter?'

'Oh yeah, boss been up a few times, isn't it absolutely magnificent? Actually …'

'Carter.'

'Right boss, sorry boss.' He read from the file. 'They are currently holding Adam Glasier, Danny Jorden, Len Jorden and Jacko Musgrove.'

'What?' Lorraine almost shouted.

'It's Jacko Musgrove, Danny and Len Jorden and Adam Glazier, it seems they found a body up there sometime last night and the Stanhope lot are checking them out.'

'What?' she repeated.

'The …'

'Yeah, yeah. Give that to me.' She held her hand out for the folder, put it on her desk, removed her white cardigan then sat down and opened it. 'Can of Diet, Carter, when you're ready please.'

When Carter returned with the requested drink, Lorraine had read the scant report. She held her hand out for the can, flicked the tab open and took a deep drink before saying, 'OK Carter, what do you think?'

He was about to open his mouth when Luke walked in. If Carter had thought it strange, them both arriving separately, he'd kept his mouth shut, and judging by the look on Luke's face was pleased that he had.

Lorraine handed the report to Luke, putting a finger to her lips for Carter to wait until Luke was finished.

A few minutes later Luke, totally businesslike, looked at Lorraine and said, 'No way. Whatever that lot were doing up there it wasn't murder. It's just like them to stumble over a body though.' He put the folder on the desk and walked over to the window.

Carter raised his eyebrows at Lorraine who frowned at him and demanded, 'Well?'

'I think the same,' he said quickly.

'Any ideas on who the victim might be?'

Luke spun round. 'You don't think for one minute that it's Andrew Knightly?'

Lorraine shrugged. 'He's been missing three days now. Where this body was found is roughly forty minutes away, if that … Of bloody course I'm thinking it might be Andrew Knightly.'

Luke gritted his teeth. *For God's sake, she's becoming obsessed with the Knightlys.* He turned back to the window and watched a pair of pigeons perched on the rugby club roof pecking at each other. He sighed. *That's me and Lorraine. Where's it all gone wrong?*

To his stiff back, Lorraine said, 'We need to pay Stanhope police a visit. They've asked for DNA of anyone missing in the area, they're convinced he's not one of theirs.'

'They can tell that, can they? A body with no head and they can tell it's not one of theirs?'

Lorraine tutted. 'Their pathologist has already estimated that the body has been there for roughly three days, that it is the body of a young male and they have no one in the area reported missing in that time, and seeing that it's a body of a teenager, it's pretty bloody obvious to me, for God's sake.'

'So what do we do now?' Luke asked, still outwardly calm and professional.

'We take some family DNA, visit Stanhope and try to convince Stanhope police that those four bloody idiots are more than likely innocent.'

As Lorraine was putting her cardigan over her shoulders Luke's mobile rang. Lorraine looked at him. 'Scottie,' he mouthed. Nodding, Lorraine sat back down. After listening for a minute Luke thanked Scottie, closed his phone and shrugged.

'No sign of anything in her blood, which means Amy wasn't

drugged, and since it doesn't look like there was much evidence of a fight ...'

'She knew him,' Lorraine jumped up. 'It was the same with Sara. It's gotta be the McCades.'

'You alright, Adam? Len?' Jacko shouted across to the opposite holding cell where Adam and Len were.

'No I'm fucking not,' Adam shouted back. 'I hate this place. We're locked up while a maniac that cuts people's fucking heads off is running loose.'

'Shut the fuck up,' a deep voice from further down the block shouted.

'Gonna make me, like, prick?' Adam shouted back defiantly.

'Shh,' Len panicked. 'You don't know how big he is, could be the size of a brick shit house for all we know, man.'

'So? We've got Jacko.'

'I heard that,' Jacko said, but he was concentrating on Danny, who was sitting with his head in his hands. 'You alright, mate?'

'Not really, Jacko, think I might have to sell Elizabeth just to bloody well make ends meet.'

'I know where you're coming from, I promised Melanie a bloody dress she's got her heart set on, now I can't come through and I'm really not looking forward to telling her.'

Danny sighed and said lightly a moment later, 'I did get an idea though when you and the rest of them were snoring your heads off in the early hours.'

'Uh oh.'

'No, hear me out Jacko ... What about gardening, you know, some of these posh houses, lot of people buying around Sunderland and Washington, some really nice places around there now, you know, and South Shields, and Tynemouth, all those places, the sky's the limit, Jacko man. A few tools, spades, wheelbarrow, you know what I mean.'

Jacko looked at him in amazement. 'Are you for real? Do you ever give up trying to make a fast buck?'

Danny replied with a shake of his head and a simple 'No.'

'Well, if you go legit for once, it might work, but first we gotta get out of this mess 'cos all I can see when I shut me eyes is that body with no head.'

CHAPTER FORTY-ONE

Carter watched Lorraine and Luke enter the Knightlys' house. With a shrug, he leaned back on the headrest. Something was very wrong between his bosses. He could sense it. Also, it had something to do with the people in that house, and he guessed that Lorraine was right about the body, but couldn't understand why Luke seemed so against her idea: it all added up.

We're missing a teenager three days now they find a teenager who's been dead three days. Simple. But why? Why all the way up Stanhope Common?

Looking in the rear-view mirror Carter straightened his hair. If he didn't get it cut soon he'd be wearing a ponytail, like Dinwall.

'Hmm ... No.' He shook his head, then turning he watched the door open and Tammy Knightly step back and let Luke and Lorraine in. When she closed the door he leaned back again and sighed, *looks like we're all going be spending the day up at Stanhope. Brilliant.*

He dug a bag of peppermint drops out of his pocket and settled back to wait for Luke and Lorraine, wondering if the endless bags of sweets he bought for these occasions could be claimed back on expenses. He smiled into the mirror as he pondered, rolling the sweet round in his mouth and rechecking his hair.

Tammy froze for a moment when she opened the door, then in a too-loud voice she shouted, 'It's the cops everybody.'

Lorraine stepped inside, but Tammy was still slow in opening the door to the sitting room and only obliged when Lorraine was practically eye to eye with her in the small hall space. Finally she opened the door and they all stepped into the sitting room. Lorraine quickly scanned around her. Stacey, Leanne, both in pretty much the same places again. But then just who she had expected to find? But why had Tammy made such a show of warning people that they were here?

'Lorraine?' Leanne said, hope in her voice.

Lorraine sat down facing Leanne while Luke positioned himself behind her chair. 'I'm sorry Leanne, but it's not good news.'

She watched as Leanne stiffened and the colour left her face. Stacey sat down quickly and Tammy's jaw clenched.

'What ... er, what do you mean, Lorraine?' Leanne whispered.

'I'm really sorry to have to tell you this, but the body of a young man has been found on Stanhope Common, he's been dead the same amount of time that Andrew has been missing.'

She sighed, feeling slightly sickly herself. She had never grown used to the deaths of others, no matter what sort of show she put on for the outside world. The depths of human depravity never failed to upset her, not like some officers she knew. She didn't think she ever would, and when it was someone she'd watched grow up, it made things even worse.

Leanne gasped and fell back in her chair, while Stacey kept flicking her eyes from one sister to another, pleading for one of them to deny it.

'It's him, isn't it? Isn't it?' Tammy suddenly yelled. 'Why don't you just say, for Christ's sake?'

Stacey started to cry, large breathtaking sobs.

'Say it,' Tammy yelled again. 'Say it!'

'We don't know,' Luke said before Lorraine could speak. 'It could be a coincidence. There's a chance it may not be him. We need some DNA to run tests.'

'What for?' Tammy whispered, quiet now and staring at Lorraine. 'You know what he looks like, Lorraine, you'll be able to tell if it's him or not, why bother with fucking tests?'

Leanne started to rock back and forth in her chair, hugging her body with her arms. 'I told youse all he was dead, didn't I?' She pressed her right hand against her heart. 'He's not here anymore. Andrew's space is empty.'

'No!' Stacey screamed and ran for the stairs.

'Why can't you identify him?' Tammy demanded again, while Leanne rocked and rocked.

Lorraine's mouth dried up. *How the hell can I tell them the real reason, even if the body is identified as Andrew? How the hell do I tell them how he died?*

'Well,' she said lamely, 'I'm afraid that everything has to be done by the book. I'm sorry.'

'It could be a tramp,' Luke offered.

'Yeah,' Tammy was sarcastic, 'and just how many fucking teenage tramps have you seen?'

CHAPTER FORTY-TWO

The cell door opened and the thickset, iron-haired officer said, 'OK, you're free to go, all of you.'

Jacko and Danny jumped up.

'Thank God,' Danny muttered. 'I'll have a lot of explaining to do when I get home, mate.'

'You and me both.' Jacko stepped into the corridor as the officer opened the cell door that had kept Adam and Len prisoner.

'What now?' Adam asked.

'Out to the desk, collect your belongings. Everything you said last night checks out.'

Told you, didn't we, didn't we?' Len said. 'So how much taxpayers' money has it cost to keep us four innocent men locked up for most of the night? Eh? And I want me shoelaces back. Bloody ridiculous if you ask me. Taking liberties.'

'Nobody's asking, so don't push it,' the officer replied, heading for a door along the corridor.

Danny poked Len. 'What did I tell you?' he hissed. 'Keep your big fat gob shut.' Len shrugged.

Outside Danny breathed deeply. 'Thank God that's over.'

'It was over the minute they found out the body had been there for three days,' Len said with feeling. 'Actually, when you think about it, we panicked for nowt.'

'Well, that's easy said with hindsight, but how the hell did we know that it had been there for three days?' Jacko pointed at the van that was parked in the corner of the yard. 'Come on, let's be getting home.'

'One thing I need to know,' Adam said turning to Len.

'Aye, what's that then?'

'When did you ever pay any taxes?'

Jacko and Danny burst out laughing as Len blustered, 'I have had proper jobs before, you know.'

Leanne stood at the kitchen window, two tablets in her right hand, a glass of water in the other. Tammy had called the doctor and he'd left the medication, but she didn't want to feel numb, she needed to be with it, not spaced out and grinning like an idiot when they came and told her that Andrew was dead.

Putting the water down and throwing the tablets into the sink, she picked a bottle of milk up that one of the others had left out the fridge again.

'Cup of tea,' Sam said in her ear.

Jumping with the sudden shock of his closeness she spilled some of the milk. As it ran down her hands it reminded her of that last morning when Andrew had pushed his bowl of cornflakes away and milk had slopped over the bowl.

'Sorry.'

'You, sorry?' She shook her head in disgust. 'You have never been sorry for anything in your life.' Turning her back on him she went into the kitchen and picked a tea towel up to dry her hand.

'Oh, but I have, Leanne,' he answered quietly.

She sighed, too worn out to even attempt to argue with him and wishing to God he would stop following her around like a dog, eager to please. 'Whatever.' She walked back into the sitting room and sat down.

She was waiting now, waiting for the knock on the door that would confirm her fears. Suddenly she felt calm. She would get this done without Sam. She would be strong enough, what difference would a death certificate make, she had lived with the knowledge for three days now, she would sort it on her own terms. If Andrew had been murdered, if it was him lying up there on that cold, windswept common then it was all Sam's fault for something he had done all those years ago.

'You can go now,' she said calmly.

'What?'

'Go back to London where you belong.'

Tammy walked in then. 'No, he won't,' she snapped, 'It's always your way Leanne, we need him here.'

Leanne shrugged. 'Where's Stacey?'

'Out for the count, she took the pills the quack gave her.'

'You should take them as well Leanne,' Sam urged. 'It could be hours yet before we find out anything.'

'Quick, Sam,' Tammy said suddenly from the window. 'Sandra Gilbride and her bunch of merry men are on their way over.'

Sam hurried upstairs and stood on the landing where he could hear everything.

'Eee pet, you alright?' Dolly Smith asked, pushing ahead of Sandra, Doris and Vanessa.

'She's fine and so am I,' Tammy said.

'I was getting round to you love, don't fret … Put the kettle on, there's a good girl.'

Coming from anyone else Tammy would have scorched the air with her reply. Instead she just shook her head and went into the kitchen.

Half an hour later after discussing everything from the weather to

Dave Ridley, anything but Andrew, they left and Sam came back downstairs.

'I see she's still bossing people around, and that lot's still a gossip crew.'

'Well, you're wrong there,' Leanne snapped.

Sam looked to Tammy to side with him and was surprised when she came out in favour of Leanne.

'Actually, Sam, they're good people. Sandra's head of the Seahills' committee and she's managing to scrape some money up off the council to get a youth club started, keep the kids off the street, between her and Vanessa things are starting to happen around here, and yes Dolly's still a bloody bossy boots, but that's Dolly. She means well.'

'OK, put in my place I guess.' Sam's mobile rang and after a series of yeses, rights and OKs he hung up, looked at his sisters and said, 'I have to go out for a while, will you be alright?'

Leanne snorted.

'Yeah, no probs, we'll be fine,' Tammy said quickly as she glowered at Leanne.

After he had gone Leanne warned, 'Don't get used to having him around, Tammy. He has another life now, pretty soon when all of this is over he'll be gone again.'

CHAPTER FORTY-THREE

The ride over to Stanhope Common had been quiet, Carter revelling in the magnificent views. Twice he had tried to draw his bosses into conversation about the history of the common and commoners' rights of grazing and other little interesting titbits he thought might interest them, but both of them had looked out of their windows and said very little to him or each other. Blissfully unaware that both Lorraine and Luke were not taking a bit of notice of his ramblings, he pulled up outside of Stanhope police station.

Inside, Lorraine introduced herself to the desk sergeant, who took her and Luke through into an office where a bald-headed man in his late forties sat behind a desk and gave them a friendly smile.

He spoke with a soft Scottish burr as he introduced himself as Detective Ross Marlow and asked them to sit down.

'Well, there have been a few changes since we last spoke on the phone a couple of hours ago.' He paused a moment, coughed, then said quickly. 'One of my officers found the head.' Lorraine raised her eyebrows as he went on. 'It was halfway up a tree in a nearby copse, and from what I've been told in a far, far worse condition than the body, those flying insects, nasty wee beggars some of them.'

'Oh, God,' Lorraine said.

'You may be able to identify him now, see if it's your missing boy. The autopsy's scheduled for four this afternoon.'

'Will that be somewhere close by?' Luke asked.

'Durham, that's a tad closer to you than us. I would have rung but the news just came in ten minutes ago, apparently the officer who found the head has been taken to hospital in shock, poor bugger, first day on the job too.'

'To be confronted with that, on your first day.' Luke shook his head in sympathy.

Unaware that three separate pairs of eyes, two blue, one a watery brown, were staring at them, the McCade clan gathered around their barbecue.

Seth, already the worse for wear, was snoring in his deckchair. A half-empty can of lager was perched precariously on his bare stomach, his sons taking bets on how long before it tipped over, while Patrick flipped a few dozen stolen beef burgers to the tune of Elvis singing 'Hound Dog'.

'Turn that fucking shit off,' Tony complained.

Doris giggled, while Dolly and Mr Skillings, who were staunch Elvis fans, tutted.

Patrick glowered at Tony, then gritted his teeth as hot fat from the burgers splattered on his hands. 'I'll fucking turn you off in a minute,' he snarled.

'Cool it guys,' Lee, who had been home for an hour, said, feeling the animosity between his father and uncle was stronger than ever.

A couple of the others looked up, momentarily distracted from their game of penny toss, which usually ended in fist fights. Seeing nothing amiss, they soon got back to the game in hand. Tony snorted, then walked over to Lee and sat down next to him.

'You certain,' he said quietly, 'that mate's gonna stick to your cover story and not chicken out?'

'Oh, he'll stick to it alright. There's nowt to tie me to Dave Ridley. This morning me mate told the coppers that he started the brawl, and the witnesses are primed and ready if the coppers persist and it goes to court. Fucking brilliant or what?' He took a joint out of his pocket and lit up.

Tony nodded his head. 'Good, 'cos with that lot up in the attic we don't want no coppers around here for any reason.' With a satisfied smirk, he drained his can of cider, crushed it flat, then threw it towards the bin, shrugging when he missed. Then he turned to Lee and snatched the joint out of his son's hand.

'Hey, that's mine, roll your fucking own, greedy bastard.'

Tony lifted his hand and slapped the back of Lee's head. The skinhead was about to yell when Seth snorted, opened his eyes and said, 'I've told youse that stuff's no bloody good, fairly rattles the brain, been saying it for years I have ...'

'Shut the fuck up,' Tony and Lee chorused.

'What did he say?' Mr Skillings hissed.

'Something about the burgers being burned,' Dolly whispered back.

'No, not him, the other one, Tony, something about a chicken, was it, and a court?'

'That'll be right, nobody else can afford chicken on the barbies except that thieving bunch of creeps,' Doris said. 'And I wish they'd turn the bloody music down so we can hear properly.'

'I just heard them swearing at Seth,' Mr Skillings said.

'If their grandmother Sadie could hear them she'd turn in her grave, decent woman she was, no bloody wonder that Patrick's wife did a runner,' Dolly said.

'Aye,' Doris agreed. 'But that Tony's wife, if she is his wife 'cos I can't remember them ever getting wed, can't even remember her bloody name now ...'

'Trisha,' Mr Skillings said.

'That's it. Well, they reckon she's as bad as the lot of them.'

'Well, this just about takes the bloody biscuit,' Jacko said from behind them.

Startled, the three of them spun round. 'Shh,' Doris said, putting her finger over her mouth.

'The three of youse'll get shushed alright if they ever catch you spying on them.'

'You just scared me out of a year's growth, Jacko lad.' Mr Skillings put his hand over his heart.

'And where've you been all night?' Doris asked.

'Tell you later.' Grinning at Mr Skillings Jacko shook his head, turned and headed back into the house just as Melanie and her friend Suzy came in from playing in the street.

'Dad!' Melanie squealed, running up to him in her own particular way, one leg dragging behind the other, with her arms outstretched.

Jacko caught her, spun her round, deposited her on the ground and squeezed her shoulder. 'Hi, munchkin.'

Suzy moved to his other side and gazed up at him. Jacko squeezed her shoulder as well and was rewarded with a huge smile, 'Aha, two little munchkins, eh? And what have you two ladies been up to?'

'Helping Sandra collect the trip money in. Sandra was happy today, nearly everybody paid ... Dad?'

'What?' Jacko asked suspiciously, knowing all too well his daughter was after something when she used that particular wheedling tone.

'Can we go to the air show tomorrow? Please Dad, we heard the planes go over today, well some of them, can we go, please? ... Honest, I won't ask for anything else, not even an ice cream. And if we go can Suzy come too, please ... Everybody at school's going, me and Suzy will be the only ones left out.'

Suzy looked expectantly at him; her eyes wide, she nodded in eager anticipation. Jacko sighed. *How the hell can I refuse?* 'Of course she can.'

Melanie clapped her hands and said excitedly, 'So we can go, really, can we?'

'Well, I said Suzy can, don't know about you though.'

'Dad!'

Jacko laughed, remembering that Danny had said he was taking his kids. *If I can hitch a lift with him then it's chips and ice cream.* He rummaged in his pocket, knowing the crumpled piece of paper was a five-pound note. There were also three pound coins and some loose change. Maybe Christina would like to come. His heart warmed when he thought of Christina, he loved her so much. Perhaps this gardening job with Danny might work out. He was sick of ducking and diving. Time to get a regular job.

Wonder if Danny would go for some kind of partnership, do it properly, a real business?

'I'm just gonna pop round and see Danny for a mo, OK pet?'

Melanie and Suzy ran happily out of the house. Suzy, way in front, suddenly slowed down as she remembered that Melanie could never keep up with her. Jacko had seen Suzy do this many times in the street and loved her for it. He looked over to where Doris and her friends still had their faces pressed against the fence. Hiding a smile and shaking his head, he left to go to Danny's.

As he was passing the Knightlys' he recognised Tammy at the window and gave her a nod. She replied with a small wave. Out of the corner of his eye he noticed the upstairs curtain move. For a moment he was startled, he could have sworn that it was a man's hand that pulled the curtain closed.

No, he told himself, *it must have been Leanne or Stacey or more than likely Stacey's boyfriend.*

Whatever, he prayed they would soon find Andrew. It wasn't so long ago that he'd gone through nearly the same trauma with Melanie. Thank God she had been found safe and well.

CHAPTER FORTY-FOUR

Luke held the heavy door open for Lorraine. She smiled. They were running a sort of truce, which certainly pleased Carter. It made his life that much easier when his bosses were friends. Luke had decided the only way forward was to hang back and let the case unfold. But he was also determined not to let go, he would keep digging while everything was fresh.

No way, he thought, watching Lorraine walk on in front of him, *is that sadistic bastard going to kill again, but why such a large gap between killings? That's a huge puzzle. And why is Lorraine so certain that the McCades are behind this? And although she's technically off the murder case she's still in charge of the Andrew Knightly case. And there's bound to be a crossover point.*

The autopsy scheduled for four o'clock was taking place at Durham, which was much closer to Houghton-le-Spring than Stanhope. It had given them a couple of hours to sort of talk. Although Lorraine had still not said much more about what had happened that night, it was like she had told him what she wanted him to know and it was now a closed book. She was still adamant, however, that Dave Ridley had not set fire to himself.

Lorraine and Luke welcomed the cold of the autopsy room when they walked in. It was much like any other and smelled exactly the same, a mix of hospital and slaughterhouse.

'Hello there,' Terri Gerritsen a well-built brunette with the largest brown eyes Luke had ever seen, smiled as she held out her hand. 'We've met before, haven't we Lorraine?' Without giving Lorraine a chance to answer and dropping her hand as if it were on fire, she swivelled on the balls of her feet to face Luke. 'But we haven't met, have we? I would certainly have remembered you.'

Luke was taken aback. Even her voice scorched the air between them. Terri Gerritsen was openly flirting with him; her eyes, which for a moment had been on his face, now rested on his crotch. She looked back at him, winked then grinned. 'Relax, Luke, I'm a happily married woman.'

Lorraine laughed. She'd half expected this from Terri, who flirted with anything in trousers. She'd told Lorraine once over coffee that she just did it to get a reaction from them.

'OK,' Terri said a moment later. 'Down to business.'

Luke glanced at Lorraine, she smiled, and smiling back he shook his head and mouthed 'For real?' which made Lorraine laugh out loud. A moment later, all frivolity forgotten, she watched as the drawer slipped open to reveal the body.

Silently Lorraine and Luke observed the headless torso as Terri moved to the feet. 'As you can, see every toe has been broken. This will have caused immeasurable pain because of all the nerve ends there. This young man has been the subject of one of the worst tortures imaginable. His fingers were also broken.' Terri moved further up the body, while Lorraine's eyes were still on the broken, twisted toes of the victim.

'Jeez,' Luke hissed.

Terri nodded and pointed at the ragged neck. 'It's my theory that whoever committed this atrocity attempted to cut the head off while the victim was still alive and screaming. With every finger and toe broken he would have been helpless.'

Lorraine stared at the ragged, curled flaps of blackened skin and knew this was another picture she would carry with her for the rest of her life. She was fast building up a good-sized portfolio. 'Why?' she muttered.

'That's your job, and I know you won't rest 'til you've found him. Because trust me, whoever did this enjoyed it, a rather unhealthy taste for torture if you ask me. It takes some time to do this sort of damage.'

'Unless there was more than one doing the job,' Lorraine said with a shrug thinking of a certain family.

'Well, that's rare. Unless ...'

But Lorraine wasn't listening, she was staring at the torso. 'What are those?' She pointed at marks on the victim's stomach.

Luke was looking intently at Lorraine, knowing exactly where she was going with this.

'Human bite marks,' Terri said.

'What?!' Lorraine asked, her stomach churning at the thought.

'Yeah, the saliva tests confirmed my suspicions.'

Lorraine shook her head. 'Jesus. I thought this was one sick bastard already. I'll get right on to it. In the meantime ...'

Terri moved to another smaller cabinet in the wall and carefully lifted what could only be the head belonging to the torso out of the cabinet. She placed it on the table, above the neck, doing her best to match up the ragged edges.

Lorraine sucked air in. It was Andrew Knightly's insect-ravaged face.

Luke swallowed hard. The disinfectant in the autopsy room failed to mask the horrendous smell. He looked at Lorraine. Her face was deathly pale. She nodded.

Lorraine had given Carter the rest of the afternoon off, he hadn't had a break in nearly two weeks, and even though he protested, Lorraine could see the tired lines around his eyes. He was taking his mother to the Sunderland Glass Centre. She wished she was going with him. He could babble as much as he wanted about anything in the world. She'd rather be going anywhere but back to the Knightlys' with the news she had to give them.

It was six thirty as they pulled up outside the house. Across the road Jacko Musgrove was walking up his path. As Lorraine stepped out of the car, she nodded, then realised as Christina Jenkins came out of the house next door that he had not been looking at her but at Christina. She was unaware that she was staring until Luke gently said her name.

'Yes, yes,' she replied, spinning round.

She sighed and headed up the path. Before they reached the door Stacey opened it, took one look at Lorraine's grim face, gasped, then fainted.

Hearing the commotion Tammy ran in from the kitchen. She looked down at her sister, who Luke was helping to sit up, and began backing away. Oblivious to what was going on across the road Jacko and Christina walked hand in hand to the bus stop.

Lorraine helped Luke pick Stacey up off the floor and together they gently eased her into the sitting room where Leanne waited for them.

'I was right wasn't I, right all along. Oh, God. Andrew.' She sat down with a soft whoosh. Lorraine sat next to her and put her arm around her. Leanne sank her head into Lorraine's shoulder. 'Did he suffer, Lorraine?' she whispered.

Oh fuck, Lorraine thought, even though she'd known the question would come. *How the hell do you tell someone that their loved one has been tortured to death? What do I say?*

Lorraine sighed. 'I'm sorry, Leanne. I'm so very, very sorry.'

'I'm sorry too, Leanne, but sadly, he did,' Luke answered for her, knowing that Lorraine was struggling.

Leanne held tightly to Lorraine, who, holding her just as tightly, looked over to Stacey, expecting her at any moment to start screaming, but Stacey sat in stunned silence staring at a spot on the wall and seeing only she knew what.

Into the silence a man's voice said quietly, 'How? How did he suffer?'

For a moment Lorraine froze. *It can't be.*

She let go of Leanne and stood up. Standing in the doorway was Sam Knightly. She had often wondered what she would do if this moment ever happened; what she would feel.

And now she knew.

Nothing.

The past was over, gone. She knew now that any feelings she might have had for Sam had died with Randy. What Sam had done had been an accident, that he had intended to catch up with Randy and give him a beating was obvious, but he had not intended to kill him. And Jacko, Jacko Musgrove was one of the best, a good person, he always had been, who had weathered bad luck after bad luck and had never changed, never become bitter. He still had a smile for anyone who needed it and he loved his daughter to bits, but he wasn't Luke. She had inadvertently brought back to life a schoolgirl crush that could have ruined everything.

She would always have a place for Jacko and Dave in her heart, maybe even a space for what Sam used to be before his parents died and he was thrust into being a surrogate father long before he was ready, but now she had a murder to sort and she would hold back nothing to find the killer of Andrew Knightly and her two friends. With every second that passed it was becoming more and more likely that it was all somehow connected.

Luke was about to speak before the silence became unbearable when Lorraine stepped forward, and for a brief space he held his breath when she said, 'Hello, Sam.'

CHAPTER FORTY-FIVE

Jacko and Christina stood at the bottom of Dave's bed. His eyes were closed and his breathing raspy. He sounded like a very old man with a heavy cold. 'Oh Jesus,' Jacko said. 'Will you look at the poor sod?'

Dave's eyes flashed open and he looked at Christina, who blushed blood red as she always did when someone looked at her for longer than a few seconds.

'How are you then, mate?'

Dave's eyes turned to Jacko. After a moment recognition dawned and he gave Jacko a lopsided smile. Jacko was sure there was more going on in his old friend's eyes than had been for some time.

'Do you know who did this, Dave?'

Christina gripped Jacko's hand tightly. She had heard the rumours that Dave had set fire to himself and thought that Jacko was being too blunt. But Jacko had never believed for one moment that Dave had done it and he refused to believe it now.

By nature Dave was gentle, he could no more hurt himself than he could hurt anyone, even if he had mental problems.

'Who done it, Dave?' Jacko repeated.

Dave stared at the cream blanket and started pulling at a thread, his fingers moving faster and faster, pulling and dragging the thread as if his very life depended on it.

'Leave it Jacko, love,' Christina whispered. 'You're only upsetting him more.'

The thread pulled right through and gathered into a ball. Dave's fingers looked for more threads.

Pretty soon there'll be no blanket left, Jacko thought, picturing a pile of threads on the floor.

'I ... We brought some grapes.' Jacko walked round to the bedside cabinet and put the grapes in an already brimming fruit bowl. 'Not gonna starve, are you? Enough bloody fruit in here to feed an army,' Jacko grinned.

A moment later he stiffened as Dave grabbed his wrist hard and said, '*Him.*'

Dave's eyes were suddenly crystal clear. As Jacko looked into their depths he felt a chill so cold come over him, which battled the hot, dry stuffiness in the room. He rubbed his arms vigorously.

'Him,' Dave repeated.

CHAPTER FORTY-SIX

Dinwall entered the station car park two seconds behind Carter, having dropped Travis off at home.

'Good day?' he said to Carter, parked two cars away, as he turned the key to lock his own car.

'Well,' Carter said, then looked around before he spoke. 'Did you know that the body up at Stanhope Common has been identified as Andrew Knightly?'

'No way man!'

'Oh aye.' Carter locked his car and followed Dinwall into the station. 'Where's Travis?'

'The soft Jessie had sand in his shoe and went home to change. There was absolutely no need to go down on the beach and look for trouble, but you know what he's like, he'd arrest a seashell if it was pointing the wrong way.'

Inside the building Dinwall and Carter headed for the canteen.

'So, any problems on the beach?'

'No, man, not even a bloody jay walker. So where's the boss and Daniels?'

'They went to give the bad news to the Knightlys. I got a phone call at the glass centre, we were on our way out anyhow, and Luke said I had to be here.'

'Yeah, me too. Wonder what'll happen.'

'Bet she's going after the McCades,' Carter nodded knowingly.

'Of course she's going after the McCades, it has to be them hasn't it, as plain as them fucking freckles on your eyelids. Who the fuck else would it be? And I bet you anything it's them responsible for Dave and not the bloody fairies. Your turn, Carter. Mine's a black coffee.'

Lorraine swallowed hard before saying, 'How are you, Sam?'

For a moment Sam didn't speak, then his voice was icy when he finally said, 'Fine. And you?'

Lorraine nodded. 'Good.' Sam had managed to conceal it well, but Lorraine had seen the flash of anger in his eyes and wondered what it was for. 'This is my second in command, Luke Daniels ... my fiancé.

If both men were a little surprised by the announcement they managed to hide it under the sudden wailing coming from Stacey. Sam moved quickly to her side, out of his pocket he took a packet of tablets.

'I'll get some water.' Lorraine hurried into the kitchen. When she returned a moment later Luke was on the phone.

'The doctor's on his way.' He put his mobile back in his pocket and gestured with his head for Sam to follow him into the kitchen.

Lorraine nodded, knowing his intentions. She turned to the sitting room and took a deep breath before going in to see Leanne and the others.

'Oh, Jesus Christ,' Sam said a few minutes later after Luke had told him everything that had been done to Andrew. He sank against the sink, ran his fingers through his hair and made no effort to stop the tears running down his face. 'He was just a kid. A fucking kid.'

The small remnants of conscience that Sam had left pricked and pricked hard. He knew he'd done pretty much the same thing, and worse, though he'd had never got his hands dirty apart from that one time, but not kids. He had never harmed a kid. Usually a slap here and there sorted any lippy ones that were in danger of becoming too big for their boots.

He wiped his eyes with the back of his hand. 'They must never know.'

Luke knew he meant his sisters and nodded. There really was no reason why they should know the finer details.

'So what now?'

'Now we try to find who did this.'

'She knows. Lorraine knows who done this ... The bastards, it's them alright, why would anyone else want to do something like this to a kid?'

'If it's them they'll pay,' Lorraine spoke from the doorway. 'Believe me.'

'You know it's the McCades.'

Lorraine looked to Sam. What she said next made him stiffen and glower at her.

'Whatever, but you are on my turf now Sam and I want no vigilante tactics of any description. And I mean it.' She left her eyes on his for a few moments longer, reinforcing what she had said, before turning to Luke. 'Time for us to get back to the station.'

Luke followed her to the car and just before they got in their eyes met across the car roof. 'Er, Lorraine, did I sleep through a few days and miss something?'

'Like what?'

'Like an engagement announcement?'

Lorraine smiled. It was the first real smile Luke had seen in days. 'Don't you want to be engaged to me?'

'Well ...' Luke grinned, then quickly ducked when she threw a pencil at him and got into the car.

CHAPTER FORTY-SEVEN

An hour later Jacko and Christina got off the bus at the stop outside of the Beehive pub and headed home. When they turned into their street they were amazed to find just about everybody outside.

'What the hell's gone on here?' Jacko said, a chill curling round his spine, as Christina gripped his hand tightly.

'Jacko,' Sandra Gilbride said from behind, hurrying to catch up with them, her plastic carrier bag banging at her side. 'It's Andrew. That body they found up on Stanhope Common. It's him.'

'Oh, no,' Christina gasped, her hand going to her mouth, tears springing instantly in her eyes.

For a long minute Jacko said nothing, then shook his head and muttered, 'The poor bastard ... Have you heard how? Why? Anything else at all?'

'No, the first thing anyone knew was when Stacey ran sobbing and screaming over to your mother's house, then a strange bloke followed her. I was standing at my gate talking to Vanessa. We didn't realise who it was at first, but your mother and Dolly did, right off ... It was Sam Knightly.'

Jacko's jaw dropped. *Jesus Christ ... Sam?*

Something very strange was happening. First Dave burned, then Andrew dead, and next Sam appears out of the blue. He swung his head in the direction of the McCades' house.

'Jacko.' Christina gently tugged at his arm.

He looked down at her and for a moment he was looking at a stranger. The only face he could see was Randy's.

'Jacko?'

He blinked, then gave her a weak smile. 'Come on love, I need a cuppa, let's see what Doris's spy ring has found out.'

He put his arm on Christina's back, easing her down the path. Outwardly he looked as calm as ever, but inside his mind was doing cartwheels. *What the hell's going on?*

Suddenly his breath caught in his throat. He'd forgotten the first ... *Amy*.

What's wrong Jacko?' Christina asked.

He stood still, his face pale.

Amy murdered. Dave attempted murder. Andrew murdered. Just who the hell was the woman found the other day?

It was all starting to add up in Jacko's mind and sent chills down his spine.

CHAPTER FORTY-EIGHT

'And you are absolutely sure about this?' Superintendent Clark asked Lorraine.

'Yes sir.'

He pulled himself upright in his seat and pondered a moment as he slowly tore the wrapper off a stick of mint chewing gum, rolled the wrapping into a ball and flicked it into the waste paper basket before putting the gum into his mouth. Watching through lowered lids Lorraine felt like strangling him.

How come it's always pompous twits like him who get into such high positions? she thought, never taking her eyes from his.

'OK,' he finally said. 'As long as you know what you are doing and as long as you know the consequences of arresting a whole family, especially if they are innocent.'

'Huh. That lot's never been innocent since the day each of them was born.' She stood firm. 'I want to go in now.'

'I thought you might. Could I suggest kid gloves?'

'With that manky lot, they'd be scruffy in minutes.'

Clark looked at her for a moment: he could never tell if Lorraine was taking him seriously.

Lorraine looked right back at him wishing for the umpteenth time that Clark had been born with a sense of humour. 'OK, then I'll get on with it.'

After she had closed the door she mouthed a silent 'Yes!' to the ceiling, then hurried down to the incident room. 'Right,' she said, walking in and facing her team. 'We go.'

'Melanie,' Doris shouted up the stairs. 'Are you up there?'

'No, Nana.'

'Don't be bloody funny, hurry along and tell Dolly and Mr Skillings to get themselves along here double quick, there's something going down out the back.'

'God Nana, you are so nosey.'

'Just do it. Unless you want daisies in your hair as well as on your dress.'

Melanie flung her head and walked out of the house. She'd heard about Andrew and both she and Suzy had frightened themselves silly speculating on different ways he could have died. Suzy had been so frightened she had gone home early. Bored on her own, Melanie had caught up with her homework. *That'll be a shock for horrible old Miss Hatford* she thought as she knocked on Mr Skillings' door, having seen Dolly walking down his path.

A few minutes later the threesome were at their usual posts at the holes in the fence. Melanie had gone upstairs to see her dad and Christina.

'Look at them three,' Jacko said from the bedroom window. 'It's hard to tell which one's got the fattest arse.'

'Nana,' Melanie giggled. 'She should have two great big massive daisies on it.'

'Melanie,' Jacko chided her, hiding a smile.

'Oh, something's happening,' Christina said.

Dinwall and four uniformed officers climbed over the high garden gate, which was locked with an unreachable heavy duty bolt, as Queen belted out 'It's a Kind Of Magic' from the stereo. Dusk was falling and most of the McCades were either blind drunk or so stoned they were seeing little green men.

Lee was facing the gate and spotted them first. His uncle Pete thought his nephew was having some sort of fit when Lee, his mouth hanging open, made a sort of strangling noise and waved his arms about and yelled for Patrick.

'What the ... Shit!' Patrick dropped his can of larger as one of the policemen ran up to him and seized his arm. 'What the fuck do you think you're doing?' he screamed, his face screwed up and full of rage. 'Trespassing bastards!'

Tony spun round in his chair. 'Fuck off. No way. We ain't done nothing.'

'Yeah, well, you're gonna have to prove that, because we're arresting the whole corrupt conniving lot of you for murder,' Dinwall said with great satisfaction as he reached for Tony's hands to cuff him.

Behind the fence the watchers gasped and looked wide eyed at each other, each wondering who could make it out to the street first with the news.

In the sitting room, Luke, Travis and two uniforms arrested three of the McCades and marched them outside to the waiting vans as Dinwall and three uniforms brought the lot from the garden.

'Is that all of them?' Lorraine asked.

'Think so,' Luke replied, keeping tight hold of Mick, who was doing his best to wriggle free. Luke tried not to breath and knew exactly why one of the WPCs wrinkled her nose as she helped lift Mick into the van and quickly slam the door behind him.

To the sound of a dozen pairs of feet kicking the floor and walls of each van, accompanied by a whole string of cursing, the drivers took off for the station.

'OK, Carter keep two officers and go through the whole house from top to bottom, every nook and cranny. Don't come back to the station until you find me something that ties this bloody lot to Andrew Knightly. Got it?'

'Sure thing boss.'

Lorraine nodded as she got into the car. 'Right,' she said to Luke. 'Let's get on with it. I expect at least one of the younger ones to crack pretty early.'

CHAPTER FORTY-NINE

Sam was watching TV a re-run of *Dad's Army*, but it could have been a repeat of last week's news for all the notice he was taking. He still wasn't over the shock of seeing Lorraine with dark hair.

The bitch. All these years. All these years I've worshipped her.

He felt his anger building. *How dare she!*

I even fucking married her lookalike for God's sake, and she dares to die her hair dark behind my back!

His sisters, all three of them exhausted, were in bed. His mind jumped from Lorraine to Andrew, as it had been doing for the last few hours, and the terrible things that had been done to him. Ten fingers and ten toes would take a good wedge of time to break.

There must have been more than one of them.

Bastards.

He sighed heavily. *The fucking kid must have suffered agonies, and all for what? A fucking accident? Jesus Christ, the kid wasn't even three years old at the fucking time.*

He knew, though, that revenge was a dish much better served cold. He'd known people who had waited twenty years or even longer to dish it out.

The bites. There was something in the back of his mind, a little maggot of a thought that wriggling away from him that he couldn't quite get hold of it. *Someone used to bite when they were kids.*

But who? Jacko, Dave, Randy?

Or was it one of the girls?

He snapped his fingers and muttered with a deep sense of shock, 'Oh my God ... It was Jacko! The bastard did lose an eye at the crash. All this time he must have been holding a grudge. Fucking hell!'

He was still lost in thought five minutes later when his mobile rang. Before he could say hello, Goth's voice came out loud and clear.

'What the fuck do you think you are doing, sending me into a fucking raid? Last time I saw that many coppers was when Tarak murdered two of his fucking slappers.'

Even if Sam didn't have things on his mind, Goth's speech would have momentarily stunned him. It was the longest string of words he had put together the whole time Sam had known him.

'What the hell are you on about?'

'Look out of your window. The whole bastard street's out.'

Sam rushed to the window and moving the curtains he saw a group of people milling about, some he recognised, others he had not seen before. Then two police vans came round the corner followed by three patrol cars. 'Eh?'

'No, not "eh?"' Goth snapped. 'The whole fucking family's in the vans, including the two you wanted me to waste.'

'OK, OK, I want you to keep low, stay in the hotel as much as you can until I need you, if you have to go out don't be seen in Houghton or Sunderland. Go to Newcastle or Durham, no, make it Middlesbrough, and I'll contact you. The coppers are obviously on the ball, but don't fret, I can reach the bastards inside, they won't last a day whatever nick they end up in.'

'Right. See you, then.'

'Yeah.'

CHAPTER FIFTY

Tony lay back in the seat, his arms draped over the side, a sneer etched on his face as he glared at Dinwall.

'I told you,' he slurred. 'We were having a barbie.'

Dinwall got up and switched the desk light on in the darkening room, twisted it so that it shone in McCade's eyes, then switched the recorder off. 'So you have a barbie every day? Expect me to believe that, do you?' Dinwall snarled back at him.

'Go get a fucking haircut. Pony tails are for girls. Fucking prick.'

'At least my hair's washed, you dirty twat, and I'll use the same shampoo to wash your mouth out if you don't clean your act up and start telling the truth.'

Tony leaned forward threateningly. 'Aye, you and whose fucking army?'

Dinwall lunged forward. Quickly, Travis threw himself between them.

'Let me at the freak, I've had hours of this shit, the murdering bastard,' Dinwall yelled.

'He's not worth your job, mate.'

'Don't play good cop bad cop with me, you pricks, think I'm still wet behind me ears, don't you. Yeah well, I'm not, and I know me rights.'

'Oh hell, not another backstreet lawyer,' Dinwall snapped. 'God help us.'

'I told you, we had a barbie, and the others will tell you the same. A lot of gobs to feed, a barbie's easy. OK, now arrest me, or let me and mine fucking well go.'

'Outside,' Dinwall said to Travis. He looked at Tony. 'Don't move.'

Tony looked at the bars on the window. 'Who d'you think I am? Fucking Houdini?'

Outside Dinwall growled, 'I could flatten the cocky git.'

'Yeah, you and me both, but we're getting nowhere, we've been going round in circles for over an hour. You know as well as I do that he'll admit to nothing even if we had it on tape. I'm gonna see how the others are doing.'

He had only taken a step when a door further down the corridor opened and Lorraine stepped out. Spotting her officers she walked up to them. 'Anything?'

Dinwall shook his head. 'It's like flogging a dead horse in there.'

'Same here, and I don't think Luke or Sanderson are fairing any better either.'

'I'm all for calling it a night,' Travis said.

Lorraine's mobile rang and with a flash of irritation she snatched it out of her pocket, looked at the number and said, 'This better be good, Carter.'

As Carter talked, her smile grew wider by the minute. Finally she said, 'Well done Carter, wrap it up and go home, you've done a damn good job.'

'Well?' Luke, who had joined the others in the corridor, asked.

Lorraine nodded at each of them. 'Got the bastards.' She clapped her hands, then went on with a huge grin, 'We've got them for another twenty-four hours at least. Carter found a whole bloody cannabis farm in the loft. He said all the plants were nearly full grown and in another couple of weeks would have been ready to hit the streets.'

'Yes, yes, *yes*!' Dinwall said heading back into the room, followed by Travis.

Lorraine went into her interview room, looked at Patrick McCade and, still smiling, said, 'I am arresting you on suspicion of drug dealing.'

'No way,' he snapped. But his face flushed, his eyes narrowed and Lorraine knew she had him on this count at least.

'Let's see you wriggle out of this one. Explain a whole cannabis farm in your loft, mate.'

Jacko, Christina and the girls finished their bags of chips sitting facing the sea. The spectacular air show had finished an hour ago but the girls were still talking excitedly about the event.

Jacko stood up. 'Right. A nice brisk walk along the beach, work those chips off, else I'll have three fatties on me hands. Come on.'

'Aww, Dad, do we have to?'

'Yes, lazy bones, the bus stop's that way anyhow.'

'Can we paddle, Dad?'

'Please,' Suzy added.

'OK, but don't get wet.'

'*Dad!*

Jacko laughed and the girls, trainers tied around their necks with the laces, ran ahead. Hand in hand with Christina, Jacko couldn't ever remember feeling happier.

Until the sun disappeared a few minutes later when Christina said, 'What did Dave mean this morning when he said "Him" as if it was somebody he knew?'

Jacko shrugged. He knew it should mean something but whatever it was kept escaping his mind. It was as if he could capture the corner of the meaning and then it was pulled out of his grasp.

With the whole McCade clan locked up for the night, Lorraine said goodnight to Luke in the car park.

'Sure you won't come back for pizza? We could pick one up on the way,' Luke asked hopefully as he looked quickly round before kissing her.

'No, love. I need to check up on the Hippy and the Rock Chick, they'll be expecting me,' she laughed. 'If I'm not in bed by a certain time they just might call the police.'

Luke sighed. 'OK, but it's not the same without you in my bed. I'll phone you later.' He smiled, 'That's if you're certain you want to go.'

Lorraine hesitated. She was certainly tempted, she wanted Luke's arms around her so badly that she ached all over.

No, everything's working out the way we planned it, could add another night on in a week or two though.

They kissed, and with a smile Lorraine got into her car and waved as Luke pulled out before her. She drove up to the gates, hesitated a moment, then instead of taking a left, which was her way home, she turned right and drove through Houghton and headed for the Seahills.

Luke frowned. *Now where the hell can she be going?*

Five minutes later, Lorraine pulled up outside of the Knightlys' house.

CHAPTER FIFTY-ONE

The sun was just going down and broad swathes of purple, red and gold covered the darkening sky.

'Magnificent,' Lorraine murmured as the door opened.

'Did I hear right?' Sam asked, his eyes twinkling as he smiled down at Lorraine.

'Not you. Look.' She stepped to one side so he could see the sky behind her.

'Yes I know, I've been watching it from the window. You forget after a time when you move away just how fantastic the sunsets can be up here.' She stepped back and ushered her into the sitting room.

Lorraine sat down. 'Girls in bed?'

'The doctor's keeping them all sedated thank God. Stacey's hysterical most of the time, Leanne's just the opposite, she sits staring into space, and Tammy, I'm afraid if Tammy got loose she'd wipe the McCades out on her own.'

Lorraine sighed. 'Oh, dear.'

'I take it you've come to tell me that the McCades have confessed? Would you like a drink, tea or something?'

'No thank you, I don't drink tea. A glass of water would be fine though.'

Sam swallowed hard. He had been praying that she hadn't changed anything else, she had never liked tea and it used to annoy him when Carol drank it. As he passed behind her on the way to the kitchen he struggled hard to stop himself from touching her. Although he was still annoyed that she had dared to change the colour of her hair. The need to be close to her was burning him up inside.

He stood by the sink for a moment, letting the tap run, until he gained control of himself. Going back into the sitting room he handed her the glass. 'The McCades?'

Lorraine blew air upwards, disturbing her fringe, as she reached for the glass. Sam's breathing quickened. She had done that the first day they had met at five years old. 'Sorry, but they all swear blind they had nothing to do with Andrew. Every bloody last one of them.'

'Bollocks Lorraine, you know as well as I do it's payback for Randy. They've been waiting for years for this. I thought it was me they would come after but they've waited haven't they, waited for Andrew to reach a similar age.'

Lorraine put her elbow on the arm of the chair and rested her chin in her hand. 'I don't know what to say. I'm certain it's them too, but …'

'But what?' Sam snapped. 'You know it's them, who the hell else would it be for Christ's sake, Lorry? Andrew had no enemies, he was a kid, what did he do to warrant an execution, because that's what it was. A fucking execution, for fuck's sake.'

'Andrew was involved with drugs, Sam. He knew other people, probably the wrong sort of people, perhaps he wanted to get away from it all.'

'From those bastards, you mean?'

'Maybes.' She debated with herself, whether to tell Sam about the cannabis farm in the McCades' attic and decided against it.

She was about to speak when Sam, who had started pacing up and down, stopped suddenly and said, 'Who found him?'

'Adam Glasier.'

'Who the hell's he?'

'A friend of Jacko's. Jacko was with him at the time. Him, Len and Danny Jorden.'

'What? Jacko was there?'

'Yes. I have a sneaky feeling they were up there sheep rustling, certainly not much else going on up there in the middle of the damn night that's for sure.'

'Now don't you think that's weird?'

'Don't for God's sake go thinking Jacko had anything to do with it.'

'Why not? He lost his eye, remember. And ask yourself this – who was the biter when we were little kids, eh? I know he bit me more than once, and the others. The bastard.'

'That is ridiculous. You know as well as I do that Jacko has always been a good person.' She shook her head in frustration. 'You are way off beam with that one, Sam.'

Sam sneered. 'Oh really? How's that then, got a soft spot for him, have you?'

Lorraine felt her face flush and she snapped, 'I don't see that's any of your busi …'

'You have, haven't you?' Sam butted in, his voice rising by the minute and his old accent breaking through. 'It was always him, wasn't it? Never Randy, even though he thought it was, certainly not Dave … I thought it might have been me, but I never stood a chance where he was, did I, eh? Not a fucking chance. Jacko all along.' He scowled at her.

Lorraine wondered where all this was leading. Sam was getting pretty het up. 'Sam, we were kids. What the hell are you talking about?'

But Sam answered with a question of his own. 'Does he know how you feel?'

'What do you mean, feel? Why should he know? Why would he want to know, for Christ's sake? It was years ago, I'm with Luke now. Look, I'm leaving. I came to tell you how far we were getting with the investigation. I don't need to hear this.'

She stood up and Sam grabbed her wrist. Lorraine froze. His grip was far stronger than it needed to be, and for a moment her heart gave a jolt of fear. Then she looked into his eyes and slowly he let go.

'Sorry,' he mumbled, dropping his gaze for a moment.

'Goodnight.' She headed for the door. 'In future I'll send Luke or one of the others with updates.'

'I named my daughter after you,' he said softly.

In the doorway Lorraine stopped. Had she heard him right? Then, gathering herself together, and without looking back, she left. She started the car and headed home. *Daughter?* she thought. *Jesus!*

No one even knows he has a daughter. No one knows what the hell he's been up to since the day he left. And calling her after me: I know friends sometimes do that, but it just doesn't feel right.

And he was jealous of Randy.

The whole situation gave her the creeps.

I should be flattered that he's called her after me.

But Sam had been so intense. The episode had given her a bad feeling. When she pulled up at home she sat for a moment.

Sam paced the floor, his mind in turmoil. 'Jacko. Fucking Jacko!'

All this time, it wasn't me at all. It was fucking Jacko.

He stopped in the middle of the room and repeatedly punched his left hand.

The bitch. All these years.

Switching off the light he went to the window and glared at the house across the road where Jacko lived. 'Bastard,' he muttered.

CHAPTER FIFTY-TWO

'Dad,' Melanie said as she chewed on her toast.

'It's bad manners to speak with your mouth full,' Doris got in before Jacko could say anything.

Melanie swallowed quickly. 'Sorry.' She smiled sweetly at Doris.

Uh oh, here we go, Doris thought, looking suspiciously at Melanie over the top of her newly prescribed National Health glasses.

Jacko folded his newspaper. 'What, pet?'

'Am I still getting the other dress?'

Doris groaned loudly as she picked up the plates and took them to the sink. 'Now where have I put the bloody washing-up liquid?'

In the fridge,' Melanie yelled, then turned quickly back to Jacko. 'Dad?'

'You shouldn't tease her like that Melanie.' Jacko tried not to smile but gave in.

'You do it too! Anyway, she secretly likes it, I know she does. So Dad, what about it?'

'Well pet, it looks like your luck's in.' He'd been waiting for this moment since last night.

'What do you mean?' Melanie's heart skipped a beat and her eyes lit up.

'Christina's dad surprised her yesterday by giving her five hundred pounds towards the wedding.'

'My God.' Doris nearly dropped the teapot on the way back in. 'Did I hear right?'

'Yeah. I could hardly believe it myself when Christina told me about it last night.'

'Don't tell me the nasty old sod's won the bloody lottery. It would just be his luck.'

'Apparently it's part of his savings.'

'That'll be right, the crafty old bugger, just like him to have a stash. Wait 'til I tell Sandra, the greedy sod wouldn't buy any raffle tickets for the kids' trip though, would he.'

'Mam! You tell nobody. I mean it. Promise.'

Deprived of a juicy bit of gossip, Doris's face fell. She sighed, then said to her waiting son, 'OK, but ...'

'No buts.'

Unable to wait any longer, Melanie butted in, 'So Dad, does that mean that I can have ...?'

'Yes, love.'

'Yes!' Melanie yelled, jumping up from the table. 'Come on Dad, else I'll be late.'

Jacko walked Melanie and Suzy to school every morning, then doubled back and walked Christina up to Houghton Library where she worked. Suzy knocked on the door just then and Melanie grabbed her bag. 'Come on Dad, see you later Nana.'

Happy because Melanie was happy, Jacko followed her outside. They headed towards the school, Melanie chatting to Suzy about her new dress. Listening to their chatter Jacko was blissfully unaware that he was being watched.

The closer Lorraine got to the station the heavier her heart felt. Peters had released half of the McCades at six this morning and she knew she would have to release the rest of them shortly. Because the house where the cannabis farm was found was Patrick's, she would be able to hang on to him for at least a few more days, and perhaps Tony, but both of them were hard nuts to crack.

Peters had phoned at seven this morning to say that there was no progress. Even the younger family members were adamant that they had not seen Andrew for over a week, a simple enough story to stick to, no elaboration, so any of them could slip up.

What if they're telling the truth? No way, it's definitely them. Who the hell else could it be? With renewed determination Lorraine went to her office.

Ten minutes later she had her team in the incident room, some of them still carrying their teas and coffees. Dinwall was chewing on a bacon sandwich.

Before Lorraine spoke, Luke brought everyone up to scratch on Amy Dawson. His speech lasted all of three minutes. He shrugged at the end. 'Basically that's about it. We are no further forward than we were fifteen years ago.'

He moved over and Lorraine took the floor. 'OK, the McCades are not budging.'

'And making a damn good job of it,' Peters put in.

'As I was about to say,' Lorraine said sharply, 'they can deny it as much as they bloody like. I want them and I'm gonna have them, OK?' She glanced at her watch. 'We have a while yet before we need to start letting the four we have left go. Get on with it, guys. We need them wearing down.'

Peters sighed, then yawned. As he followed Sanderson and the others out, Lorraine said, 'Peters, not you, I think you will be better off at home in bed. We may need you back on duty tonight.'

'Oh thanks, boss,' he said, relief showing on his face. 'I'll get right off.' He hurried past her as if he was frightened that at any moment she just might change her mind.

'Luke, me and you are going to the hospital. If we can get Dave to identify one of the McCades as his attacker it'll give us more to hold them on.'

'OK. I'll just get the car keys.'

'What's the matter?' she asked as Luke brushed past her.

He hesitated a moment, knowing she would not like what he was going to say, then said it anyhow because he had to. 'I've been giving it some thought, Lorraine. What if it's not them?'

'What do you mean, not them? Of course it's them.' Suddenly she didn't know what to do with her hands. She could kill for a cigarette.

'I'm just worried you're setting yourself up for a fall if it's not them, Lorraine. You know fine well even though he's sanctioned it Clark will wriggle out and leave you high and dry, that's all.' He held his palms up.

'Of course it's them.' She turned and headed out of the building. With a shrug Luke followed her. 'And somehow' she said before she got into the car 'Amy and Sara are tied in with this. I'm certain.'

Luke nodded as she started the engine. It had crossed his mind too, but he just couldn't make the leap to tie it all in.

Jacko and Christina turned the corner and stopped outside the library doors.

Jacko rested his hands on her waist and said, 'OK, I'll see you tonight, love, I've got some things to sort out with Danny. It's looking good, though he still keeps trying to keep it on the fiddle when I want to go legit, but I'm working on it and who knows, one day we might even be able to afford our own house. Len says there's grants and things you can get to start off with.'

Christina smiled up at him. Whatever Jacko did was fine by her, she loved him so much she'd live in a cave with him if she had to.

'I'd better go in now Jacko. There's a new book delivery due in and the van'll be here anytime now.'

'OK, babes.' Jacko bent down to kiss her smiling lips. A second before their lips met there was a loud bang and a moment later Jacko collapsed in a ball at her feet.

Shocked, Christina got down on her knees. 'Jacko? What's wrong? Jacko?' Gently she shook him, fearing a heart attack. 'Jacko? Please talk to me! *Please*, Jacko.'

It was then that she saw the blood. For a moment she was too shocked to do anything, then she started screaming. Within seconds she was surrounded by people, a young man used his mobile to call an ambulance and a woman hurried forward.

'I'm a nurse,' she said as she felt for a pulse.

After a moment she looked at Christina. 'He's alive, and I think he's been shot.'

'Shot?' The word buzzed rapidly around the crowd, which dispersed as quickly as it had formed.

The young man with the mobile stepped into the library and shouted 'The ambulance is on its way' before disappearing up the escalator.

'Shot?' Christina sobbed, her eyes wide with disbelief. 'But who would want to shoot my Jacko? Why? Jacko never hurt anybody. He's a good man my Jacko, ask anybody, we're gonna get married, aren't we, Jacko? Talk to me Jacko ... Jacko?'

The nurse had no answer. She nervously looked around before taking her cardigan off and using it to staunch the bleeding. But it was soaked in seconds. Seeing this, Christina started to scream again, she was still screaming a few minutes later when the ambulance arrived.

The medics jumped out and ran towards them, carrying a stretcher.

'Gunshot wound to the neck,' the nurse said as the medics put the stretcher on the ground and carefully eased Jacko on to it.

'How long has he been unconscious?' the first medic asked.

'Almost immediately,' the nurse replied, picking up her bag and following them.

Christina held tightly on to Jacko's hand as they lifted the stretcher on to the ambulance. 'Is he going to be alright?' she asked, her voice trembling.

'Well, he's going to the best place, OK love? And the doctors will be waiting for him. Hop on board, we'll get some drips into him then be one our way, OK?'

Terrified for the life of the only man she had ever loved, the only man she would ever love, Christina nodded grimly as she held on to Jacko.

CHAPTER FIFTY-THREE

Dave was sitting up in bed when Lorraine and Luke walked into his room. Propped up on his pillows, he looked only marginally better than he had two days ago, but he was conscious and his colour, though far from good, was certainly better than it had been.

'You don't look too pleased to see me, old mate.' Lorraine smiled at him, but Dave just stared straight ahead.

'Hello, Dave. How are you?' Luke asked in an effort to divert Dave's piercing gaze, but it didn't work.

Lorraine moved to the side of Dave's bed and picked up his hand. It was ice cold. She rubbed it between both of hers. 'My, you're freezing, Dave, but it's red hot in here!'

'Probably all the stuff they'll have him on,' Luke nodded.

'Is there anything I can get you, Dave?' Lorraine smiled.

'Him. *Him!*' Dave suddenly shouted like a tourette's victim.

'Who, Dave? Who? What are you talking about?'

'Him!' he shouted again, imploring Lorraine to understand with his eyes.

'Him!' he repeated, and again, 'Him!' His eyes were beginning to bulge with the effort he was using to get his message across.

Lorraine's phone rang, startling all of them. As she pulled it out of her pocket Dave started blinking rapidly and began counting on his fingers over and over. Lorraine gestured with her head for Luke to take care of Dave while she went into the corridor.

A blonde nurse pushing a trolley was just about ask who she was and whether she should be in Dave's room when Lorraine flashed her badge. A moment later Lorraine shouted 'What?' causing the nurse, who had moved on, to jump and turn quickly, giving Lorraine a furious glare.

Ignoring her, Lorraine listened for a few more minutes before going back into Dave's room. Luke had hold of Dave's hands and was trying to sooth him.

'Sorry Dave, but we have to go now. I promise we'll be back to see you. Luke ...' She motioned with her head towards the door.

'OK.' Luke patted Dave's arm. 'Calm down mate, I'll send the nurse in.'

Dave watched them go, mouthing weakly to their backs as they disappeared into the corridor, 'Him, him, him.'

'What's up?' Luke asked as he hurried to keep up with Lorraine, who was heading at a fast pace for the lift.

'Jacko Musgrove has been shot,' she said, her face ashen as she pressed the button for the lift to move.

'What's he after now?' Dolly said, watching Carter get out of his panda car and pause a minute to complement Mr Skillings on the beautiful smell of his roses before walking down the path.

'Who's after what?' Doris asked, coming in from the kitchen holding a carrot in one hand and a knife in the other.

'That ginger copper, the one with all the freckles, the one that's about to knock on the door.'

'Oh.' Doris dropped the carrot and knife on to the settee. 'Coppers at the door is nowt but bad news.' She hurried through into the small hallway, reaching the door just as Carter knocked.

'What's the matter?' she snapped as she yanked the door open. 'Oh, God, is it our Melanie?'

'Can I come in?' Carter asked.

'It's our Jacko, then. What's he done now?' Doris's heart began to pound and she clutched her chest. 'He's alright, isn't he?'

'Come in, officer,' Dolly said, taking Doris by her elbow and easing her through into the sitting room.

'I'm sorry to tell you this, Mrs Musgrove, but Jacko's had a sort of accident.'

'A sort of accident?' Doris gasped. 'What's "a sort of accident" mean?'

Carter licked his lips. He hated to be the bearer of bad news. It was the one part of the job he didn't like. There was no way of dressing a shooting up at all. He'd gone through it over and over in his head on the way here. In the end he said the only words he could. 'I'm so sorry to have to tell you this, but ... he's been shot.'

'Shot?' Dolly gasped. Doris for the moment couldn't get her mind round the word 'shot' and everything that it implied, and what the hell was this young man doing standing in the middle of her sitting room telling her that her son, her Jacko, had been shot?

'No.' Doris shook her head. 'No. You've got it wrong. Nobody would shoot my Jacko. He's a good lad, my Jacko. No.'

'Is he ... Is he ...?' Dolly, horrified, couldn't bring herself to say the word.

CHAPTER FIFTY-FOUR

Sam flipped his mobile shut and smiled.

He watched as Doris, shrugging into her coat, followed Carter up the path, and Dolly shouted for Mr Skillings.

He sighed as Mr Skillings hobbled up his path to meet Doris at the gate. He'd been a good bloke, Mr Skillings, helped a lot of people on the Seahills. And now he was a crippled old wreck of a man clinging on for God knows what.

'Is that all you do all day, stare out of that bloody window?' Leanne said from behind him.

Sam spun round. He didn't like anyone coming up on him like that. It was a survival instinct, one of the reasons why in most places he would only sit facing the door with his back against the wall. It came naturally.

Forcing a smile, he said, 'You're up and about early enough, Leanne.'

'The vicar's coming today, or had you forgotten already? Things to arrange, flowers, hymns, service, that sort of stuff. The undertaker's coming as well.'

Sam swallowed hard. He didn't like the way she had said that, no real emotion behind the words, just a flat sentence that sort of finished off their brother's life. As if she just didn't care anymore. Andrew was gone, end of story.

'So what are you planning?' he snapped, then felt a twinge of conscience when she cringed.

Shit! She's still under sedation. That's why she's so calm, so cold.

'I'm sorry,' he offered.

'Sorry? Oh yeah. Well, that means everything, doesn't it. Sam's sorry. Seeing as you're probably to blame for all of this, that's rich. Oh boy, that's certainly rich.'

'Me?'

'Yes. You. I've got a good idea what went on that night and it was your fault. You've always been the same. If you can't have it your way then you're not playing. It's always you.'

'What's all the shouting about?' Tammy demanded, walking into the room, her mane of black hair tangled about her head and her eyes full of sleep.

'It's sorted,' Sam shouted at Leanne, ignoring Tammy as she threw herself on the settee.

'What with?' Leanne retorted. 'More fucking violence? Then they'll retaliate again, with who? Who's next, Sam, because of your selfishness? Who's next? Me? Tammy? Stacey? ... Who?'

CHAPTER FIFTY-FIVE

Lorraine hurried into casualty not knowing if Jacko was alive or dead or why anyone in their right mind would want to shoot him. Looking around for a nurse or someone with some authority, she saw no one, so she pushed the trauma room door open and was stopped in her tracks by a tall grey-haired male nurse.

'Excuse me. I am Detective Inspector Lorraine Hunt, if you don't mind.'

'You're still not allowed in here.'

Frustrated, Lorraine stepped back. 'At least tell me if he's still alive,'

'Yes, just. He's lost a lot of blood though, and I'm afraid he's far from out of the woods, but we're working on him now. If you take a seat in the waiting room we'll let you know as soon as we can.'

'And it was a gun shot.'

'Afraid so.' He gave a quick half-smile and a nod as he closed the door.

'Guess we're gonna have to wait, boss.' Luke smiled at the stubborn set of her face. 'Come on.'

He led the way into the waiting room where they found a white-faced Christina, accompanied by a young WPC, sitting in the corner. As they approached her Doris, followed by Dolly with Carter bringing up the rear, came rushing in.

'What's happened?' Doris begged of Christina as they all converged.

'I don't know,' Christina sobbed, overwhelmed to be the centre of attention. 'I ... I was just going into work when he went down and ... and there was blood all over.'

'Oh my God,' Doris sobbed as loudly as Christina. A moment later she started to sway and, putting their arms around her, Luke and Carter managed to manoeuvre her into a seat.

Before Lorraine could ask the WPC said, 'She knows nothing, boss, it came out of the blue.'

'OK, Cartwright, stay with them. Luke ...' Lorraine nodded to the door.

Outside she watched a youth with a cut and bruised face light a cigarette up under a NO SMOKING sign. It took all of her willpower not to snatch it out of his hand and take a few deep draws as she and Luke passed.

When they were out of range of anyone's hearing she looked around then hissed quickly, 'What the hell's going on, Luke? Why would the McCades shoot Jacko? None of it makes any sense.'

But Luke had no answers for her. Nothing was making any sense. Again he wondered if he had the full story of what went on that night.

'For Christ's sake.' Lorraine looked back at the hospital doors. 'He was nearly as much a victim that night as Randy was.'

Before he could say anything Lorraine's mobile rang. 'Yes?' she said, snapping it open. A moment later she squealed 'What?' in disbelief. Before she could say more she was cut off. 'I don't bloody believe it. No way. He's finally lost the plot.'

A few seconds later Luke's mobile rang. He had much the same reaction as Lorraine. 'What?' He stood open mouthed as Lorraine shook her head.

'No way,' she said, her mouth set in the stubborn line that Luke knew so well.

Luke listened for another minute before snapping his mobile shut and putting it in his pocket. 'He's adamant.'

'He's a fucking idiot, that's what he is.'

'I suppose his reasoning does make a sort of sense.'

'A sort of sense?' Lorraine spat the words at him with the rapid fire of a machine gun. 'You're as far off your trolley as he is if you agree with him. I've never heard anything so bloody ridiculous in my life. Jesus Christ!'

'Well, orders are orders, and whether you like it or not, he just might be right. Think about it. Clark's convinced your life's in danger. He's put two and two together. It's all your friends, Lorraine, and what happened to Jacko has sealed it. Short of locking you up in a cell the best he can do is confine you to your house under guard.'

'Under guard,' she muttered, glaring at the driver of the riot van as it arrived with two squad cars, one in front and one behind it.

Mr Skillings had been left in charge of Melanie. He watched as she tried to keep up with Suzy, the pair of them chatting and skipping as they came along from Suzy's house. *Two bonnier little lassies would be hard to find*, he thought, snapping two yellow rose buds off and removing the thorns just as the girls reached him.

'Hi Mr Skillings,' they sang together, before looking at each other and giggling.

'Hello, girls.' He presented each of them with a rose, which they accepted with grace, smiles and more giggles. 'For the two prettiest young ladies on the Seahills.' He gave them a lopsided bow that made them laugh even louder.

'Er, we need to go inside, Melanie. I have something to tell you, dear,' he said as he slowly straightened up.

Melanie's smile melted as quickly as a dropped ice cube, forgotten and left on the bench in a hot kitchen. 'What's the matter?' she asked as they walked down the path. She felt a strange sensation in her chest that she had no words for, but she knew something was not right and dreaded what Mr Skillings was going to tell her.

Mr Skillings didn't answer but waited until they were all inside and seated.

'Where's Nana?' Melanie suddenly shouted before he had a chance to say anything. 'Where is she? There's something wrong with Nana, isn't there, Mr Skillings?'

She jumped up and the yellow rose fell to the floor. Her foot crushed the heavily scented petals that peeped out from under her shoe. 'Tell me what's wrong with Nana.' Tears sprung into her eyes. 'Mr Skillings?' she sobbed.

Mr Skillings felt the lump in his throat. *What can I say?*

Melanie was imploring him. The need to know was burning.

Clearing his throat, he said the only thing he could.

'I'm sorry pet. But it's not Nana, it's, it's your dad ...' Melanie's face registered abject horror and he hurried on. 'But I think he's probably gonna be alright. You know big strong Jacko, why aye, he'll be alright, don't you worry pet.'

'Dad? My dad? What's the matter with my dad?' Melanie's voice grew weaker and Suzy, to whom Jacko was like a favourite uncle, burst out crying.

'Er, he ... he's had a sort of accident.' *No way can I tell her that her dad's been shot, the poor bairn looks close enough to fainting as it is.* 'I'm sure he'll be alright, we just have to wait until Nana gets back from the hospital. OK, pet?'

She sat down. 'My dad,' she murmured, and shook her head in denial. 'My dad? No. My dad's big and strong he wouldn't have an accident. Impossible for my dad to have an accident. What sort of an accident?' She looked at Mr Skillings expectantly.

'I'm not quite sure yet, love.' He sat between both girls and put his arms around them. He didn't know what else to do except to pray that Jacko was alright and that Doris would get home from the hospital soon. It seemed to him that the Seahills was under a huge black cloud, what with poor Andrew Knightly and now Jacko. He sighed. *When was it all going to end?*

CHAPTER FIFTY-SIX

Surrounded by her squad, Lorraine stormed down the path.

The door was opened before she could touch the handle and Peggy greeted her. 'Here's a right state of affairs, bonny lass. But don't worry, I sent that nice young copper to the shop for a pack of Diet Coke so you won't get thirsty, love.'

Lorraine glared at Luke, then swung her gaze to the ceiling. 'For God's sake give me strength.'

Trying not to smile, Luke said, 'She means well ... pet.'

'Ugggh.' Lorraine threw herself into the chair by the fireside.

Sitting down opposite her, Peggy looked from Luke to Lorraine. 'Isn't this exciting?'

'Er ... No.' Lorraine turned to Luke. 'How long am I supposed to put up with this?'

'As long as it takes to catch whoever it is.'

'I've told you who it is.'

'Well, for some reason Clark thinks otherwise.'

'It can't be anyone else.' Lorraine felt herself becoming more angry by the minute and, trying to control herself, she muttered, 'Why can't the dimwit see what's under his bloody huge beak of a nose?'

Luke shrugged. 'Sometimes, Lorry, you can be too close to the wood, if you know what I mean?'

'Cup of tea anybody?' Mavis asked, sweeping in regally, the gold embroidery on her green gypsy skirt catching the light.

Lorraine jumped up quickly. 'I'm taking a shower, OK? It's too damned hot.' But it was nowhere near as hot as she felt inside. In danger of blowing and not in the mood for taking prisoners, she headed quickly for the stairs.

'Just a minute.' Luke was just as quick getting out of his own chair.

'What?'

'We'll have to check the place out.'

'Oh, for God's sake, it'll already have been done if I know Sanderson. And the Hippy and the Rock Chick have been in all day, haven't you girls?'

Wide eyed, Peggy and Mavis nodded in unison, as if both of them suddenly realised just how serious this was and that Lorraine might be in danger even if she swore adamantly that she was not.

'Just being cautious, boss,' Luke said. 'Travis, go with Peters and check it out.'

'You have to let them do their job, love,' Mavis said, handing Lorraine a can. 'You would have done the same if it was one of the others.'

'Yeah, but it's not one of them, is it? It's me! And bloody stupid Clark's crazy ideas. Boy, when he gets them he gets them big time.'

'Guess it's pizza all round then.' Peggy rubbed her hands together. 'All these lovely men, got to be fed.'

Lorraine looked at Peggy and shook her head. 'You're beyond belief, Peg, you know that? Beyond belief.'

'I do,' Mavis said over her shoulder as she went back into the kitchen. 'I certainly know that.'

'All clear,' Peters shouted down the stairs.

'Huh.' Lorraine shot Luke a dirty look then headed up. Duke unwound himself from his favourite sleeping place and padded after her.

'I'm allergic to dogs,' Peters said.

'Tough,' Lorraine replied, slamming the bathroom door behind her.

Duke sat down outside the door and thumped his tail at Peters.

'Piss off, dog,' Peters said, moving to the far end of the landing.

'I heard that,' Lorraine shouted as she took her clothes off and stepped into the shower.

CHAPTER FIFTY-SEVEN

He watched the bathroom light go on and spat in the long grass. He could see her shape through his army night glasses and she was splendid, as she always had been.

He stepped back without making a sound as he heard the policeman moving towards him.

Fools. So predictable.

Every half hour they swept the place, passing in a full circle not far from where he stood. The breeze was blowing in his face, carrying his scent away from the dogs. But the blood of the four dead rabbits hidden at points on the other side tantalised the dogs' noses, momentarily drawing them away from the scent of man. *Ha. Fools. Don't they know that no matter how well trained the animal is the scent of blood will get them every time, passed down from the very first wolf that howled at the moon over its first kill?*

CHAPTER FIFTY-EIGHT

Mr Skillings had fed the girls beans on toast and was washing the dishes as the sun began to set. He was worried sick because there had been no news from the hospital yet. *Although some say that no news is good news*, he thought, *and Doris hasn't got a phone, so maybes Jacko's alright.*

'Hello there!' Mr Skillings jumped as the voice came from the back door as it opened.

'Robbie Lumsdon,' he chided. 'You nearly stunted two years' worth of me growth there.'

Robbie grinned. 'You stopped growing two centuries ago, Mr Skillings.'

'Not quite. Cheeky puppy.'

Robbie shrugged and, smiling, said, 'I've come for our Suzy. I thought Doris would be in. Me mam and Sandra said someone's been shot up Houghton and she wondered if Doris ...' His words trailed off as Mr Skillings put his hand over Robbie's mouth and pointed into the sitting room with his other hand.

'No,' he mouthed when Mr Skillings dropped his hand. 'Not Doris?'

'Jacko,' Mr Skillings whispered. 'And that's all I know. I wondered where everyone's been today, usually there's someone knocking about, but I've never seen a soul for hours. I didn't want to upset the kids by making a big fuss. They think Jacko's been in an accident.'

'Jesus. Should I take them along to our house? Melanie can sleep with our Suzy.'

'I was hoping for that. Do you think you can ask Sandra to call the hospital see if she can find out anything, then phone me a taxi, 'cos Doris must be in a terrible way.'

'Why aye, no bother, I'll go now.' Robbie spun round and quickly ran out to the gate just as a patrol car pulled up.

Mr Skillings had followed Robbie out and, walking up the path, watched as Carter jumped out and helped Doris out of the car as Dolly got out the other side. 'Don't bother with the taxi, son, they're back.'

Robbie nodded as he hurried home.

'How is he?' Mr Skillings asked, concern etched on his weather-beaten face.

Doris took one look at her old friend and burst into tears.

It was full dark a half an hour later when Sam came home.

'Where have you been?' Leanne demanded.

Sam gave her a look that alternated between scornful and smug, his eyes cold. Leanne had seen that look before. 'Not that it's any business of yours, but I've been to see a friend.'

'You have no friends round here.'

He shrugged. 'True.'

'You'd better not be planning anything, I mean it, Sam. When you're long gone we still have to live here.'

'Come and live with me then, all of you. I have a huge house. You'll love it.'

'No way.'

'Why?' Sam was warming to the idea of having his sisters live with him. He had been thinking of it for days, as an alternative to the plan he had made already. He was just wondering when the right time to broach the subject would be.

'Why? There you go again, thinking of yourself like you always have. We have lives here, Stacey's getting married soon, or have you forgotten already that you've met her man? A dentist. A good, honest job. Something I have a feeling that you've never had in your whole bloody life.'

Sam glared at her for a long moment, saying nothing, then, his tone bitter, he snapped, 'As soon as the funeral's over I'll be out of your hair. I do have other commitments.'

Leanne gave a hollow laugh. 'Yeah, and I can well imagine what those are.'

'I have a daughter.' He walked out of the room, leaving Leanne staring open mouthed after him.

'What?' she blustered following him into the kitchen, where she repeated herself.

Sam turned, and leaning his back against the sink he folded his arms across his chest. 'Her name is Lorraine.'

If the fact that he had a daughter had stumped Leanne, the name he had given her made her blood run cold.

CHAPTER FIFTY-NINE

Lorraine pulled a pale blue sleeveless T-shirt over her head, then fastened the button on her white cotton skirt before throwing herself on to her bed, putting her hands behind her head and staring at the ceiling. She could hear Duke snuffling at the door and Peters whisper 'Go away.'

She allowed herself a small smile and toyed with the idea of letting Duke in, even though he was barred from the bedrooms. He could obviously sense that something was troubling her. *Dogs are good at that, sometimes better than people.*

God, I hope Jacko's alright.

If Luke hadn't been so over the bloody top with his determination to get me home, I might have had time to talk to people.

Why would the McCades want Jacko dead? He was there that night, but only to try to help.

Shit. Clark's let all the McCades go.

The fucking idiot.

Oh, to hell with this.

She got off the bed and went downstairs, Duke padding at her side. In the sitting room Luke, Travis and Sanderson were sitting on the settee with Peggy in the middle of them, looking through photograph albums. Dinwall was leaning against the wall staring out of the window. She was about to say something to him when her mind skittered back to the albums.

Oh my God. They've got the bloody baby pics out. I'll kill the pair of them. How embarrassing.

'Mother!'

'What?' Mavis shouted from the kitchen.

'Oh, don't get your knickers in a twist,' Peggy said. 'It was me that got them out, not your mam.'

Lorraine gritted her teeth as Sanderson said, 'What a little cutie you were, boss!'

'Huh.'

'Who's this, Lorraine?' Luke held a photograph up. 'I can recognise Jacko and Dave and I'm guessing the other two must be Randy and Sam. But who's the guy in the background?'

Lorraine took the photo from Luke's hand. 'Oh, him.'

'Him?'

Dinwall showed a sudden interest in what was going on. He looked over Lorraine's shoulder 'Ah, now I see who's who. Wow, boss, nice legs. By the way, Dave has the same picture.'

Ignoring Dinwall, Lorraine answered Luke. 'Yeah, he used to follow us around, we tried, all of us, to be his friend, but there was always something about him, no one really liked him. And we sort of nick-named him "Him". One of us would look round and say, "It's Him".'

'Him?' Luke repeated, looking oddly at Lorraine.

'What?'

'Give me a look?' Travis took the photo.

A moment later Lorraine snapped her fingers. 'Dave, Dave kept saying Him, over and over. He was trying to tell us something.'

'So, you think this Him has got a real name?' asked Sanderson.

'Darren Watts,' Lorraine sighed.

'You think he might be the murderer?'

'But why?' Lorraine took the photograph off Travis. She shook her head. 'No, there's no reason. No reason at all.'

'Think you might be wrong there, boss. He might have been harbouring a grudge all this time, especially if he wanted to be one of the gang and you lot wouldn't let him. It's been known before.'

Lorraine still wasn't convinced. 'But why, for God's sake? And that's downright creepy if you bloody well ask me.'

'He always was a creepy little bastard,' Peggy put in. 'Same as his mother. Urgh.' She shuddered.

'Yes, I remember him hanging around a lot. He used to come to the door and ask where you were. I never thought much of it at the time,' Mavis added.

'So that's how he managed to turn up most of the places we went.' She looked sideways at her mother. 'God, we used to think it was weird. Amy especially couldn't stand him, she used to practically moan in his face, and more than once she told him to piss off. The lights would go on in the pictures and there he was, sitting behind us. Creepy. But I've never seen him for years.' Lorraine looked from Mavis to Peggy.

'Didn't the family emigrate to New Zealand?' Peggy said, after a moment's thought.

'That's right Peg, shortly after that little boy from Dairy Lane went missing. Remember, wasn't Darren Watts pulled in because he'd been seen in the area talking to kids?'

'I remember now,' Sanderson said. 'Yeah, there was a Peeping Tom in the area as well, he disappeared when the Watts family emigrated. There was speculation at the time but no proof.'

'Oh, I never did like the little creep,' Peggy put in.

Mavis looked at Peggy with a raised eyebrow and said, 'Would that have something to do with the time his mother pulled most of your hair out at the Christmas party way back in, oh, God knows when? You were only a baby though, Lorraine.' Mavis smiled at her daughter who was gritting her teeth as she slowly counted to ten. 'You won't remember Peggy's bald patches.'

'Oh Mavis, she never did!' Peggy said indignantly, patting her hair.

Before Mavis could say anything else and Lorraine could explode every which way, Luke stood up. 'Right. So where do we go from here?'

'From what I can see this bloke seems as likely a candidate as any of the McCades,' Sanderson said and nodded as they all looked at Lorraine, one arm across her chest, the other arm resting on it. She sucked her middle finger for a moment.

Then, putting her hands behind her back, she said, 'OK, you all seem to want to go with this idea, and yes, there have been crazier reasons for murder. And Brenda Sweeny swore 'til the day she died that there was another bike there that night. It could have been him. But shit, we weren't really that bad to him, for God's sake, just didn't want him around. That happens all the time. I mean, if you can't choose who the hell you want to be friends with without somebody holding a grudge, what the hell can you do? We never ...' She paused a moment, remembering one time when Randy and Sam threw stones at Darren Watts.

She felt guilt pricking at her heart, her breath caught in her throat as she thought, *Can all of this, all these deaths be my fault? I ... We, we were only ten years old for Christ's sake.*

The rest of us laughed though, laughed at the stone throwing, laughed when he ran away crying, bleeding ... Then that other time he followed us down to the beck and Sam pushed him in, we all laughed then ... Jesus.

She sighed again, and looking at them all, the sadness evident in her eyes, she said, 'Guess Clark didn't get where he was by being an arsehole all of the time. He's adamant that it's not the McCades and he just might be right on this one. I'll phone Carter, see if he can find out where Darren Watts is at this moment in time. He's our computer expert. He can find anyone on that thing.'

CHAPTER SIXTY

'Nana, Nana!' Melanie had spotted the police car pull up outside and she hurried up the path after Mr Skillings, Suzy trailing behind her. 'Nana.' Before Doris could answer Mr Skillings' question about Jacko Melanie threw herself at her.

'Where's me dad?' Melanie wailed, tears streaming down her face. 'What's the matter with him?'

Mr Skillings held his breath as Suzy squeezed his hand. They waited, Melanie's heart pounding in her chest, the fear of the unknown making her feel light headed.

'Nana?' she whispered.

Doris straightened up, looked at her granddaughter and smiled. 'He's gonna be alright, Melanie love. Your dad is gonna be just fine.'

Carter handed Doris her bag as his phone rang. He flipped it open. 'Hi boss … Yes, yes boss, Jacko's alright … Gonna be just fine. They've kept him in, probably be home in a day or two.'

He watched as they all walked down the path. At the door, Doris turned. 'Cup of tea, son?'

'No thanks Doris, gotta get back to work.'

'OK.' She waved her hand. 'Thank you.'

Nodding and smiling, Carter waved back. 'You still there boss? Sorry 'bout that. Just saying ... Yes, yes, I'm sure he's gonna be alright, the bullet ripped open the back of the neck and shoulder and tore a lot of muscle. The scar will be just awful, Doris says. What? OK, OK ... Darren Watts. Right. I'm on it.'

Lorraine closed her phone and smiled at the others. 'Jacko's going to be alright.'

'Well thank God. For a minute there I thought we might be going to a funeral instead of a wedding.' Peggy nodded at Mavis, who tutted at her before going back into the kitchen.

'Didn't you have something else to do?' Lorraine asked Peggy, one eyebrow raised.

'Who, me?'

'Yeah, Peg, this is police business.'

'Why, I was gonna join the coppers once over, you know. I ...'

'Aye, in your dreams. Go.'

Shrugging and pulling a face at Lorraine, Peggy got up and followed Mavis into the kitchen, winking at Dinwall on the way. He blushed scarlet as she passed by him.

'Right guys, we need to do some serious tossing around here. OK.' She held her hands up. 'I may have been wrong about the McCades, but at least we have the worst two of them for drug offences and no doubt we'll be able to tie a few more into the operation.'

'It all seems feasible to me,' Luke said.

'But why Andrew for God's sake, and why in such a terrible way?' Sighing, Lorraine sat down on the settee next to Luke.

'Probably because he couldn't get to Sam. He'll have known how Randy died and what he did to Andrew was geared to have us believe that the McCades were seeking vengeance,' Sanderson said.

'So, he's killed Andrew for Sam. If it is him, he must have murdered Sara first the night of the accident … Then Amy … He's tried to kill Dave and Jacko, and that leaves …'

Luke reached for her hand.

She nodded. 'Me.'

'I wonder, why wait all this time, and did he really kill Sara?' Luke frowned.

'It's a pattern which isn't a pattern,' Sanderson added. 'If you see what I mean. Most serial killers follow the same MO, but every single killing and attempted killing has been different, apart from the women. If I remember rightly, both of them poor girls were practically bitten to death. Now, to me, that's the action of a very angry person.'

Again feeling the swift pangs of guilt, Lorraine shuddered at the picture in her head, then said, as if talking to herself, 'Andrew was bitten the same place as the girls, over and over.'

'Oh. I didn't know,' Sanderson said.

'We just got some of the results through,' Luke added.

The phone rang and Lorraine hastily snatched it up. 'What?' she said after a moment. By the tone of her voice, Luke and Sanderson knew it was something serious. Putting the phone down, she looked at both men and said in a hushed voice, 'He was also raped.'

Sam slipped his jacket on. A wind from the North Sea had sprung up, turning what had been a very warm day into a chilly evening.

Watching him, Leanne said, 'Where are you going now? You haven't been back half an hour.'

'A surprise, Leanne, OK? Just leave it, will you? I won't be long.'

She didn't answer, just watched helplessly as he walked out the door.

No change there. She sighed as she sat back in her chair. She was so exhausted she really couldn't care where he went. *He can take the whole of the flaming McCade clan on by himself if that's what he wants.* She shook her head, feeling completely adrift. She was preparing to bury her brother, who had been more like her son, and whatever Sam did now would be as much use to any of them as an ant trying to bring a mountain down.

Carter closed his laptop and sat for a moment. 'Hmm,' he muttered. 'Better get to the boss with this lot.'

Ten minutes later, in his eagerness, he shut the car door on his little finger. He bit off a scream but couldn't stop his finger from finding his mouth. 'Ow, ow, *ow*' he mumbled as he hurried up the path.

'Ah, good. Carter, what have you got for us?' Lorraine said after Peggy let him in, only to be shooed back into the kitchen. Lorraine turned back to Carter. 'But first Carter, please, what exactly happened to Jacko and how bad is it?'

'Right, boss. Judging by what I got from Christina, though she was a bit hysterical, Jacko is one hell of a lucky man. That bullet was going right for his head, but at the exact moment he leaned over to kiss Christina, the bullet missed his head and made a half-inch groove from his left shoulder to his right.'

'God, I bet that's bloody painful,' Dinwall said.

'Master of the obvious, aren't you?' Peters sneered.

'OK, *OK.* Let's get on with it,' Lorraine said, thinking she was going to have to sort those two out sooner rather than later. The barbs were getting deeper all the time. 'Carter?'

'Well, boss.' Carter could feel all the eyes in the room on him and forgetting the pain in his finger he began: 'Darren Watts moved to New Zealand shortly after his nineteenth birthday with his parents and younger sister. Blenheim, a city in Marlborough, which is in the north east of the South Island.' He checked quickly with his eyes to make certain everyone was listening while Lorraine silently urged him to hurry up.

'There was a few accusations hurled his way over the five-year period they lived in Blenheim, mostly to do with staring in windows, and twice he was accused of following women home. Then his father died ...'

'How?' Lorraine asked quickly.

'He was shot accidentally, so the mother swore in court, and the entry wound looked as if it could have been an accident.'

'Shot!' Luke and Sanderson echoed.

'He's the one,' Dinwall stated adamantly.

Lorraine chewed on her lip, then dry-washed her face, praying for a cigarette. 'OK, what happened next?'

'Mother and son moved to the North Island, a town called Inglewood, population in 2004 was 2800 souls.'

'Like we needed to know that,' Dinwall muttered, to be silenced by a look from Lorraine.

Carter shrugged. 'A few years later Watts disappeared and no one's heard from him since.'

Travis stood up. 'He's our man, boss. Seems like every other day you're hearing about shootings and things like that 'cos a spoilt brat spits his dummy out as he couldn't get his own bloody way. Why should the rest of us suffer for twats like that?'

'Well, there's always more to it than that ...'

'No boss, you're wrong. What it always boils down to is that some pathetic creep can't stand to hear the truth, that either his wife or girlfriend doesn't want him no more, so he goes on the rampage and fucking well kills everybody in sight. Or in this case, just because you lot didn't want to be his friend. Fucking pathetic if you ask me.'

'Guess that's it, in a nutshell,' Sanderson said, nodding his head while thinking *There's an awful lot of sense in what Travis's just come out with.*

'In the meantime,' he went on, 'this nutter's out there with a gun. His plan to get the McCades and the Knightlys warring backfired. So to my mind he's gonna be very angry.'

In the ensuing silence Duke drew their attention by wining and scratching at the door. Carter jumped up. 'I'll take him out, boss.'

Her mind on other things, Lorraine nodded.

'Goody two-shoes,' Peters hissed as Carter walked past him, then he squealed loudly a moment later when Peggy, coming in from the kitchen, winked at Carter and accidentally spilt a glass of water down Peters' back.

Outside, Carter took Duke along to the edge of Russell Woods. The dog had growled softly ever since they had left the house. A few minutes later he stopped and began pulling back on his lead in an attempt to go home. Carter turned and looked at him. 'What's up, boy?' he turned back at the house.

It was then that the lights went out. Blinking quickly, Carter was left with an after image.

Duke's tugging became stronger. The dog was now frantically twisting his head from side to side, trying to slip his lead. 'OK. We'll go back.' Carter was feeling apprehensive himself now. Duke was seriously spooking him out.

'What the hell?' Luke said as the lights went out and Peggy gave an ear-splitting scream.

'Shush, Peg. We have a house full of coppers; what the hell can happen? Now get the candles out of the drawer next to you,' Mavis said.

'For God's sake, I can't even see the bloody drawer,' Peggy answered, panicking as Sanderson came rushing in. 'What if it's him, come to bite us or chop our bloody heads off?' Even though she'd been sent to the kitchen Peggy's ear had been firmly attached to the other side of the door. Terrified, she reached out for Mavis.

'Where's the fuse box?' Sanderson asked before dropping to the floor a moment later and shouting, 'Down, everybody! *Down!* as gunfire erupted all around them.

In the sitting room Luke pushed Lorraine on to the floor and threw himself on top of her.

Lorraine's heart was pounding, worried sick for her mother, and Peggy's screams did nothing to take the fear away as she hit the floor.

The sound was deafening and seemed to go on forever. Bullet after bullet, six sharp bursts, a minor pause, then again. Lorraine reckoned in a few minutes he had pumped the contents of three guns into the house and she had heard at least two of her men yell out in pain.

'Duke!' Carter shouted as Duke slipped his lead and headed for home with the speed of a greyhound. Carter took off after him, pulling his phone out as he ran. 'Help, help! Emergency backup needed ... Gunshots now at Mulberry Cottage, west of the Seahills. DI Hunt's house. Quick!'

He reached the house just as Duke launched himself at a man, a gun turned on him. 'No!' Carter yelled as the man, brought down to his knees by Duke, began to twist his arm to turn the gun on the dog.

When the shooting stopped Lorraine could hear her mother and Peggy whimpering in the kitchen.

'Is anyone hurt?' she asked in a loud whisper, as she crawled from underneath Luke.

'Me,' a voice she recognised as Sanderson's said practically in her ear. 'The bastard got my leg.'

'Hold on Sandy, I'm certain Carter will have phoned for help ... Can anyone find their mobiles without making themselves a target, just in case? And be careful of glass, all the windows are shattered.' They all knew what she meant by 'just in case'. 'Mother, are you and Peg alright?'

'Yes, love. I'm fine. Peg bashed her head on the corner of the drawer but she's alright.'

'No, I'm not,' Peggy said indignantly. 'I'll probably need bloody stitches. Ten at least. If I have a scar when we get out of here I swear I'll strangle the mad bastard.'

'I've got my phone, boss,' Sanderson said, and Lorraine could hear the pain in his voice.

Ignoring Peggy because she knew that her godmother was a master of exaggeration, Lorraine said, 'Good Sanderson, make the call ... Dinwall, Travis, Peters?' Then her heart skipped a beat. 'Luke?'

CHAPTER SIXTY-ONE

'I won't be long,' Sam said to Goth as he held out his hand to help the other occupant out of the car, his eyes scouring the darkness across the fields in the general direction of Russell Woods.

A minute later Leanne, Tammy and Stacey looked up from another TV quiz show that none of them had been interested in as Sam entered the room. At his side was a small girl with long blonde bunches that nearly reached her waist. The girl's large blue eyes stared nervously at them.

'Hi, girls. This is your niece, Lorraine.'

Tammy's eyebrows rose as she mouthed, 'Creepy or what?' to Stacey.

Leanne found her voice, though it was full of amazement. 'Hello love, come on in, sit down, next to your Auntie Stacey.' Over the child's head she glared at Sam.

Shyly giving a backward glance at her father, who nodded and smiled at her, Lorraine did as she was told.

When she sat down, Tammy put her arm around the small girl's shoulders and embraced her. 'Welcome, pet. I bet you're as shocked as we are. Now, who is it that you remind me of ...?' She turned her face and scowled darkly at Sam.

Sam ignored her and gestured with his head for Leanne to follow him into the kitchen. Reluctantly, wondering what was coming now, Leanne rose and followed him.

'So, your name's Lorraine, is it?' Tammy asked when Sam closed the kitchen door behind them.

'Mummy used to call me Sophia,' Lorraine offered with a tiny smile, before quickly adding, 'when Daddy wasn't there.'

'Did she now? Well pet, how about we call you Sophia then? It's a much nicer name. Don't you think so, Stacey?'

'I suppose so,' Stacey answered, praying inside that Tammy wasn't going to use the child as a pawn against Sam.

'OK, Sophia it is then. Oh, by the way, where is your mam?' Tammy smiled.

Stacey shook her head at her sister and quickly asked if Lorraine/Sophia would like some pop and a biscuit.

When the child said yes, Stacey went into the kitchen, just in time to hear what Sam was saying to Leanne.

'I have to go Leanne, now.' He pulled a fat brown envelope out of his pocket and held it out. 'This is for my Lorraine. I need you to take her in, Leanne. It's not safe in London, certainly not in the circles I move in. If something ever happens to me she has no one. She could end up anywhere.'

'Where's her mother?' Leanne snapped, still in shock at this new turn of events. She guessed rightly that Tammy hadn't known about Lorraine: that news she would never have been able to keep to herself.

'Long gone. She was no good, a fat lazy cow, and a filthy drug addict to boot. She never wanted Lorraine, ever. She never cared one jot about her and honestly, she used to disappear for days at a time.

Spending most of those days looking at the world through the bottom of a bottle.'

Leanne snorted. Like he would allow that to happen. Sam took it the other way though, and thinking Leanne was agreeing with him, he went on, 'She's a good kid, Leanne, I know she'll be better off here with you than down there. Don't worry, I'll send money and visit regularly ...'

'Yeah, I just bet you will.'

'I promise.'

'Ha.' Leanne remembered a promise made years ago, a promise that she had known from the beginning he wouldn't be able to keep, and she couldn't see this one being any different.

Sam was backing out the door. 'So it's OK? I know she won't make up for the loss of Andrew ... But she'll bring her own love, you'll see.'

'How dare you,' Leanne shouted.

But Sam was gone. Again.

As instructed, Goth had kept the engine running. Sam hurried down the path. Jumping quickly into the car he said, 'You know where he is. Move.'

CHAPTER SIXTY-TWO

Carter was screaming 'No, *no!*' as he ran forward, but still the gun kept turning towards the dog. Bending quickly he picked up a large rock, and from eight feet away he hurled it at Watts with all the force he could muster. He had aimed for the gunman's head, but the rock caught the gun barrel with enough force to knock it out of his hand. Then suddenly a blow to the back of Carter's head brought him to his knees and sent him reeling into unconsciousness.

It took Sam three strides to reach Watts, and pointing the gun at his head he said, 'I should have guessed in the beginning it was you, but time dims a lot of things. A lot of people would be alive now if I had. Should have finished you off that night, you bastard ...'

Watts sniggered. 'Perhaps you should have.'

'Cocky bastard,' Sam growled. 'Why the kid, eh? Why the fucking kid? You didn't even know him.' He hit Watts with a crushing blow across his face, the gun barrel slicing a hole in his cheek. 'Bastard. That's for Jacko.'

As Watts, his eyes burning with pain, grabbed his face, Sam gripped him by his neck. 'This is for Dave.' He squeezed hard, then harder, the veins standing out on his hand. Watts began to choke.

His legs started to buckle. Just before he hit the ground Sam shot him between the legs. 'And that's for the girls.'

Watts curled into a ball as Sam put the gun between his eyes. Blinking to get rid of the tears, but unwavering, he pulled the trigger, 'And that's for Andrew.'

Watts died instantly.

A low growl bubbled deep in Duke's throat.

'Good dog,' Sam said, backing into the car. Not looking at Goth but admiring at his handiwork lying on the road he said, 'Go.'

Goth didn't have to be told twice. He sped off towards Houghton-le-Spring and the southbound motorway, the sound of sirens coming from the opposite direction urging him on.

Duke backed into the field, keeping a wary eye on the prone body as if, on some subliminal level, the dog understood just how evil the human in front of him had been.

Those inside who were alive and conscious cringed when they heard more shots, fearing it was starting over again.

'Luke,' Lorraine shook him. 'Luke. Please, *Luke*.'

'I'm alright, boss,' Dinwall said slowly. 'I think a bullet grazed my brow, sort of stunned me for a minute. I can't hear Travis though.'

'Oh, shit.' Her hands were anxiously feeling Luke's wrist for a pulse as her heart pounded with fear in her ears. 'Peters, you all right? Answer me, for God's sake.'

A match flared in the kitchen doorway. 'Put that out,' Dinwall said. 'We don't want to be seen.'

'Sorry,' Peggy whispered, quickly blowing the match out, then 'Thank fucking God,' as the sound of sirens reached them.

'Coming in, boss,' Carter yelled as he shouldered the door open. He had regained consciousness, taken one look at Watts' body, hastily glanced around, wondered who the gunman was and if he was still around, but knowing he was needed he'd gathered all the courage he could muster and hurried to the cottage, getting there moments before Duke and the squad cars. 'It's alright, everything's under control ... Boss? It was Watts, boss. The bastard's dead,' Carter said.

Lorraine's heart lurched, picturing Watts as he'd been when they were teenagers and wondering briefly if it was something they'd done to turn him into the monster he became. 'Did you kill him?'

'No, boss. Somebody knocked me out. When I came to, Watts was already dead.'

'Any idea?'

'Sorry, boss.'

'Can I light the candles now the cavalry's here?' Peggy asked, but Mavis had already started to light them.

'Over here with the candles,' Lorraine shouted. 'Be careful. There's glass all over.'

Mavis had scented candles everywhere in the room and within moments there was enough light to see by. The extent of the damage was revealed: the two main windows were totally gone, there were bullet holes all around the walls and hardly an ornament nor lampshade had escaped. The television screen was shattered and whole chunks of the settee had been gouged out.

Frantically she looked round for her daughter. 'Lorraine?' she whimpered.

'I'm alright Mam, but I'm worried about Luke. If you could just get some of this bloody glass off me so that I can move.'

As Mavis and Peggy went to her the ambulance men arrived, closely followed by two uniformed officers and Clark.

'See to my men first,' Lorraine insisted, trying hard to keep a grip on herself, as dreading the worst she put her head on Luke's chest.

'I think Peters is dead, boss,' Sanderson said quietly.

'Oh, God. No,' Lorraine's mind flashed back a few moments to the noise and the flare of the gun and prayed that Peters was the only one. She pushed the sadness aside to deal with later.

'No,' Dinwall groaned. There was no love lost between the two, but Peters had been a fellow officer who didn't deserve to die, especially at the hands of a bastard who couldn't get on with the rest of the world.

'I'm alright, boss ... I think,' Travis said from the corner of the room. 'Though something...' he moaned loudly, then fell silent.

'Don't any of you move,' the ambulance man shouted as Dinwall and Sanderson started to drag themselves over to where Peters lay.

'I want the whole lot in the hospital,' Clark said, glass crunching under his feet as he moved to Lorraine.

A moment before he got there Luke whispered in Lorraine's ear, 'Marry me.'

'What?' she squealed.

'What's the matter?' Mavis hurried to her daughter to be stopped halfway by a medic.

'I'm alright, Mam.' The heavy table leg had taken half a dozen bullets before hitting Luke on the back of his head and knocking him out. She was praying hard that he didn't have concussion and wouldn't forget everything he'd just said when the morning came.

As Sam and Goth were passing the petrol station at Carville, near Durham, Goth was reminded of the time a few years ago when he'd used a poisoned dart to kill Alf. There were not many people in this world that Goth liked, and certainly not the man sitting next to him. But Alf had been pretty much alright, fair in everything he did. He hadn't wanted to kill him, but orders were orders. It was a case of kill or be killed, nothing personal.

And one day – he glanced out the corner of his eyes at Sam, who was reading a newspaper – *one day, you smug bastard, it will be your turn.*

As he headed on to the M1 he turned his face away from Sam and allowed himself a small smile. The latest offer from Billy Jean had been good, but not good enough.

Twenty-four hours later, Luke served up his special spaghetti bolognaise to a very subdued team. Travis was still in the hospital a bullet had lodged in his shoulder, but the doctors expected him to make a full recovery.

Sanderson sat with his leg on a stool and accepted a bowl from Selina, thinking of Peters and the day he'd started in the force alongside the dead officer. A lot of years gone by, Peters had not been easy to get on with, but not even Lorraine had known the sadness Peters lived with daily, Peters had kept his home life personal, an alcoholic wife and dead daughter had been the route of his problems, the tears Sanderson blinked back for his dead comrade were really for the young man who had started off with dreams that never came true.

Peggy patted the bandage around her head, covering the one stitch the doctor had deemed, after some gentle persuasion from her, to administer. She had added the large bandage herself and was now giving Clark the eye as he stood up to toast the bravery of everyone in the room.

Lorraine smiled sadly at Luke, who was standing next to Peggy. He nodded and smiled back.

Hmm, she thought disappointedly, distracted a moment from Clark's speech, she gave a quiet sigh. *Looks like Luke can't even remember asking me to marry him. Damn.*

ABOUT SHEILA QUIGLEY

Sheila Quigley has had various jobs ranging from the bad to the ridiculous and all the in-betweens: machinist, presser, double glazing sales person, market stall holder and frozen food sales person amongst many. The hardest of these was picking tatties to put shoes on the kids' feet, at a time when the weekly dole money for a family of two adults and three little girls was ten pounds.

She now has nine grandchildren (six boys and three girls), four children (three daughters and one son) and two sons-in-law.

An awful lot of tatties are eaten at family dinners.

ACKNOWLEDGEMENTS

Good friends indeed, especially in need: Diane Allen, Paul Blezard, Maureen Carter, Tess Gerritsen, Alex Hippisley-Cox, Margaret Hutchinson, Matt Hilton, Denise Hilton, Paul Lanagan, Eileen McKnight Smith, Dorothy McKnight Smith, Ken McCoy, Valerie Myers, Adrian Magson, Anne Magson, Michael Quigley, Sarah Raine and Kevin Wignall.

You all know why. Thank you.